WHAT
THE
TREES
KNOW

NANCEE CAIN

SERRATED EDGE
PUBLISHING

Serrated Edge Publishing
PO Box 969 Jasper, AL 35502

WWW.NANCEECAIN.COM

First published September 2021

ISBN: 978-0-9995362-8-5

Editor: Jessica Royer Ocken
Line Editor: Colleen KeoughWagner
Cover Designer: Gina Dickerson of RoseWolf Design
Interior Book Designer: Gina Dickerson of RoseWolf Design

FOR THOSE WHO BELIEVE IN MAGIC.

CHAPTER ONE

2001
SKYLAR

"THIS IS YOUR new home, my sweet girl."

Mrs. Jackson turns up a driveway toward the biggest house I've ever seen. It's white with pale blue shutters that match the ceiling of the wraparound porch and the ceiling on the smaller balcony above it. Part of the house even looks like a castle with a round turret. I clutch the stuffed cat she gave me, wondering if I'm dreaming. *I'm going to live here?*

Movement on the porch catches my attention. It's a boy sitting on a swing. He's older than me and giving me the stink eye. Lifting my chin, I glare back. Mrs. Jackson drives around the side of the house and parks the old black Cadillac in a detached garage that looks like it used to be a barn. I unbuckle my seatbelt and follow her toward the back porch. A strand of her long gray hair blows free in the breeze, and her patterned skirt swishes back and forth. She's carrying sacks with the new clothes she bought me on the way home from the hospital. On her back porch, there are carved pumpkins on a hay bale.

"Jedidiah," she yells.

An older girl comes out the door, and Mrs. Jackson hands

her some money. "Thank you for staying with Jedidiah. He didn't try to set the place on fire, did he?"

The girl stares at me for a minute and then looks away. I inch behind Mrs. Jackson to hide.

Her laugh sounds nervous. "No, ma'am. Thank you. Anytime you need a babysitter, er, just call me." She stares at me again before getting in her car and leaving.

Mrs. Jackson brushes her hand down my hair. "Don't mind her. Folks around here aren't used to new people." The bracelets on Mrs. Jackson's arm clink and clank as she raises her other arm and motions toward the dark forest behind the house. "Don't you be going back yonder. You'll get lost, you hear me?"

I nod. She doesn't have to worry. I don't want to leave her side. With her, I feel safe.

She shouts again. "Jedidiah!"

The sullen boy rounds the corner. His brown hair is standing on end, and his clothes look like he slept in them. He's taller than me and seems ready to bolt for the forbidden woods at any minute.

"Why did you have to have Clara come babysit?" he asks. "I'm almost grown."

"There you are. You're still just a youngin', and it's my job to make sure you make it to adulthood. Now turn that frown upside down, boy. What if your face froze that way? You'll never get through life looking like that. I've told you, life is too short to be unhappy. Now lookie here—I've brought you someone to play with," Mrs. Jackson says cheerfully.

"It's a girl," he spits, wrinkling his nose. "And she's just a baby."

I look up and glare at him. *I'm* not *a baby.*

"Well, aren't you observant." Mrs. Jackson chuckles. "Jane, this is Jedidiah…" She pauses and cocks her head to the side, studying me like those doctors did in the hospital.

2

I look down at the ground, my stomach feeling topsy-turvy.

She squats in front of me, taking my cheek in her hand. "Look at me, my dear."

I reluctantly look at her. She's smiling. The lines by her cornflower-blue eyes crinkle. My mama never smiled. I take my finger and trace her lips. She smiles wider, and my stomach settles a little.

"The name Jane does not suit you. What would you like your name to be? You can choose anything you like."

The boy beside me gasps and crosses his arms. "How come she gets to choose her name? That's not fair. If I could choose another name, it sure as heck wouldn't be *Jedidiah*. I want to be Mike."

"Mike? That's boring and common. We Jacksons are anything but common. You have a wonderful name, Jedidiah. This little girl has no name."

I press my lips together, not saying a word. *I do have a name, but I'll never tell it, even though I want to. I promised…* My chest tightens, and I look up to gulp some air.

Above us, a bird soars through the air. It's the biggest and most beautiful bird I've ever seen, and I point at it, wondering what kind it is. *Maybe if I just point, that's not the same as telling.*

Mrs. Jackson chuckles. "That's perfect. Your eyes are the color of the sky. How about we call you Skylar? Do you like it?"

I shrug, more interested in the bird dipping and floating through the air. I wonder what it would be like to be that bird, free and flying without being afraid.

"That's a dumb name," Jedidiah proclaims, bringing my attention back to him.

"You mind your manners, young man, or I'll tan your hide. You and Skylar are family now."

"My family's dead!" the boy yells. His face scrunches as if he's trying not to cry, and his fists clench.

I step back, feeling his pain. *Literally.* It cuts deep, and I can't seem to catch my breath. I tug at the high collar of my new shirt.

"Nice, slow breaths, Skylar. Breathe in through your nose and out through your mouth. You're fine," Mrs. Jackson coos, handing the sacks with my new clothes to the rude boy. She strokes my back and shows me how to breathe.

"What's wrong with her? Is she crazy? Look at her eyes! The whites are red, like a vampire's."

"Jedidiah, that's not nice," Mrs. Jackson barks.

I breathe like she told me, and I feel better. The boy's frowning at me, but it's different from before, more sad than mad. He's suffering some deep hurt, just like me. Feeling sorry for him, I offer him my stuffed cat. Sneering, he knocks it to the ground.

"I don't need your stupid ol' stuffed animal. I don't need *nothing* or *nobody.*" He looks ready to either hit something or cry.

"Jedidiah! I'm your grandmother, and we're family, whether you like it or not." Mrs. Jackson's face softens, and the sharpness leaves her voice. "All we have left in this world is each other. Your parents dying isn't what we wanted to happen. But it's life, and we have to accept it and move on. Skylar doesn't have anyone either. We need to take care of her. Of each other. That's what family does."

His gray-green eyes are watery, and one tear slips down his flushed cheek, which he dashes away. He quickly bends over, as if embarrassed, and picks up my stuffed cat. Pulling a twig off, he hands it back to me.

He sighs and glances at his grandmother. "If you're Queenie, she's Princess. And I wanna be called Jed." He drops the sacks of clothes and runs off toward the forest where "Queenie" just forbade me to go.

To my surprise, she doesn't go after him or yell for him to stop. She just watches him disappear. "If that boy doesn't learn to deal with life, he's gonna have a heap of hurt."

He already does.

She strokes my hair. "He's not like us, Skylar."

I look up at her, wondering what she means.

"We know things…and it's our duty to bring relief to folks who are suffering, like him. I'll teach you how. Someday, he's gonna appreciate you. You're going to save him." She smiles. "Princess fits you, too, Skylar. It will be your special nickname. My real name is Guinevere, but Jedidiah has always called me Queenie."

I smile at the woman, hoping I can trust her. Queenie fits her better than Mrs. Jackson or Guinevere. But I'll never call her anything.

I'll never speak.

I promised I wouldn't.

JED

A girl? And not even a girl my age. This Jane/Skylar/Princess is just a baby with her dumb stuffed animal. She's little and couldn't be more than five. And I'm ten. What was Queenie thinking, bringing *her* home for *me* to play with? Heck, I'd rather play with Caleb, and he can't do much because of his asthma and his bossy ol' mama.

I wonder where she'll sleep. Maybe I can convince Queenie to give her the stupid, girly turret room that was my Aunt Charlotte's. I hate that room; it's creepy as all get-out. Aunt

Charlotte died long before I was ever born, and Queenie kept that room like some sort of shrine.

I'd never even met my grandmother until last month at my parents' funeral. Dad used to say she was "batshit crazy," and he was right. She fancies herself some sort of conduit to the other side, like a walkie-talkie to the dead. Caleb's dad, Pastor Buzbee, calls it "innocent parlor tricks," whatever a parlor is. I'd ask Queenie, but she always makes me look up words I don't know.

This is all my dad's fault. If he hadn't insisted on taking my mom to New York City for their anniversary, they wouldn't have been killed at the World Trade Center. Guilty for this bad thought, I march around spewing out every cuss word I know. Something scampers through the woods, probably startled by my hootin' and hollerin'.

I let out a deep breath and pick up a rock, skimming it four times across the water. I love the woods. They're my sanctuary, where I come to get away from Queenie. The sun's setting, and I pause to watch a moment as the light paints colors on the stream. Then, instead of going back home, I climb up the mountain and down into the holler to the cabin I discovered last week.

It's creepy but a good place to hide out. I'll show Queenie I don't need her or that new kid. I'll just live here on my own. When I asked Queenie about this place, she told me it was the original house her great-grandpa had built a gazillion years ago. Even though it's spooky, I've homesteaded it as mine.

Yesterday I brought an old sleeping bag I'd found in the attic and left it here. I also have food and bottles of water I'd brought from the pantry over the last few days. I light the candle with a match I stole from Pastor Buzbee's church. I could've lifted 'em from Queenie's, but I didn't want to push my luck. The food was no biggie. I told her I was hungry. But she's a sharp old woman and would've missed the matches. She's all the time lighting candles and mumbling nonsense.

The flame flickers to life and snaps and fizzles. It smells musty in here, but I don't care. I'm not going home to that stupid, girly room. Or to be nice to my new "family." *I don't need nobody.*

Snuggling in the sleeping bag, I open a bag of chips, pausing every few bites to listen for Queenie hollering my name. Surely she's worried by now. All I hear is an owl and other creatures outside the cabin. Maybe I didn't think this plan through. I shoulda brought a gun. Queenie has a pistol in the top of her closet. Polishing off the chips and water, I blow out the candle and lie awake, imagining Queenie organizing a search party for me. I bet she's sorry now for bringing that new kid home to live with us. She's supposed to be taking care of *me*. She'll be so relieved when I return. She'll probably cry all kinds of happy tears and make me my favorite peach cobbler...

What if Queenie loves this girl more than me?

I roll over, shivering. If I die out here, it will serve her right and make her regret treating me so badly. Maybe she'll ask Pastor Buzbee to preach a nice funeral.

Like Mom and Dad's...

I cover my face and give in to a good cry, missing them so much. *Why? Why did they have to die and leave me all alone?*

Outside the cabin, I hear some twigs cracking. I start to call out to Queenie...but don't. What if it's a bear looking for something to eat? I pull the top of my sleeping bag over my head. I want to go home, but I'm too scared of what's out there. Instead, I close my eyes and recite the twenty-third Psalm that Caleb taught me...

JED

After a restless night, I haul myself outta bed to take a leak. The sun's just rising, and it's cold. My teeth chatter as I write my name with my stream. I'm kinda disappointed no one came looking for me. I guess Queenie's all talk about caring about me and us being "family." I'll just go back, pack my things, and be on my way. Somehow I'll find my way back to Asheville, where I used to live.

Cold, sleepy, and hungry, I creep in the back door. Queenie's sitting at the kitchen table, drinking her coffee and looking at playing cards she's laid out. There are dark circles under her eyes, and she's wearing the same clothes she had on yesterday.

"You hungry?" she asks without looking at me.

The baby isn't here. *Good.* Maybe Queenie hauled her off somewhere.

"Yes, ma'am." I throw myself in the chair opposite her and cross my arms. "I was gone all night."

"I know."

"Weren't you the least bit worried about me?"

"I'll always worry about you, Jedidiah. But not for the reasons you think. I knew you needed some time to think. That's not a bad thing, thinking. You should do it more often." Gathering the cards, she puts them back in the box that stinks of herbs. She wasn't playing solitaire; she thinks she's some kind of fortune-teller.

"Skylar's still asleep in the bedroom on the third floor. Why don't you go ask her to please come down for breakfast?"

I wrinkle my nose and sigh. "Why did she have to come here? And why can't she have Aunt Charlotte's room?" I tilt my chair back, looking around the cluttered kitchen.

It isn't dirty, but there are pots of plants everywhere and weird religious symbols on the walls. Drying herbs hang from the ceiling, and a mortar and pestle sit on the counter next to bottles of disgusting potions. Folks come to the back door and barter with Queenie for spells and the so-called medicines she concocts. I don't know why—for the most part they're gross smelling. I can only imagine how bad they taste. I dunno why they don't just go to the pharmacy like *normal* people. This place is like living in that old show *The Twilight Zone*. It wouldn't surprise me if some of the folks around here were aliens, which would be pretty cool, actually.

"Jedidiah, put the chair back on all four legs and sit up straight. Do you want to break your fool neck? And be nice. Something bad happened to Skylar. She needs us. It's as simple as that." She places bacon in the microwave that looks out of place in this old-fashioned kitchen. I wish it was as neat as Mrs. Buzbee's and smelled of home-baked goodies like hers does.

"Why does she have those creepy red vampire eyes?"

"While I do admire your imagination, she is *not* a vampire. She was hurt, and it broke the vessels in her eyes. They'll heal with time."

I quit tilting the chair and slink down in my seat. "Ain't she got no family?"

"*Ain't* you got no learnin'?" she rebukes. When I don't reply, she raises one eyebrow. "And sit up, don't slump." Queenie checks on the pan of cat-head biscuits in the oven.

"Doesn't Skylar have a real name or anybody else she could go live with?" I ask, sitting up, trying not to act interested.

"Not that we know of. She was dubbed a Jane Doe following the accident."

I lean forward, really interested now as Queenie prepares to cook some eggs. "What kind of accident? Was it a car accident or a terrorist attack like what happened to my mom and dad?"

"No, she nearly drowned, and there's no record of her anywhere. She's special. And she needs us. I want you to man up and be kind to her."

The microwave dings, and I hop up. Using a potholder, I remove the bacon and place it on the old wooden farmhouse kitchen table. It's smooth, and I like the pattern of the wood grain.

Queenie whips some eggs and pours them into a hot skillet. "Run and get her. And be nice or *else*."

The food smells good, and my stomach growls. Hunger overrules principle, so I trudge upstairs to the room on the third floor. The door is open, and I peek in.

Huge bloodshot blue eyes peer at me from under a blanket pulled up over Skylar's nose. Her long blond hair is a tangled mess on her pillow.

"Queenie says to get your butt up and come eat." Her stuffed cat is on the floor. Remembering I'm supposed to be nice, I pick it up and hand it to her.

"What's your real name?" I press. "You can call me Jed."

She blinks but doesn't say a word.

"How old are you? I'm ten."

She watches me. It feels weird, me doing all the talking.

"Cat got your tongue?" I ask.

She lowers the blanket enough to stick her tongue out at me. Then she holds up five fingers.

"Just what I thought, a baby. Get your tail up or you'll get in trouble. Are you coming?"

She shrugs.

"Fine. I was told to come get you for breakfast, but if you don't wanna come downstairs, I don't care. Just means more for me to eat." As I'm leaving, I turn back around and whisper, "But just so you know, Queenie's a witch, and she'll cook you in the oven like her biscuits if you don't obey her."

Her eyes widen and go so black there's hardly any blue left. I grin and run downstairs. My job here is done, and I'm hungry.

A few minutes later, my stomach's growling, and the food's getting cold. "Why can't we eat? I *told* her to get her butt down here." Fiddling with my fork, I glare at my grandmother.

"Because we're a family, and we eat together." She turns and yells, "Skylar, come eat breakfast."

I cross my arms and stare at the doorway, trying that mental-telepathy stuff for the brat to hurry up and make an appearance. Finally, she peeks around the door. I'm tempted to yell *boo*, but the lecture sure to follow would delay breakfast even more.

"There you are. I know you're still settling in, but from now on, you be on time and dressed for meals or go hungry, young lady." Queenie motions for her to take a seat.

"Hurry up, I'm starv—" I stop and stare at Skylar's neck above her pink nightgown. It's green, yellow, and light purple. Yesterday she had on a high-collared shirt, and I didn't notice the bruising. I cut my eyes to my grandmother, who shoots me a warning look. Skylar, in turn, is looking at Queenie like she's scared to death. I feel bad for being so hateful and telling her Queenie would hurt her.

I pat the place next to me. "You can sit here, Princess."

She bites her lip, and instead of sitting, she sidles in close to me. I inch over so we can share a chair. Queenie's face relaxes as she hands Skylar the bowl of fluffy scrambled eggs. Skylar has a death grip on her stuffed cat.

I lean over and whisper, "I was just kidding earlier. She's a good witch, like Glinda in *The Wizard of Oz*."

Queenie's eyebrows rise, and she smiles, but she doesn't say a word. Next to me, Skylar relaxes, puts her stuffed cat in the chair she should be sitting in, and serves herself some breakfast.

"So you're five years old? When's your birthday?" I ask around my biscuit.

"Don't talk with your mouth full," Queenie admonishes. "And Skylar isn't a talker. The doctor said you were around five or six. You're a tiny thing, like a little bird."

Skylar drops her fork and grips the table, as if she's seen a spook or something.

"Why don't you talk? Does it hurt?" I point at her neck.

She stares at her plate like she hasn't heard me.

"I reckon she'll talk when she has something to say. Don't be so nosy, Jedidiah. Since we don't know when Skylar's birthday is, we're making today her new birthday. I've invited the Buzbees over for lunch after they get out of church."

"Is she gonna get presents?"

Queenie smiles. "Of course." She leans over and strokes Skylar's hair. "You're safe here, my darling girl. No one will ever hurt you again."

The kid doesn't look like she believes Queenie, so I try to take her mind off whatever's upset her.

"But I don't have any money for a present." While I feel bad for her, I'm kinda peeved Skylar gets to have a birthday with presents when it may not even be her birthday.

"The best presents don't cost money. They come from the heart. You'll think of something—"

The doorbell rings, and we all pause. "He's here," Queenie says sunnily, getting up to answer the door.

I wonder who's calling this early. Most of our neighbors are at church. Maybe it's one of the heathens wanting a voodoo spell. Curious, I follow her, with Skylar right behind me.

"Hello." Queenie motions the stranger into the house.

Good grief. Even I know letting this man in the house is dumb. He's a stranger. *Or is he?* After all, Queenie knew it was a man at the door. Mentally I cue the spine-chilling music.

My mom and dad taught me about stranger danger. I ease over to the end table and pick up the glass paperweight, ready to hurl it if needed. I'll show Queenie I can protect my family. I'll probably make the paper when I save us from a serial killer. Shoot, they might even have a parade in my honor…

"Mrs. Jackson." The man holds out his hand, and Queenie shakes it. He shifts from foot to foot, scrunching the cap. He's a big man with short gray hair. His mouth hangs open a little, and spittle drools from his lower lip. He's probably thinking Queenie looks weird. People always stare at my crazy grandmother. His dark eyes zero in on Skylar. Behind me, she grasps my belt loop. I can feel her shaking, so I move her behind me, giving the stranger my best don't-mess-with-me glare.

"Come in, Darrell. I appreciate the help you're going to give me. The house next door has stood empty for a year. It needs a tenant to keep from going into disrepair. Are you hungry?"

The man hangs his head, fingering the cap in his beefy hands. "Yes'm, I could stand to eat."

"You don't gotta stand. We have chairs," I pipe in, still trying to figure this guy out.

"Jedidiah, don't be impertinent."

"Let's have breakfast and talk about what your job would entail." Queenie closes the door and walks past me, taking the paperweight from my hand and putting it back on the table.

Darrell shuffles behind her, surreptitiously looking at Skylar, who shrinks closer to me. A fierce need to protect her swells within me.

Darrell waits until Queenie is seated at the table before sitting. She looks sharply at Skylar and me as we hang at the doorway. "Are you two done eating? If so, run along and play, but stay out of those woods. I have some business to talk over with Darrell. He's going to be our new neighbor and help me look after this place."

I look over at Skylar, who seems ready to bolt. Taking her hand in mine, I lead her to the stairs so she can go get dressed. If

Queenie gets murdered by this stranger, that's her business. I'm makin' it my responsibility to take care of Princess.

CHAPTER TWO

SKYLAR

AROUND LUNCHTIME, I look around the kitchen and wonder if I'm dreaming—not the scary nightmares I have about him but a good dream, where monsters don't hurt you. I pinch myself, and it hurts, so I must be awake. This is real. Not only do I have a nice home, but Queenie has planned a party for me. Today isn't my real birthday. I'm five; I'll be six in a few weeks on Halloween. But I haven't corrected Queenie. She's an adult, and you're supposed to do what adults say. If you don't, bad things happen.

Pink balloons sway above the kitchen chairs. Some of them have princesses on them. On the table, there's a white cake with pink roses. There's writing on it, but I don't know what it says. Next to the cake are brightly wrapped presents. *How did this happen? Magic?* I bite my lip, trying to contain my excitement. I've never had a birthday party, and presents were rare, even on Christmas because Santa isn't real. Last year Mommy bought me a cupcake on my birthday. It had a candy pumpkin on it and was chocolate with bright orange icing. I snuck it out of the garbage after *he* threw it away, mad because it wasn't his beer.

But I'm not going to think about *him*. Or Mommy.

Jed inches to the table, his finger hovering over the icing on the edge of the cake. He spent the morning with Darrell trying to find out if he's a *cereal* killer. Which seems silly. If we eat cereal, aren't we all cereal killers? Jed says he isn't, but I'm not so sure. A murky pink light surrounds Darrell, and it's confusing. Queenie always has red and white lights around her, like a candy cane. Grays and browns follow Jed.

"Jedidiah Lafayette Jackson, touch that cake before company gets here and you won't be having any." Queenie's back is toward us as she makes sandwiches for the party.

Jedidiah must be right; she *has* to be a witch. How else did she know he was going to sneak some icing?

Wrinkling his nose, he stuffs his hands in his pockets. "When are they gonna get here?"

"I reckon when they get here and not a minute before."

Jed rolls his eyes.

"Roll those eyes one more time…" she warns.

Definitely a witch.

She turns around and smiles at me. Today she's wearing a bright green dress. The fake pink flowers stuck in her gray hair match her lipstick. Around her neck are some multicolored beads. When she sees me admiring them, she takes a purple, a green, and a gold strand off and gently wraps them around my sore neck. I run my finger across them, feeling special.

The doorbell rings, and Jed races to get it. At the same time, the back door opens. I grip the chair, nervous with everything going on at once.

Queenie turns and almost drops the plate of sandwiches. "Dammit, Darrell. Don't sneak up like that. Wipe those feet and go wash up for the party."

Eyes wide, Jed snickers and mouths from the doorway, *She said dammit.*

Darrell nods at Queenie and smiles at me, but I don't smile back. This morning, I watched from my bedroom as he moved into the little house next door. There's something about him that doesn't feel right.

Behind Jed, a man and woman walk into the kitchen, followed by a thin boy with hair not quite as blond as mine. He sounds funny when he breathes and shoves his glasses up his nose. "Hey, Jed. Have you done your social studies homework yet?"

"Caleb." Jed acknowledges him with an added light punch to his arm. "Nope. I'll do it before class. Homework is stupid."

As Queenie makes introductions among the adults, Jed swipes some icing off the back of the cake. The dressed-up lady speaks really loud and really slow to Darrell, who nods and appears as uncomfortable as I am. She's tall and slender and dressed in a fancy pale blue dress with pearls. The man is a taller version of his son, but without glasses and with better teeth. He shakes Darrell's hand and invites him to church.

"Skylar, this is Pastor and Mrs. Buzbee and their son, Caleb. He's in Jedidiah's class at school but is a couple of years younger."

"We missed you all in church today." Pastor Buzbee smiles wide.

"Caleb is a *prodigy*," his mama brags.

I have no idea what that is, but it must be pretty special, judging by the way she's looking at him.

Mrs. Buzbee glances around the kitchen, her smile fading as her nose wrinkles. The kitchen smells like cake, so it can't be because it smells bad. In her hand is a wrapped present. When her gaze lands on me, her mouth drops open.

"Oh dear God," she gasps, and tears fill her eyes.

Embarrassed, I move my beads up to cover the bruises on my neck. Caleb's father smiles and holds out his hand for a shake. I clutch Kitty and look away, wishing I could sink through the floor and disappear. I don't like being the center of all this attention.

"Be polite and shake hands, Skylar."

"It's fine, Guinevere. She doesn't know me." He drops his hand, still smiling.

I look up and catch Queenie raising an eyebrow at Jed, who has a bit of icing on his upper lip. I motion to him, and he licks it off, grinning.

Everyone gathers at the table and sits. I wish they'd quit staring at me. Thankfully, they start passing the food around, and the attention moves away from me. Mrs. Buzbee shakes her head at Caleb and hands him a brown paper bag.

"There's no poison in the sandwiches, Eleanor," Queenie states matter-of-factly.

I blink. *Poison? Like the apple in* Snow White?

Mrs. Buzbee's chin juts toward the ceiling. "You know Caleb has allergies. And your great-grandmother poisoned my great-aunt's second cousin."

"Eleanor..." Pastor Buzbee frowns.

"Really? I wanna hear more about this," Jed says, leaning forward.

"That's just hearsay. Our families aren't the Hatfields and McCoys, Ellie. And I know Caleb has allergies. Therefore, there are no nuts." Under her breath she mutters, "Unless you count the ones sitting at this table."

"Don't call me Ellie," the minister's wife huffs.

"Do you mind if I offer a prayer, Guinevere?" Pastor Buzbee interjects smoothly as he squeezes his wife's hand.

"Go right ahead. You know me. I say it can't hurt. Christian, Hindu, Hebrew, or Muslim?"

The man laughs. "Christian."

Beside me, Jed snort-laughs. Caleb pushes the glasses up his nose and stares longingly at the sandwiches rounding the table. His front teeth have a gap between them that reminds me of the carved pumpkin on the porch.

We all hold hands—Jed's to my left, and Caleb's on my right. As the minister thanks God for the food, Jed tickles my palm, while Caleb softly squeezes my hand.

Finally, the prayer ends, and Darrell adds a loud "Amen!"

I jump, and Jed chuckles. "Whoa, Dammit Darrell. I think they heard you all the way over in Asheville."

"Jedidiah!" Queenie rebukes. "Another outburst like that and you will be excused from the table without cake."

"You called him that!" Jed protests.

Queenie's mouth thins, and one eyebrow goes up. Jed's right, but he shouldn't talk to adults like this. He might get hit.

Mrs. Buzbee huffs and opens her mouth, but the minister shakes his head, looking stern.

Darrell's face is red, and it's now strangely quiet at the table. I kind of feel sorry for him, but at least the attention isn't on me.

"Let's eat," Queenie interjects, motioning to the food.

"Yes, everything looks delicious," Pastor Buzbee says, nudging his wife's arm.

"Tell us about yourself, Skylar. Are you glad to be here?" Mrs. Buzbee asks. She's staring at me like I've got two heads.

"She doesn't talk," Jed replies for me. Just when I'm grateful for his support, he adds, "She's weird, and Dam, er, Darrell doesn't talk much either. But he's super smart about plants and stuff."

"At least she has manners," Queenie reprimands. "Your commentary on folks is uninvited, Jedidiah. Darrell is a brilliant horticulturist, and Skylar will talk when she's good and ready."

Not happening. I promised...

Caleb nibbles on his fruit and cheese but continues to eyeball the food being passed around the table. The adults talk as we eat. I chew carefully because my throat hurts, and my tummy feels flippy-floppy with all these people watching me. Beside me, Caleb picks at his food, too. Actually, I think his grapes and cheese look good. Seeing me watching, he gives me a few, but they're too hard to swallow. Jed has inhaled two sandwiches before I've even eaten half of one. Queenie calls him Hoover, but I don't know if that's a nickname or not.

It's finally time for the cake. The conversation at the table goes quiet, and all eyes turn to me. I grip Kitty tighter.

Queenie lights the candles on the pretty dessert. "Skylar is the newest member of my family. And today we're celebrating her birthday as a Jackson. All right, my darling girl, blow out the candles and make a wish! Your birthday wish is powerful. We'll open presents afterward."

The heat from the candles is nothing compared to my hot cheeks when everyone sings "Happy Birthday." I blow out the candles, wishing to stay with Queenie forever. She moves the cake and starts cutting slices for everyone.

"For the little girl." Darrell digs into his pocket and pulls out a plastic black cat that's missing an ear. "This was my baby sister's."

What happened to his sister? The way he stares at me makes me squirm, but I know I should be thankful for the gift. After all, it must've meant something to him if he's kept it all these years. I give him a small smile, and he squeezes my hand when I take the cat. I snatch my hand back and sit on it.

Mrs. Buzbee reaches across the table and places a brightly wrapped package with a big bow in front of my plate. I don't want to ruin it by ripping it. It's too pretty to open.

"Hurry up," Jed complains.

"Patience is a virtue, Jedidiah," Mrs. Buzbee says.

"Guess that makes me a sinner, because I *for sure* don't have any patience. I don't much see a need for it," Jed boasts.

Caleb gasps, his head turning back and forth between his

mother and Jed.

"Jed, why don't you hush now and let Skylar open her presents," Queenie interrupts.

"Really," Mrs. Buzbee huffs. "If Caleb ever spoke to an adult like that—"

Pastor Buzbee places his hand on hers and shakes his head. She quits talking, and Queenie kicks Jed under the table. I sit still, watching everyone, ready to run and take cover if need be. When adults get to arguing like this, bad things follow.

But this time, nothing happens, so I begin carefully unwrapping the present. I want to save the paper and the bow. Inside is a leather-bound book. I thumb through it, disappointed there aren't many pictures. I smile and nod my thanks to the Buzbees. Queenie passes pieces of the cake around the table.

"We'll get your name engraved on the cover of your Bible, if you'd like," Pastor Buzbee offers.

I swallow my fear and shake my head, holding it close to me. *No one can know my name...*

Pastor Buzbee chuckles. "It's fine, Skylar. You don't have to give it up. I hope you enjoy it and will come to Sunday school."

"If she wants to go, she can, but yours won't be the only church she attends. I want her well-rounded, Preacher," Queenie says as we start eating the cake.

"Oh, for goodness' sake, what are you going to do, Guinevere, send her over to the snake handlers?" Mrs. Buzbee huffs.

I take a bite of my cake. It's pink and tastes like strawberries. The inside is soft and goes down easy with my milk. I've never had anything that tastes this good. No wonder Jed tried to sneak some earlier.

Jed stops shoveling cake into his mouth and looks up. "Snake handlers? Real snakes? In a church? I wanna go!"

"Jed, we'll discuss this later. But, yes, if that's where you want to go, I don't care," Queenie says.

Caleb pipes up, "Can I go, too, Daddy?"

"Absolutely not!" Mrs. Buzbee's eyes bug out as if one of those snakes were slithering across the table toward her.

Next, I open another book from Queenie. This one has lots of pictures of princesses and castles. I like it better than the book of words called a Bible. I also get some new clothes. I can't imagine why I'd need them. It seems silly to have so many; I can only wear one outfit at a time.

The last present is from Jed. He wrapped it in a leaf and tied it with a string. Inside I find a blue car that fits in the palm of my hand.

"Jedidiah, what a lovely gift," Queenie says. "I'm proud of you. That's your favorite car."

Jed nods, looking kind of sad. I offer it back to him.

"No, you keep it. I'm too old to play with toys. But don't lose it, okay?"

I smile and place the little black cat on top of the car, moving it back and forth on the table in front of me.

"Can we go outside, Queenie?" Jedidiah asks.

"The question is *may* we go outside," Queenie corrects.

"Actually, we need to be going." Mrs. Buzbee stands. "Thank you for inviting us, but Caleb needs to rest before church tonight."

"Let the boy go outside, my dear. He'll be fine." Pastor Buzbee pats her hand and motions with his head for Caleb to go.

He and Jed clamber out of their chairs. "Come on, Skylar," Caleb calls.

Mrs. Buzbee yells, "Stay on the porch, Caleb! And carry your inhaler."

We hurry outside, and Caleb throws himself on the wooden

swing. "Sit with me, Skylar." He grins for the first time since he got here.

Jed starts walking on the porch rail like a circus performer. Holding Kitty, I sit next to Caleb, nearly tipping us over in the process.

He shoves his glasses up his nose and stares at me. "What happened to your neck?"

"She nearly drowned," Jed answers for me, wobbling to keep his balance.

Caleb's brown eyes widen behind his thick glasses. "Were you scared?"

I shrug. *It was beyond scary. But I'll never tell.*

"Of course she was scared, ya moron!" Jed jumps from the rail, landing in front of us. Startled, Caleb yelps.

"She was kidnapped by pirates."

"Pirates? In North Carolina?" Caleb gasps, looking back at me. His mouth has dropped.

"Sure. It happened at Nag's Head, 'cause girls do nothing but nag, nag, nag. They told her to shut up, and she didn't—so they made her walk the plank."

I'm not sure who's more dumbfounded by this story, Caleb or me.

Caleb turns back to me and croaks, "What did they look like?"

I shrug. *How should I know?*

"How would she know? She was blindfolded. Pirates aren't stupid, ya know."

"Wow…" Caleb pushes his glasses up his nose and starts coughing and wheezing. Taking something out of his shirt pocket, he puts it in his mouth and squirts it.

I glare at Jed for telling this whopper fib, wondering if it's made Caleb sick. Instead of looking worried, Jed grins like he's ready to bust a gut laughing.

I offer Kitty to Caleb, to help him feel better. But he shakes his head.

"I'm okay. I have asthma and have to use this inhaler to breathe." Caleb takes my hand. "I'm glad you're okay. That must've been scary."

You have no idea...

I squeeze his hand back. Pale green lights swirl around him. I like him; Jed shouldn't be so mean. Caleb's hand is warm and soothing, like Queenie's was when she sat with me at the hospital. It's a comforting feeling, and I don't want to let go.

My mother's hand was always cold and would sometimes shake when she touched me. Blackness always surrounded her...until she was covered in red blood. Shoving the painful memory aside and feeling curious, I jump up and take Jed's hand. A spark of electricity jolts between us, and he jumps back as if burned. His energy is wild and surges through me. Something draws me to reach out for his hand again. He grabs mine and squeezes it tight. The only comparison I can come up with is we're like the black and white dog magnets on Queenie's refrigerator. She let me play with them after breakfast, and they chased each other and then ran away. She said it was magic. Jed lets go and hops back on the railing.

Mrs. Buzbee appears at the front door. "Caleb, say goodbye. It's time for you to go home and take a nap."

"A nap? Only babies take naps," Jed grumbles.

Caleb looks sad, but he obeys. Feeling sorry for him, I hop off the swing and give him a hug.

He hugs me back and whispers, "I'm glad the pirates didn't kill you."

Laughing, Jed falls backward off the railing into the bushes. "Son of a bitch!"

"Jedidiah, get off your butt and go pick your own switch!" Queenie hollers.

Mrs. Buzbee fusses about bad influences—whatever that is—but it must be *really* bad, because she hustles Caleb to the car without even saying goodbye.

Pastor Buzbee stops in front of me. "I'm glad you're here, Skylar. It was nice to meet you."

I like him as much as I like Caleb. Bright white light surrounds him. Behind him, Darrell puts on his cap and nods at me. Instinctively, I back up a step and then turn to run and help Jed find this thing called a switch.

SKYLAR

"And they lived happily ever after." At bedtime, Queenie closes my new book and kisses my cheek.

I hug her. This has been the best day I can remember in a long time. Turning on my night-light, she blows me another kiss and leaves. I wait awhile, letting the house get quiet before getting up to look out my window. This morning I watched Darrell move in. Tonight he's got a shovel and is digging in his yard. *Who works in their yard at night?*

I tiptoe down the stairs to find Jed. At first I don't see him, because he's leaning out his window, the one that overlooks the front yard. He's smoking a cigarette. When he hears me, he jumps and cracks his head. Something falls to the ground outside.

"Ouch!" He rubs the back of his head and glares at me. "If Queenie wakes up from that screen falling, we're both dead meat."

I wrinkle my nose because the smoke stinks. He flicks the cigarette out the window and closes it.

"What are you doing up, Princess?"

I motion for him to follow me.

"Why?"

I point toward my room.

"The bogeyman up there?"

I nod and head toward my room.

"Hella cool." He follows.

He stops me midway up the stairs and points to the far-right side of the step. "Step over here. The left side squeaks," he whispers. "Remember, think right, step light."

I hesitantly tiptoe up the right side of the staircase, take him to my window, and point.

He looks out and whispers, "What the heck is he doing? You reckon he's burying a body?"

My heart races so fast I can't breathe. Black spots dance before my eyes, and I start panting for air, clawing at the neck of my nightgown.

"Whoa, I was kidding." Jed takes my hand and guides me to the bed. "Hey, calm down. Do I need to get Queenie?"

I shake my head, holding on to his hand as hard as I can. *Don't tell, don't tell…*

"Let go. You're pulling my arm hair. Look, Dammit Darrell's just a tad tetched, is all. He's probably planting petunias or something." He starts to leave, but I tug him back, shaking my head, silently begging him not to leave.

"I think I need to get Queenie. You're acting all baby-girly."

I bite my trembling lip and try to blink the tears away, but I don't let go. He sighs and sits on the side of my bed.

"Okay. I'll stay, but you gotta turn that dumb night-light off. I can't sleep unless it's dark. Ain't nothing gonna get us."

I'm scared of the dark, but with Jed here, I think I'll be okay. I nod. We crawl under the covers, and he snaps off the light. I inch closer to him, and he groans.

"Hey, get on your own side. Haven't ya ever heard of personal space?" Taking Kitty, he places my stuffed animal between us and rolls to the far edge of the bed.

I sniffle and dash my tears away.

"Ain't nothing gonna happen to you. Like I told ya, Queenie's a witch. A good witch. She probably has all kinds of spells protecting this house. And you're a princess. You ever hear of anything bad happenin' to princesses? I mean permanent bad. They always come out okay, right? You'll be fine. You've got me." He rolls over and starts snoring.

I wrap my arm around Kitty and pray Jed's right.

CHAPTER THREE

JED

YAWNING, I WANDER to the window, happy for a Monday off. I love having a long weekend. I'm not much for school—not like Caleb, who loves it. I'd rather be outside fishing or exploring the woods. The sun's just coming up, and I see Darrell back at it, digging. He now has a square plot that looks like it's gonna be a garden, not a grave. Still asleep, Skylar turns over, hugging her stuffed cat. I wonder what happened to her. I'm pretty sure she can speak, 'cause last night she whimpered in her sleep and hit at the air like a ghost was chokin' her. *Who would hurt a little kid?*

I sneak downstairs, avoiding another squeaky step. Folks in town say this place is haunted. They may be right, which would be pretty cool. Queenie will whip my butt if she finds out I stole a cigarette from Darrell and smoked it last night. But the screen is gone, and I gotta find it. I start searching the bushes.

"Here."

I spin around, my heart pounding like a woodpecker on a tree. Darrell's standing there holding the screen and a ladder.

I swallow my nervousness. "Uh, thanks. I think the wind blew it off last night."

Darrell glances to the ground at the cigarette butt I flicked out the window last night.

I look him straight in the eye, hoping he believes me or, at the very least, won't rat me out. "I, uh, was looking at the, er, weeds that need to be pulled from around these bushes, and I'm thinking the shrubs need to be trimmed, too. Only, I'm not really sure how to do it, to be honest." *That's about the only true statement I've made.*

He stares at me, and I haven't got a clue if he's bought my story. He talks only marginally more than Skylar does. The entire time I spent with him yesterday, he didn't say anything except about plants.

At last he says, "Hold the ladder."

I'm on it like stink on poop. Maybe it'll keep him from telling on me. I hold the sides as he climbs up. Queenie walks out on the front porch.

"What in tarnation is going on out here?"

"I'm helping Darrell," I offer. Brown-nosing is an art form I'm perfecting.

"Good. You can help him around the yard, too. Idle hands are the devil's workshop. You wouldn't want to go up in smoke, would you? Y'all come in for some breakfast when you're done."

"Yard work? But it's a holiday! I was gonna go fishing."

She walks back in the house.

I glare at Darrell, wondering if he told on me. *But he didn't know for sure. Maybe she really* is *a witch.*

He attaches the screen and climbs down.

"Thank you," I tell him.

His face is unreadable. "I'll help you, if you help me," he says. His eyes squint slightly.

"Uh, sure. What time?" I wonder if I'll still have time to fish. I'm starting to think that cigarette wasn't worth all this trouble.

"After breakfast. Maybe we can fish when we're done?"

"Sure." I'll show him my *second* favorite place. No way am I giving all my secrets away.

Darrell puts the ladder away, and we head to the kitchen. Princess is dressed in clothes as mixed up as Queenie's and setting the table. Her eyes shift from Darrell to Queenie and back to me. Her hands shake as she folds the paper napkins the way Queenie likes 'em.

Wearing overalls and a neon-pink blouse, Queenie brings a bowl of scrambled eggs and some biscuits to the table. Behind her back, I snitch a piece of ham off a platter.

"What are your plans for today, Darrell?" Queenie asks as she takes a seat.

"Why did ya dig up the ground last night? That was kinda creepy," I add.

Skylar's eyes round at my question, and she starts shaking like Old Man Crump, who has some disease that makes it where he can't stop twitching. Biting her lip, she looks ready to cry. That doesn't deter me. I can't help it if she's a crybaby and scared of her own shadow. I'm *helping* her, showing her how to get what she wants.

I shrug. "What? You want to know, too." Sharing the blame is another talent I'm honing. Besides, if she won't talk, I will.

"Impertinence is not attractive, Jedidiah. Sit, Skylar. A biscuit, Darrell?" She hands him the plate. They're big, brown, and perfect. I love mine slathered with honey and butter.

"Thank you, Mrs. Jackson. I just about got my garden plot ready to add the manure. It will make for a good garden next year. I'm gonna work on the apiaries, too."

I wrinkle my nose. *He's planting shit?* "What's an apiary?"

"Look it up," Queenie says.

I hate when she does that. Why can't she just tell me?

"Beehives," Darrell answers.

I knew I liked him.

Skylar stares at her plate. *She's so weird.*

"Ain't ya gonna eat your biscuit?" I ask with my mouth full. If she isn't, I'll gladly eat hers.

Her gaze darts toward Darrell and then back to her plate. I'm disappointed when she picks up her dry biscuit and nibbles at it. *Such a waste.*

Queenie raps the table, getting my attention. "After you help Darrell, I want you to write, 'I will never use the word *ain't*,' fifty times."

"Oh man, that sucks."

"Indeed, your language skills do." She looks sharply at Skylar. "Is there something wrong with your breakfast? Sorry for the interruption, Darrell."

Skylar shakes her head, and her knuckles blanch holding that stuffed cat.

"Today I'm going to put your garden to bed, too." Darrell looks over at me. "And the shrubs around your house need weeding and mulching. And me and Jed want to fish."

It's the most he's ever said. I wonder if Queenie's gonna correct him and tell him it shoulda been *Jed and I want to fish.*

My grandmother nods. "You need to clean the bird feeders and turn the birdbath over, too. We'll have a frost soon."

"Yes, ma'am."

Skylar's leg is bouncin' ninety-to-nothing under the table.

"If ya need to go pee, just ask to be excused," I tell her.

Eyes wide, she stills but doesn't say a word.

"Why won't you talk?" I press.

Queenie drums her fingers. "Because she doesn't want to. When you and Darrell are done eating, you both may be excused."

"She's weird. Everybody around here is about two cents short of a dollar. No wonder my daddy never wanted to come here."

Queenie flinches, and I shut up, feeling bad for my low

blow.

"You can add 'I will not call Skylar weird' to your fifty lines. This makes a grand total of one hundred. Would you like to add more?"

I glare and shake my head. *I need to learn to keep my big fat mouth shut.*

She waves me away. "Now go."

Clearly amused at my expense, Darrell stands. He's grinning from ear to ear. "Thank you for breakfast. It was good."

"You're welcome, Darrell. I hope your good manners rub off on Jed."

I scowl and follow him before Queenie comes up with more dumb punishments.

I can't wait to get away from this place.

SKYLAR

Queenie stands, pours another cup of coffee, and refreshes hers. The feathers she's braided into her hair wave with her movements. Coming back to the table, she adds lots of milk and sugar to the extra cup and hands it to me.

"Crumble up your biscuit in the coffee. My grandmother used to call it soaky bread. Try it. It's good. You don't eat enough to keep a gnat alive, but it will get easier to swallow, I promise."

Doing as she said, I take a bite. It *is* good and goes down my sore throat easily. I smile and dig in, feeling more relaxed without Darrell being here and Jed asking questions.

"Skylar, you've been through a lot. There's nothing I can do about the past. But you're safe here. I won't let anything bad happen to you as long as there is breath in my body." She pulls something from her pocket and hands it to me. It's a necklace with a silver dragonfly and a black stone. It's the prettiest thing I've ever seen.

"I've infused this necklace with good, positive, protective energy during a full moon. You're like a dragonfly, Skylar. They're born in or near water…"

I shake my head. I hate water.

Queenie continues, "And they symbolize renewal and transformation. They've been around for over three hundred million years. They're extraordinary, just like you. Whatever happened to you was not the end. It was a new beginning. Someday you'll understand just how special you are."

I run a finger over the shiny, rough black stone.

"That's black tourmaline. Its property is to protect." She takes the necklace and places it around my neck, where it joins the bright beads she gave me on my new birthday. "You're going to help so many. I foresee great things for you, Skylar. Don't be afraid to embrace this new life. You hold the power." She taps my chest right over my heart.

Looking into her eyes, I trust her. And wearing this necklace, it feels like a weight has been removed from my shoulders. I blink back tears. Rubbing the charm and stone between my fingers, I start to believe in the power of magic. And love.

Hopping off my chair, I throw my arms around Queenie's neck and hug her tight.

"My sweet girl," she whispers, returning my hug.

I promise myself from this day forward, I'll do anything for this woman. She saved me. And even though Darrell makes the hair on my arms stand on end, if she trusts him, I will, too. I vow to be just like Queenie when I grow up.

Together we clear the table. She starts telling me what all the potted plants in the window are and what they're used for. After the dishes are done, Queenie puts me in her lap, and we start looking at a big, old book. In it are drawings of plants, moons, and strange symbols with lots of writing.

"This grimoire holds so much knowledge. Some of it has been handed down for generations. You may look at it anytime you like. See this? It tells me how to make a special tea for Caleb. It will help him breathe easier. And don't you be payin' no mind to what Eleanor Buzbee said about my great-grandmother. She was a great healer, but some conditions just can't be healed. Her great-whatever died from drinking his own tainted homebrew."

She points at another picture. "And this right here shows how to make the knots for a witch's ladder. It's a powerful spell I'll teach you when you're older." She turns the page.

Jed was right! She is *a witch!* But I know she's a good witch. I can feel it. The next page is just a bunch of words. I really prefer the princess book Queenie gave me, but I don't want to hurt her feelings. I point at the writing, wondering what the words are.

"Don't you worry; I'll teach you to read. And after you get settled in, you'll go to school and make lots of new friends."

I bite my lip. I don't want to leave this house.

"Speaking of friends, Pastor Buzbee is bringing Caleb over to visit in a bit. You two can play while the good reverend attempts to talk me into heaven. But first, let's make Caleb's tea together. When you infuse your own good energy into a mixture, it makes it work even better."

I watch as she mixes a variety of dried plants in a stone bowl. Using something she calls a pestle, she starts pounding the herbs and talking softly.

She sees me watching her and smiles. "I'm putting a healing

spell on the herbs for Caleb."

I nod, going over the words silently. I'm excited when she allows me to help smoosh the leaves in the stone bowl. They smell funny.

After the tea is made and placed in tiny cloth bags, she says, "Now go brush your teeth. Caleb will be here soon. Scoot."

I hurry upstairs, making sure to step right and light. Caleb's nice, and I'm excited he's coming over. Running to the bathroom, I brush my teeth and hair, but I don't look in the mirror.

Don't look... The voice from my past echoes, and the room closes in on me. I duck down, making myself as small as possible. My hand's shaking as I rub the black stone in my necklace. Downstairs the doorbell rings. *He's not here. I'm safe.*

I inch my way down the steps as Queenie shuts the door behind Pastor Buzbee and Caleb. She looks up and smiles.

"There she is. Why don't you two go play on the porch?"

"What toys do you wanna play with?" Caleb asks.

"You don't need toys. Use your imagination, Caleb. Coffee, Pastor? Or tea and tarot?"

Pastor Buzbee chuckles. "Coffee or tea is fine. No tarot."

Caleb and I go sit on the wooden swing, and he carefully places the knit afghan around our shoulders. He shoves his glasses up his nose. On the table next to the swing is a board with writing on it and something that looks like a triangle.

"I had fun at your party yesterday," he says, looking me over. "Ya know, plaid doesn't really go with stripes."

Looking down at my red plaid shirt and striped leggings, I shrug, wondering why not.

"Do you really not talk?"

I shake my head, dreading the questions. Through the open windows come the strains of gospel music. Last night after supper, Queenie played music from India. I like all of it.

"Can you read?"

Again, I shake my head no.

He picks up the board. "I can teach you your ABCs with this. It's kinda cool. See? That's an *A*." He takes my finger and points to a letter. We get to the letter *S*, which he says is the first letter of my name, and the front door opens.

His father hurries over and takes the board from Caleb. "I don't think your mother would understand you playing with a Ouija board, son."

"I was teaching Skylar her ABCs."

His father smiles. "I know. Maybe we can find those magnets that used to be on our refrigerator for her. Why don't you just sit and talk?"

"But she doesn't *talk*."

"Son." Pastor Buzbee doesn't look mad, but it's the same kind of look Queenie gives Jed.

"*Okay*. I'll talk for both of us," Caleb says.

His father goes back inside with the Ouija board and the triangle. "This is superstitious nonsense, Guinevere," he says, closing the door.

"I've got plenty to talk about, and being an only child, I don't really have anyone to talk to," Caleb says. He points toward Darrell's backyard and laughs. "Jed doesn't look very happy working in that garden. Mama won't let me do stuff like that because of my asthma. But it's okay because I'm really smart. I got to skip two grades. I wonder if there are worms in the dirt. Worms are good for a garden. Wanna know why? Because they dig tunnels, which lets the air and water get to the plants. And they eat dead leaves. And their poop is like fertilizer."

I give him a questioning look. *How does he know all of this?*

"I read a lot. You can learn anything in books. When you read, you can go anywhere and be anything…" He sighs and adds, "Not stuck sitting around being sick. I could read to you, too. I like reading. And I'll help you learn how. My mama says I shouldn't be around Darrell. I guess Mrs. Jackson thinks he's okay?"

I wonder why his mama told him that. *Does Darrell give her the creeps, too?*

"Will you be going to school?"

I bite my lip. I don't want to leave Queenie. I shake my head.

"It's okay. Some kids homeschool. Mama wanted to do that with me, but my daddy said I need to learn to socialize on account of me being so smart and sickly."

Overhead, the big bird I saw yesterday soars. I point at it and look at Caleb.

"That's a bald eagle. Did you know it's our national bird? He isn't really bald, though. He has white feathers on his head."

I watch the bird, loving how he glides above the treetops. The wind blows, and the trees whisper as the branches sway. They're telling me I'm safe here. I relax and smile at my new friend.

For the next two hours, we swing, and Caleb talks. I like having a friend. And he doesn't ask questions like Jed does. He just tells me stuff and teaches me how to play rock, paper, scissors. It's fun, and I like it when I win. It's getting warm, and we crawl out from under the afghan. The sun makes the leaves bright and shiny. Caleb is telling me where Halloween came from and that his mama thinks it's evil.

Jed approaches, all sweaty and stinky. I wrinkle my nose.

"Whatcha lazy asses doin'?"

"Just talking." Caleb pushes the swing with his foot. "And you shouldn't say *a-s-s*."

"Whatever." Jed frowns and points at me. "She talked?"

"Well, *no*. But she's a good listener. I talked for both of us. I was telling her about the benefits of worms in a garden. Did you find a lot? If so, that's really good for the soil. Want me to help you with your homework? It's really not that hard."

"Oh brother. I told ya, I'll do it before class. I like having a long weekend off. I wish I didn't have to go to school tomorrow. I'd rather be learning stuff from Darrell. He's a little off in the head, but he's okay. He knows all about gardening—real gardening, not that stinky herb stuff Queenie does. Darrell and I are going fishing. Y'all wanna go?" Jed hops up on the porch railing and starts swinging around the post.

"You shouldn't say someone's 'off.' That isn't nice. Maybe he has a disability. We're all God's children and special in our own way. What about the worms? Did ya find any?"

Jed looks at me and smirks. "Yeah, there were plenty of worms. I didn't find any *dead bodies* like Sky thought might be there, but, then again, they may be buried really deep."

He proceeds to sing about worms crawling in and out of dead people's mouths.

"That's gross," Caleb says, laughing.

"I'm just keeping it real." Jed's arms flail, and he does several funny moves, but he doesn't fall off.

Queenie steps out onto the porch with Pastor Buzbee.

"Thank you for the coffee and interesting discussion, Guinevere. And I appreciate the tea for Caleb's asthma. You ready to go, son?"

"Yes, sir. Thank you, Mrs. Jackson. Bye, Jed. Bye, Sky."

His smile brightens his face, even if his teeth are crooked. I like his eyes, too. Behind his glasses, they're the color of hot chocolate.

Queenie ruffles Caleb's hair. "You can call me Queenie, Caleb. And come visit any time you like. It does a boy good to get outside in the sunshine and fresh air. Jedidiah? Don't you have some lines to be writing? Finish them, and then you can go fishing."

Beside me, Jed scowls. "I hate this place."

"Well, when you're eighteen, you can leave. But until then, you'll do as I say. Now go."

"I hate you, and I can't wait to grow up. When I do, I'll leave and never come back. *Ever!*" He goes inside, slamming the door behind him.

"I'm sure he didn't mean it," Pastor Buzbee offers.

Queenie smiles. "Oh, I'm quite sure he did. But he'll be back. Mark my words."

CHAPTER FOUR

2009, EIGHT YEARS LATER
SKYLAR

"CALEB'S HERE," QUEENIE calls from downstairs.

I finish applying my lip gloss and fix my loose braid. My stomach cramps, and I'm feeling out of sorts. I'd rather stay in bed and read, but I promised Caleb I'd see him today before the bonfire tonight. I apply some lavender oil on my wrists to try to calm my nerves. Making my way down the stairs, I run into Jed coming out of his bedroom. I pause, unwilling to go down the stairs with him. It's bad luck. He's wearing jeans with no shirt and smells of sunblock. Working with Darrell this summer has made his muscles stand out and the veins on his arms cord. He hasn't shaved, and the scruff gives him a dangerous look. He's "gorgeous" according to all the girls in town. Stella, in particular, talks about him nonstop and flirts outrageously with him.

"What's your hurry, Princess?" He frowns and motions me ahead. "Are you already dressed for the summer silliness tonight? Whoa, wait a minute… Are you wearing makeup?" He pinches my hot cheek, and I slap his hand away.

I glance down at my white peasant blouse and skirt. I'm

tired of everyone treating me like a little girl and decided to dress up and try the makeup I bought at the drugstore yesterday. I speed down the steps, now feeling self-conscious. My effort was wasted. Jed still thinks of me as a *kid*, even though I'll be fourteen in a few months.

"Afternoon, Queenie. What's the purple flower? It's pretty," Caleb says, closing the front door behind him. "And go ahead and tell me its properties, because I know you don't plant anything without a purpose." In contrast to Jed, he's clean-shaven and dressed in khaki pants and a button-down shirt with the sleeves rolled up. He looks very conservative standing next to Queenie, who's sporting colorful yarn dreads in her gray hair that match her tie-dyed caftan.

"Back in the day, it treated heart dropsy," Queenie explains. "But it has to be used very carefully because of the potential side effects. It can slow the heart down, make the mouth go numb, and the person can even have hallucinations."

"That sounds kind of dangerous," he comments.

"It's why no decent herbalist uses it anymore. I have Darrell plant it because I think it's pretty. See the shape? The flower looks like the finger of a glove. Folks around here still call it witch's glove. Actually, *that's* why I plant it." Queenie cackles and nudges Caleb's arm. He laughs.

Behind me, Jed mutters, "Oh brother, Queenie and her hoodoo horticulture." He calls out, "Hey, Caleb. Wanna go fishing?"

"Not today, thanks. My asthma's been acting up. I'm going to take it easy. Maybe next time, but I appreciate you asking me."

"Your loss. Hey, Queenie, I'm gonna go try to catch some supper," Jed says.

"Chores done?"

"Yes'm." He pulls my braid. "I know better than to even ask

41

you. I'll see if Darrell wants to join me."

Jed hangs with Darrell a lot, but the man still bothers me on some level. He's full of secrets. *I can sense it.* The back door slams as Jed leaves.

Queenie gathers her purse and basket of potions. "I have some errands to run. Skylar, you need to be home by supper. Even though it's the longest day of the year, guests will be arriving around six. Caleb, you're welcome to join us if you'd like."

"Thank you, Mrs. Jackson. I, uh, appreciate the invite, but, well, Mom says I can't come... Skylar and I will stick close to the house." He smiles and jingles the change in his pocket.

Nervous energy swirls around him in a kaleidoscope of color. I hide my disappointment. I thought we might go for a ride into town and get ice cream. He got his driver's license a few months ago. Instead, he opens the door and motions me toward the front porch swing, our favorite place to visit. We talk, or sometimes Caleb reads to me. He doesn't even mind reading what Jed calls "girly books," like my favorite romances.

Lately, we've been holding hands, and he's been telling me about his plans for the future. He wants to be a pharmacist. Being smart in books, I know he'll do well. I'll miss him when he leaves for college. He's always been easy to be around.

Queenie waves as she drives off, leaving us alone.

We sit and swing, not saying a word. I can hear Jed whistling as he and Darrell head into the forest. Over the years, Jed's sometimes asked me to go with him to his special cabin, where he likes to get away from Queenie. But years ago, I promised Queenie I'd stay out of the woods, so I never venture into them unless she goes with me. Besides, there's a river just over the mountain, and I don't like it. Even the sound of it makes me shake and takes me back to the scariest night of my life. I much prefer staying close to home.

Caleb clears his throat and takes my hand. I give it a squeeze. Maybe today's the day he'll kiss me. I know he wants to, but he seems nervous. The bees hum as they dip into the various flowers planted near the house. There's a strange feeling in the air today—I sense something momentous is about to happen. Plus, when I threw my cards last night, they told me a life-changing event is in my future. I wish I'd had a chance to ask Queenie about it.

It's Midsummer Eve, and colored ribbons flutter from the maypole Darrell erected in the yard. Tonight we'll host a bonfire and dance around the pole. It's one of my favorite celebrations. Friends will bring dishes for a potluck supper, and the curious will drive by to see if we're having some pagan sex festival. Jed threatened to run around naked, just to give them a show, which earned him a tongue-lashing from Queenie at breakfast—and piqued my interest.

"You look really pretty today, Skylar," Caleb says.

Heat spreads across my cheeks, and I stare at our hands clasped together. I sign, *Thank you*. I point at the pole and then him.

"I'm sorry I can't come. I want to. But my mom…she doesn't…" He frowns. "You know how she is. She's kind of straightlaced."

Kind of? Mrs. Buzbee is nice enough, but she's judgmental if something doesn't fall in line with her beliefs.

I'm glad Caleb's more like his dad. I squeeze his hand. I've done readings and seen that, indeed, our lives are intermeshed. Again I wonder if he's going to kiss me. I hope so. He's thoughtful, interesting, and fun. I've been biding my time and trying to encourage him gently. Performing a love spell is out of the question. They never work the way you want them to. But if this boy doesn't kiss me soon…I might just have to initiate the kiss myself.

Caleb's thumb rubs my ring finger. "Even though I'm graduating from high school in a couple of weeks, my mother says I'm still too young to get serious about a girl." He shifts to face me and takes both of my hands in his. I lean forward, ready.

"But sometimes she's wrong…"

I grin and nod. Before I lose my courage, I lean in and kiss him. Our eyes are open, and his are so wide and dark it's like looking down a well. His lips remain closed, but his breathing is erratic.

He blinks and pulls away, his face red. Biting his lip, he mumbles, "Sorry about the braces."

He lets go of my hands to cup my face. His hands are soft, his touch gentle.

"I love you," he whispers.

I smile and lower my eyes, a little unnerved by the intensity in his. I do love him, and I wanted him to kiss me, but I'm unsure if my feelings are as strong as his. I'm curious more than anything. *Maybe it takes time…* Or perhaps it's because I feel out of sorts in general.

"If I asked you to do something for me, would you?" He shoves his glasses up his nose.

I nod. Caleb is, after all, my best friend, aside from Jed.

"Come with me?" He stands and holds out his hand.

I take it and follow him off the front porch. I don't feel well, but maybe an ice cream would help. And I like riding in Caleb's car with the top down and the wind blowing in my hair. It makes me feel like a bird soaring in the air.

But instead of walking to his car, we head toward the back of the house, up the path into the woods. I hesitate.

"Come on, it's cooler in the forest. We can gather some honeysuckle vines and make crowns for your party tonight."

I shrug. Why not? Jed was supposed to gather some, but

knowing him, he'll get caught up in fishing and forget. This will keep him from getting in trouble with Queenie. We head up the trail that leads to the river. I grab some honeysuckle vine and twist it into a crown. Caleb places it on my head.

"Pretty. You look like a woodland princess."

In the distance, I hear the water from the river and Jed laughing. We pull more honeysuckle vines for the crowns, going deeper into the woods. A briar snags my skirt. Caleb stops to unhook it. Again, he cups my face in his hands. The wind ruffles his light brown hair, and a sheen of sweat dots his upper lip. Caleb still looks like a boy, unlike Jed.

"Do you trust me?" he asks softly.

I nod, but my heart races.

He smiles. "There's more vines, but they're close to the river."

I shake my head.

"It'll be okay, I promise."

I'm afraid, but I trust him. Besides, if I want to be grown up, I need to act like an adult and not give in to my childish fears. We hike up the mountain and then down the steep path toward the riverbank. I remind myself this isn't a lake. It's daylight, not dark. And I've been here with Queenie and Jed a few times, and nothing bad happened. It's different water than the inky darkness of my nightmares.

But ten feet from the rushing water, I stop.

"Isn't it pretty?" Caleb asks.

The roar of the river contends with the pounding fear erupting from deep within me. I feel sick to my stomach and want to go home and lie down. Shaking my head, I point back toward the house.

"There's nothing to be afraid of. Look, we'll just sit here on this rock, weave the honeysuckle crowns, and listen to the river. It's a lot cooler than on the porch. And, uh, I want to talk to you…"

I point at the dirt, not wanting to get my clothes dirty.

"Not a problem. I'll be a modern-day Sir Walter Raleigh. Only, you're a princess, not a queen," he teases, unbuttoning his shirt. He carefully places it on the ground for me to sit on. Scooping my skirt, I gingerly sit and stare at the water, willing my heart to slow down and trying to shut out the memories.

Caleb sits beside me and hands me one of the fragrant vines he's pulled. "Feeling better?"

I shrug.

"My dad says it's best to face your fears head-on," he comments. "You've never told me what happened to you, but I know it was bad. I remember the bruises on your neck and your eyes being all bloodshot…"

I move to get up. I will *never* discuss this.

He catches my hand. "No, please—don't leave. I'm just trying to explain that I know how it feels to be terrified. When I have an asthma attack and can't catch my breath, it's really scary until my inhaler works. My heart pounds, and it feels like I'm trying to suck air through a clogged straw. But it's *less* scary when someone is there with me, talking to me."

I stare at the water, focusing on the way it flows around the rocks and how the color changes from the center to the bank.

My hands tremble as memories of dark, still water surface.

Caleb hands me a vine. "Don't think about bad stuff. Make another honeysuckle crown. Keep busy, and I'll tell you why I love the water."

I glance over at him and start weaving the honeysuckles together. They smell heavenly.

"Water is cleansing and is the basis for all life. Nothing quenches thirst like water. I sneak down to the river without my mom knowing, because she worries too much. I do my best thinking when I'm floating and staring at the sky. My dad baptized me in this river." He picks up a rock and skims it across the water, making it jump three times before sinking.

"He'd baptize you, too, if you wanted. If you were to be baptized, I think my mom would come around and not be so adamant that we not date."

The trees rustle, issuing a warning. I shake my head. I've had enough, and my stomach's hurting just thinking about being in that water. I stand up, ready to leave.

"Please don't go. I love you, Skylar. I love you no matter what, even if you never get baptized—oh, uh…" His eyes widen, and his cheeks turn beet red. He jumps to his feet, looking at the ground, clearly embarrassed about something. "Skylar, I think you're right. We need to go home."

I stomp my foot, not understanding this turn in his attitude.

"It's okay. What's happening is natural. You're a girl…" He points at the back of my skirt.

Twisting it around to the front, I see the blood. *Of all the times for me to have my first cycle…* Humiliation burns my cheeks. Mortified, I run up the mountain but trip on a root and tumble back down. Desperate, I reach for a branch but miss.

"Skylar!" Caleb runs toward me as I fall into the water.

My past mingles with the present.

JED

I don't know what's making that racket downriver, but it isn't helping our luck fishing.

"I'm gonna go check it out. Watch my pole," I tell Darrell as

I head downstream. Rounding the curve, I see Caleb on his knees on the bank of the river. *What the hell is he doing? Praying?* My annoyance turns to concern when I realize he's hovering over Sky. *What are they doing here? She's terrified of water...*

I take off at a run through the underbrush. I don't think my feet even touch the ground as fear propels me forward. Caleb looks up when he hears me approach. Behind his crooked glasses, his eyes are red, and he's blubbering like he's lost his best friend. *Is she dead?*

My heart sinks to the pit of my stomach, and I double my effort to get there even faster, ignoring the branches slapping my face and the thorns ripping my flesh and clothes. I drop to my knees beside them. I can't make out what Caleb's saying for the roaring in my head. I grab her from him, more scared than I've ever been in my life.

"Hey…hey, Princess. It's me, Jed. You okay?" I manage to gasp, brushing the hair off her ice-cold face.

Her eyes flutter open, but they're so dilated I can barely see the blue rim of her irises.

"What the hell happened? Why are you two here?" I ask Caleb, who's sniffling. I start rubbing Skylar's arms, trying to get some circulation going in her limbs. She's so stiff I'm almost afraid I'm going to break her.

"I-I didn't hurt her. She slipped down the hill and went face-first into the water."

"I don't know what's going on, but I'm taking her home."

Darrell comes barreling through the woods toward us.

"What happened?" he asks, panting.

"That's the million-dollar question," I say, rising to my feet with Sky in my arms.

"Nothing," Caleb says. "I mean, she fell…"

Darrell's eyes narrow, and he points. "Blood."

I lower her to her feet and see a faint bloodstain on her torn skirt. I look at Caleb and notice he isn't wearing a shirt...

I see red just before my temper explodes like dynamite. "Darrell, take Sky home."

Princess is shaking her head, but I'm not interested in explanations.

Just retribution.

I take off after Caleb, who's running for his life.

SKYLAR

Sitting on the balcony porch swing, I hear the ribbons on the maypole flutter, and by the front porchlight, I see the unlit bonfire pyre. The party was canceled. And it's my fault. Downstairs, Pastor Buzbee and Queenie are in a serious discussion, and Mrs. Buzbee is still crying.

Jed sits beside me, openly smoking a cigarette, his leg bouncing with nervousness. Usually, he only smokes out in the woods. Queenie and I both know he does it because his clothes stink. However, I don't think she'll fuss at him tonight. There are more serious things going on.

I'm scared. Before Queenie sent us upstairs, Pastor Buzbee and Mrs. Buzbee arrived, and Caleb's mama wants Jed to go to jail. I wrap my arms around Jed, burying my face in his shoulder, scared to let him go.

"It isn't your fault, Princess."

The door closes, and it's an ominous sound. Silently we watch the Buzbees drive away.

"Jedidiah," Queenie calls. "Come downstairs."

His hand trembles as he stubs out the cigarette. Pressing a kiss on top of my head, he gets up and leaves.

CHAPTER FIVE

2019, TEN YEARS LATER
SKYLAR

THE HOUSE CREAKS and groans as the storm rages outside. Through the back window, lightning flashes across the ominous sky, followed by an instantaneous crack of thunder. I jump, nearly tripping over the black cat weaving in and out of my legs. A scratching noise sounds like an army of rats is invading, but it's only the trees brushing the house, propelled by the howling wind. I shiver and pick up Widdershins, stroking his soft black fur. He chirps and purrs his appreciation.

"You should be like a tree, Skylar," Queenie says from the kitchen table behind me. "Don't fight the storm. Bend with it, and you'll be all right."

Unless the storm topples you to the ground… I turn away from the window, keeping my thoughts to myself like I always do.

Collapsing into the kitchen chair across from Queenie, I watch the candle flame flicker. This old house needs weatherizing, along with updating, but Queenie refuses. She says it's a waste of money. Even though she has money, she's become more paranoid the last couple of months. She no longer puts it in the bank, choosing to have me or Darrell bury it out back. Even Pastor Buzbee seems worried. At her seventy-sixth birthday party last month, he mentioned his concern about her rapidly deteriorating memory and irrational moods.

She shuffles the cards like a casino dealer as another boom of thunder rattles the potted plants on the windowsill. I sigh, wishing the lights would come back on. No one should be up at four in the morning, especially without coffee.

Queenie gasps, and I turn my attention to the cards spread across the table. She's been throwing cards to pass the time. Queenie uses a regular deck. Personally, I prefer my brightly colored tarot cards that visually tell a story. On the table is a past-present-future spread. The indicator card is a Jack of Clubs, and it's placed above the Ace of Spades, Five of Spades, and Ten of Spades. These cards represent change, fear, and grief. It's an unpleasant reading, full of darkness.

Queenie drops the cards, visibly shaken. "What's that fool boy gotten into?" she mutters.

I bite my lip, worried. *Jed.* My mind is already racing, trying to figure out what I can do to protect him.

After a moment she clears her throat, back to her no-nonsense self. She gathers the cards, but her trembling hands speak volumes. She pulls her faded blue robe tight over her thin shoulders.

She's as concerned as I am.

"Not that Jedidiah would ever call and let us know anything. You can't fix stubbornness." Leveling her gaze with mine, she points at me. "No interfering, missy. You know we don't do that."

I nod. Since I've lived here, I've never lied to Queenie. But I do so now, crossing my fingers under the table.

SKYLAR

The storm moved on in the middle of the day, and after lunch and her nap, Queenie insisted we go visit an old friend to deliver some honey. Despite my urging her to leave while it was still light out, Queenie accepted the invitation to stay for supper. Autumn's here now, and while the night is warm, the days are getting shorter and shorter.

Now Queenie and I are winding down a steep mountain road as we finally head home, and I press my right foot into the floorboard, as if I could magically brake the car from the passenger seat. Her mental acuity has faded this evening, as it often does after sunset. When this happens, she gets even more cantankerous than usual, due to her deep-rooted fears about her fading memory. It's rumored her mama went crazy right before she died at the ripe old age of ninety-nine.

"When did this road get so hard to navigate?" Queenie mutters.

The car jolts as she hits a pothole the size of a possum, reinforcing our precarious situation. I motion for her to turn on her bright lights, but she pushes my hand away.

My mind wandered all day, worrying about Jed and the reading this morning. And because I was too preoccupied to monitor Queenie's erratic driving on the way back home, we're lost. Concerned for our safety, I visualize a protective shield around the car. It wouldn't take much for us to run off the road and flip down the mountainside.

I motion for Queenie to pull over, but she refuses, slapping my hand away. Luckily, her bad leg isn't the one on the gas pedal. With her slower reflexes, I pray we don't have to stop suddenly. She's driving ten miles per hour, so it really isn't *much* of a concern.

"Hands off the driver, Charlotte," Queenie says.

I sigh. Although I've felt her dead daughter's presence at home, she *isn't* in this car. Queenie slows until we're barely moving. Bright lights flash behind us, but that doesn't faze her in the least. The driver zips around us, leaning on the horn.

"Carelessness!" She points her finger at the disappearing vehicle, and we swerve onto the shoulder.

Closing my eyes, I send a prayer to *whomever* is listening and grip the Lordy bar. That's the name Jed gave the handle above the passenger seat window when Queenie was teaching him to drive. He'd drive so fast she'd grab it and scream, "Oh Lordy!" Jed's driving was more fun than any ride at the state fair. He used to look at me in the rearview mirror and wink, and I'd grin back.

I miss him so much it hurts, and after the reading this morning, uneasiness layers onto my wistfulness like the fog hovering in the valley.

"I better not ever catch you driving like that, young lady." Queenie clicks her tongue against her teeth. Her admonishment snaps me back to the present.

I have no idea if she's talking to me or if she still thinks I'm Charlotte. I never bothered to get my driver's license, but nobody seems to care. It's rare I get behind the wheel; Queenie has Darrell do most of her errands. Before he left for the army, Jed took me out in a field and taught me the rudiments of driving while he imparted all kinds of words of wisdom on how to survive living with Queenie.

Queenie once again veers off the road, and I grab the Lordy bar as she corrects her steering. Blue lights flash behind us, and I offer a silent thank-you. Swearing under her breath, Queenie pulls over, cuts the engine, and waits, tapping her thumbs against the steering wheel. Sheriff Rogers approaches with his son, Kip, who is also his deputy.

"What do you want?" Queenie asks sharply.

Sheriff Rogers shines his flashlight into the car and peers at us. "Evenin', Mrs. Jackson, Skylar. Everything okay?"

"Of course everything's okay. We're just out...going..." Queenie pauses and huffs her annoyance. "Where were we going, Skylar? Oh, wait. *Home.* We're going home. Now get that light out of my eyes, you idgit."

The sheriff moves the light to my face. I bite my lip and barely shake my head, silently beseeching him for help.

"I see." He snaps off the flashlight, and the tension eases from my shoulders. Everybody around here knows about Queenie's deteriorating mind.

"Home sounds like a right good place to be on a night like this," he continues. "It's kinda foggy on these roads and a bit dangerous. Why don't you let me drive you home, Mrs. Jackson? Kip can follow to give me a lift back."

"You just want to date my daughter. You don't fool me for one minute. Charlotte is *not* interested in you."

"Yes, ma'am. I understand. But I'd sure like a piece of your famous blueberry cake. You know, the one you shoulda won a blue ribbon for a few years back. I'm not sayin' Mrs. Buzbee's carrot cake ain't good; I'm just partial to yours. Please, Mrs. Jackson? Skylar can ride in the back seat or with Kip."

Queenie harrumphs. "That woman bribed the judges. That ribbon should've been mine. Get in." The sheriff gently helps her around to the passenger's seat, not bothering to get her walker from the back. I shake my head. Mrs. Buzbee sends her disgusting carrot cake over every week with Pastor Buzbee. Queenie would never admit it, but she loves it. However, we end up throwing most of it away since she's the only one who eats it.

I'm grateful the sheriff understands our predicament, but there's no way I'm getting in a car with Kip. He never looks me in the face, choosing to always stare at my breasts. I ignore the creep motioning me to the squad car and move to our backseat. Tonight's incident firms my decision. I can't deal with Queenie by myself for much longer. It's time I summon Jed home. Maybe doing so will keep him from whatever trouble awaits him in the future.

Thankfully, Queenie forgets about the nonexistent blueberry cake by the time we arrive at the house. She hasn't cooked in over a year. She's combative and irritable, and once the sheriff leaves, it takes me an hour to finally get her settled in bed.

As soon as her sleeping pill kicks in, I sneak into the kitchen. Looking in Queenie's supply cabinet, I choose the Come to Me oil. Shoving my guilt aside, I grab it and run upstairs, stepping light to the right. On my bedside table, I place my favorite picture of Jed, a button from one of his old shirts, and a candlestick. Using a straight pin, I carve his name into a brown candle and smear it with a smidge of oil. I light the candle and circle the flame with my hands three times, silently entreating, *Come home safe…*

SKYLAR

Two days later, Queenie peers into the fragile teacup. Her white brows knit together. "I'm afraid our nice, quiet life is about to be turned on end."

It's been unseasonably warm this week, but today a breeze ruffles the curtains. The cooler air has a different feel to it this morning, one of anticipation and hope. *He's coming!* I refrain from doing a happy dance. Queenie can't know about my summoning spell.

She pulls off her bright pink reading glasses, and her lips flatten. "It seems Jedidiah will be here soon. I don't know why. It isn't like he's given a gnat's breath of concern about us since he left home. I never should've put that boy down as next of kin on those forms at that quack doctor's office. It's all a conspiracy to put me in the home. I'm surprised the little ingrate even remembers where we live."

I smile. "That boy" is now twenty-eight, and she still loves him fiercely.

"Ma'am?" Darrell appears in the doorway, cap in hand, his dark, enigmatic eyes looking everywhere but at me. Spit sparkles on his lower lip. Some things never change. Although he's never been anything but polite and helpful, something about him continues to unnerve me. It isn't the fact he won't look me in the eye—that's normal. It's because I can't read him. Therefore, I don't fully trust him. His aura is sullied and full of secrets.

"Yes, come in and wipe your mouth. What do you want?" Queenie asks.

He pulls the blue bandana out of his back pocket and mops his lips. "I finished the yard work, ma'am. Do you have the grocery list ready?"

"What yard work?"

"Raking and mulching. I've already had the soil tested and amended with compost. There's gonna be a frost on the pumpkin soon, Mrs. Jackson."

"Frost on the pumpkin? What month is this?" She fumbles in her purse and pulls out last year's calendar.

"October, ma'am." Darrell glances my way before lowering his eyes back to the floor.

Ignoring her harmless nattering, I pull a smooth pebble from my pocket, rubbing it with my thumb until my heart quits pounding like a jackhammer. Ten years ago, Jed slung his duffel on his shoulder. A breeze mussed his brown hair, and he looked both scared and excited. Handing me the blue lace agate, he said, *"Here ya go, Princess. I know you believe in this abracadabra stuff. This is a magic stone. Rub it when you feel stressed, and it'll make the scary thoughts and feelings go away."* He then kissed my forehead and whispered, *"Mind Queenie, even if she is a crazy old bat."*

I always carry the rock with me. It's as important as the dragonfly pendant I wear.

I hand Darrell his check along with some cash and the list. He gives a curt nod and leaves as quietly as he crept in. When Queenie refuses more tea, I glance at her cup and confirm her reading. The doctor's office didn't contact Jed—that's just Queenie's paranoia—but I hope she doesn't see that I did a summoning spell.

Widdershins jumps in her lap, demanding attention by butting her with his head.

"The doctors told me that boy isn't right in the head after serving overseas. I bet he thinks I'm dying and this is his golden opportunity to get his hands on my money. Well, I've got news for Jedidiah Lafayette Jackson. I'm not so near death as he hopes." She sniffs with righteous indignation and sits up straighter. "And I'm certainly not so dotty that I can't handle my own affairs."

The cat meows, trying to divert her attention back to what's important. I don't point out that Jed doesn't need her money. His trust fund makes him financially secure for the rest of his life.

Queenie's on a roll now. "Maybe that nosy Pastor Buzbee called Jedidiah. See if I ever invite him back over for tea to discuss diversity in beliefs. No, sirree. Always telling me *I* need Jesus. Why, I've known Jesus longer than that man's been alive. And the nerve of him suggesting I need to be in an old folks' home. Who would take care of you? Jesus? I don't see his Lord and Savior paying the bills. I'm saner than these idiots who believe everything the government tells them.

"That son of his—what's his name? Is he ever gonna propose?" She pauses a moment. "*Caleb.* That's his name. He needs to grow a backbone and just go ahead and marry you. Surely he realizes his mama will never accept you into the family. She's the worst kind of hypocrite and always has been. But he's a grown man and needs to stand on his own two feet."

I hide my smile. Queenie acts tough, but she's a marshmallow on the inside. Look between the pages of both her Bible and grimoire and you'll find drawings, letters, pictures, and pressed flowers from Jed and me. And she's fond of both Pastor Buzbee *and* Caleb. But she's right…Caleb's mother dislikes me intensely. Though she's never been anything but polite to me, it's just a feeling I get. Her smile is never sincere. Besides, I'm in no hurry to get married. Queenie needs me.

Anyway, Caleb just recently moved back to the area, and we're rekindling our friendship slowly. He does everything carefully and methodically. He hasn't brought up a future together since the disastrous day ten years ago that changed everything. We just live in the moment and enjoy one another's company.

Appearing lost, Queenie scans the room as if she hasn't lived here all of her life. This vacant look of hers scares me. I'm terrified there will come a day when she won't come back from the distant world of the ancestors. Their whispers from the past draw her more and more frequently from the here and now.

But after a moment, she picks up her knitting and smiles, her eyes now clearer and more focused. Her momentary brain fog has lifted. Widdershins bats at the knitting needles and yarn, but she ignores him and continues fussing.

"I have no idea when Jedidiah will arrive. He refuses to use his phone, which surprises me considering the number of girlie magazines I used to find under his mattress. I'd think that sexy-texting business would be right up his alley."

Tickled, I accidentally snort tea up my nose. Queenie hands me a used tissue, which I stuff in my pocket, preferring my sleeve. We wouldn't be able to receive a text even if Jed sent one, as we only have an old-fashioned landline. Caleb has suggested more than once that I get a cell phone, but any time I've broached the subject with Queenie, she says it's an unnecessary expense and that technology squashes creativity.

"It's chilly in here. Is the heat on? Close that window, girl. Are you trying to kill me? Have you turned the soup down to simmer? I'm sure that rascal will show up hungry. That boy's never missed a meal in his life. It's all the bloody government's fault…"

I nod, closing the window. Moving the cat, I tuck Queenie's blanket around her lap. She reaches beside her and conceals her pistol underneath it. I leave it alone. I'm terrified of guns, but I've hidden the bullets. If the empty gun makes her feel safer, so be it.

"If the president would quit catering to big business…"

I nod, prepared for the daily rant about the evils of big government and how her fifth great-grandfather fought to free us from King George's tyranny. She goes on for twenty minutes as I mentally prepare the menu for when Jed arrives.

"Skylar, are you paying attention?"

Skylar. Sometimes I wish someone would call me by my real name. But that girl only exists in my occasional nightmares. Only her ghost remains, a body with no soul.

I shake my head and avert my eyes. I hate disappointing Queenie. Her bony hand captures mine, giving it a gentle squeeze. I never disagree with her because I love this woman more than life itself. Her perceived eccentricity has been a small price to pay for the love and security she's given me. Almost twenty years ago, Guinevere Lafayette Jackson gave a scared, broken girl a chance to find at least a modicum of peace in the mountains of North Carolina.

"Honey, look at me."

I pull my gaze to hers, ignoring the distant inner voice from my past—the one that screams, *"Don't look at me. Quit fuckin' lookin' at me."* Queenie smiles, and her rheumy blue eyes crinkle in her lined face. The vague memory of dark, empty eyes filled with hate recedes.

She pats my hand. "It's fine, dear. I always assume your silence signals agreement with my opinions. It's why I love you like a grandchild. Better, actually. You know you're my favorite. You don't mind the nattering of a foolish old woman."

I smile, knowing both statements are false. She's anything but a fool, and before he left, I heard her tell Jedidiah he was her favorite, too. Flipping on the old television, she begins barking answers back at her favorite game show. The soup is already simmering in the kitchen, so I run upstairs to prepare Jed's room.

She might say she's angry with him, but I know otherwise. His picture remains by her bedside, and every night she kisses her fingers and touches it. Personally, I hate that photo of the boy in green fatigues, his wavy brown hair shorn in an army buzz cut. His green-gray eyes appear lifeless and resigned. It's a look of mere existence, and not at all how I remember him.

When I think about Jed—which is often—I remember the carefree boy who'd rather be outside climbing trees than in the house, the hellion who'd run circles around Queenie and never think twice about it, always pushing the boundaries. *My* favorite picture of Jed is the one I used to summon him home. In the photo, he's pushing me in the old swing. I'm high in the air, eyes wide and a little terrified, but his head is thrown back, and he's laughing. After he left, it was his deep, robust laugh I missed most.

The floorboards creak as I enter his room, not an uncommon occurrence in this old house. I remove the dustcovers and get busy cleaning. I used to envy him for having this turret room. It reminded me of Rapunzel's castle. Sunlight beams through the leaded windows, adding warmth to the pale blue ceiling painted with puffy white clouds. He inherited his Aunt Charlotte's room after his parents died. The pain and suffering we'd both endured prior to coming to Queenie's is what bonded us. We understood fear and feelings of abandonment. So did Queenie, since she'd lost her husband and both children. It's what made us all family.

In contrast, my cozy bedroom on the third floor has a low, slanted ceiling. I've decorated it with treasures I've found in the attic. At night, Jed and I used to slip out my window to sit on the roof so he could sneak a smoke. To keep me from tattling, he'd bribe me with stories. My favorite was when he told me I was a princess in hiding to keep the evil troll from finding me. He always made himself the fearless prince. Goose bumps would dance across my skin whenever he told that story. It's funny how there's always truth in fiction.

These days the stories persist in my dreams, and in them my prince has wavy brown hair, a soft southern drawl, and eyes the color of moss on river rocks.

CHAPTER SIX

SKYLAR

I SIT AT Queenie's feet with my arms wrapped around my knees as she reads to me. She's done this almost every night since I came to live here. I think, in some ways, she's never acknowledged that I've grown up, but I don't mind. We're in the middle of the old fairy-tale book she gave me on my first so-called birthday at her house. The pages are now yellowed and brittle because the book was hers when she was a little girl. I've always loved the colorful, delicate painted illustrations. Tonight, she's reading one of my favorites, "Beauty and the Beast."

Queenie finishes the story, and I help her into bed, careful to place her gun in the nightstand. Once she's settled, I do my nightly check to make sure the doors are locked and the protective key spells are in place, and I prepare the coffee pot for tomorrow. Nervous excitement has me scrubbing an already clean counter. *Will Jed have changed much?* I hope his hair has grown out some. *What if he has a girlfriend? What if he's married?* That last thought dampens my enthusiasm, but I chide myself for being a selfish girl. He's a grown man. It's natural that he might have a girlfriend or a wife.

And I have Caleb. Since he moved back home, he calls or sees me every day. It's nice…but I don't know exactly what path our renewed friendship is going to take.

Leaving the kitchen, I pause outside Queenie's door and listen. Reassured by her soft snores, I quietly climb the stairs—stepping right—with Widdershins following on my heels. One of the reasons Queenie put me on the third floor is there's no bathtub in this bathroom. When I first arrived here, I was terrified of bathing, but with her reassurance and patience, showering became easier. However, to this day, being submerged in water is unthinkable for me. Finishing my shower, I slip into my simple cotton gown, avoiding the mirror. Some habits have been harder to break.

Ugly, hateful girl.

I snap off the light, and the negative thought disappears. Kneeling beside my bed, I pull out my duct-taped cigar box. Darrell gave it to me not long after he'd arrived. It's my nightly ritual to look inside and take mental inventory of all my favorite possessions. I remove the dragonfly necklace Queenie gave me from my neck and place it in the box beside Jed's old blue car and the one-eared black cat, various crystals, a worn deck of tarot cards, a crow's feather, and my treasured Winnie-the-Pooh figures that Jed whittled for me. The newest item is a seashell Caleb brought me from the beach. He told me the ocean is beautiful and you can taste the salt in the air. He wants to take me there someday, and I long to see it, provided I don't have to go in. These trinkets would mean nothing to anyone else, but to me, they're treasures. I carefully repack the box and slip it back under my mattress for safekeeping.

Wide awake, I lie down and stare at the dragonfly night-light. *Something's wrong.* I can feel it. Jed should've been here by now. A knot of worry and anticipation twists my stomach. How will Jed's visit alter our lives? Will he be upset by the changes in Queenie? In me? Will he and Queenie still fuss and fight?

Death has no power over me, but anger unsettles and upsets

me. With Queenie's paranoia growing each day, I pray I didn't make a mistake summoning him. Their relationship has always been like oil and vinegar. But I need help—she's deteriorating faster than she should, and I don't understand why. I need Jed to get things back to normal. I don't have any friends except Caleb to ask for help; I hate to be a bother. Besides, Queenie's always wanted us to be self-sufficient.

Living where we do, it's a necessity. Only the trees really know our business. The busybody neighbors in the area just think they do, and the closest small town is fifteen miles from here. Caleb has told me about life in a big city, and while it sounds interesting, I don't think I'd fit in with the hustle and bustle.

Those who don't know me would probably think my life is boring living on the mountain.

Those who fear my special abilities would say it's extraordinary.

I like to think of it as monotony with a touch of idiosyncrasy. And that works fine for me. I had enough of the unexpected in my life a long time ago.

Realizing sleep isn't going to happen anytime soon, I sneak downstairs to the second-floor balcony, careful to avoid the squeaky step. Queenie's sleeping medication makes her almost comatose, but I don't want to risk waking her.

Autumn once again teases. The night air is crisp after the unexpected warm spell. I rub the chill bumps on my arms, regretting not wearing my robe and slippers. Luckily, I keep a quilt out here. The moon is almost full, but mostly hidden behind the trees.

The hair on the back of my neck rises, but before I can react, a large hand covers my mouth, snapping my head back. I dig my nails into the arm holding the cold blade pressed to my throat.

"Don't move and don't scream or I'll kill you. Nod if you understand." The whispered warning freezes me in place as I recall another threat in the middle of the night…

The man is standing so close his facial hair tickles my neck. He smells of clean air, alcohol, woods, and raw masculinity. Something's not quite right, but familiarity calms my fear, replacing it with annoyance. *Jed.*

I try motioning to signal I won't speak.

"Stop," he hisses, squeezing my cheeks tighter.

I wince. This is going too far. Attempting to elbow him, I fight to get free, clawing at his arm and kicking his shin.

"Shit," he grunts.

The hand covering my mouth moves over my nose, too. Sheer panic makes me struggle harder, to no avail. He's too strong. I'm not even in a position where I can knee him, and my bare foot throbs from stomping on his hard boot.

"Goddammit, follow directions and you won't get hurt. If you understand, *answer me with a nod.* If you don't, I'll have no qualms about slitting your throat."

I stop fighting. *Tobacco.* That's what's missing—the smell of cigarettes. The knife presses harder.

"Nod if you understand."

The calmness of his voice unnerves me more than the blade at my throat. True fear slithers through my veins. He's a trained killer. Queenie said he went crazy after returning from serving overseas.

But Jed knows me.

Obviously, I no longer know him.

66

JED

My inebriated fog lifts slowly as my head pounds in time with my heart. The woman in my arms stops struggling, and I squelch my rising panic. *What have I done?* I'll be lucky not to end up in jail for assault and battery and whatever other charges she throws at me. *Who the hell is she?* Damn, I wish I hadn't finished that flask. I know better; I have multiple scars to prove it.

Drinking and PTSD don't mix.

Like a dumbass, I ran out of gas and ended up hiking the last few miles to Queenie's. Not wanting to listen to my grandmother rant about me showing up so late, I climbed the rose trellis to sleep on the porch. Exhausted and startled awake, I've overreacted, and my army survival skills kicked in full throttle.

My heart's still hammering like a piston in overdrive as I suppress the vivid, detailed memories of being ambushed. Forcing air into my lungs, I take a deep breath and plan my next move. With one hand, I sheath my knife, keeping a tight grip over her mouth. I know I should let her go, but if she screams, I'm toast. Queenie will likely call the cops just for disturbing her sleep. Still holding my hand over the young woman's mouth, I turn her to face me. Hopefully, intimidation will keep her silent. I'm still trying to figure out who Queenie's got staying with her aside from Princess.

"I'm going to remove my hand. Promise me you're not going to scream. Nod if you understand."

She nods, and I slowly remove my hand, ready to stifle her if necessary. She jerks away and slaps my face. *Hard.*

I rub my jaw, glaring at her, trying to make out her features without the benefit of any light. First thing on the to-do list:

have a dusk-to-dawn light installed out here. Her ragged breathing matches mine as she crosses her arms, tapping one foot with what can only be perceived as annoyance. *Who is she? Only Queenie and Sky should be here...*

Holy shit. "Princess?"

She strikes a match and lights a candle. The air is infused with some abhorrent smell, probably one of Queenie's voodoo concoctions. It provides just enough light for me to see Sky throw out her arms, palms up, in an exaggerated what-the-hell motion. Before I can react, she circles her finger next to her temple in the universal *crazy* sign.

I wince. Truth hurts. Glancing around, I realize nothing's changed except the girl in front of me. The porch ceiling is still painted haint blue, as are the shutters and doors to this mausoleum. The weathered siding needs a fresh coat of white paint, and the swing's cushion and quilt are frayed.

"Sky, listen to me—"

She puts her finger to her lips, blows out the candle, and slips inside the house. Her gown whips as she scurries toward that god-awful turret room.

Fast on her heels, I desperately whisper, "No, wait. Stop."

Ignoring me, she flicks on the light.

Jesus H. Christ. I'm in a fuckin' time warp. My room's reverted back to a teenaged girl's bedroom from another era. My posters and stolen road signs are gone. Instead, staring at me from over the antique mahogany bed are those piss-poor replicas of *Pinkie* and *The Blue Boy*. On the nightstand is the hobnailed glass lamp with its hideous lace shade. My crazy grandmother always wanted this room kept as a shrine to Charlotte, the aunt I never knew. We had countless arguments about the décor. It's one of the reasons I always preferred being outdoors, and in nice weather I slept in a hammock I'd strung up on the porch.

They say you can't go home again. Staring at this cloying

room, I understand why.

Sky points toward the bed, but I give it only a cursory glance. I'm too busy staring at the changes in my little shadow. She's no longer the scrawny, pigtailed brat who used to follow me everywhere. Before me stands a beautiful young woman with tangled blond hair and—judging by the silhouette behind her gown—curves in all the right places. She has to be, what? Twenty-four now?

For a split second she looks me in the eye before her long lashes lower over her pink cheeks. She's never liked making eye contact, and heaviness settles in my chest. I've seen that same haunted expression innumerable times overseas. It's the knowing look of an old soul, someone who knows life is not kind, much less fair.

After I left here and went to that godforsaken beige land on behalf of Uncle Sam, I often looked up at the blue sky, missing Princess and Queenie. But my homesickness passed, and the longer I stayed, more and more of it was replaced by an overwhelming black depression. Maybe that's why I've come home to Appalachia. I've missed the color of life.

Skylar shifts and sighs.

Crap, I've zoned out again.

Her lips have settled into a straight line, and she folds her arms under the breasts she didn't have ten years ago. The material stretches tight, displaying hard nipples. I react like any normal male and stare a minute longer than society would deem proper, then immediately chastise myself.

I pull my gaze from her heaving chest to her dilated eyes, and a darker pink infuses her cheeks. The energy between us is akin to what I used to feel as a sniper zeroing in on my target. I'm the hunter; she's the prey. Her throat bobbles, and she steps back.

For God's sake, this is Skylar. She's like a sister! I don't want her scared of me. I throw my hands out where she can see them. "Shhh." *What the fuck, dumbass?* Why am I telling a girl who never speaks to shush? I really need to sober up. "I'm sorry. I promise, I'm not going to hurt you."

She raises one skeptical eyebrow and points to the knife strapped at my waist.

"Look, you caught me unaware, and I overreacted. Don't tell, and I promise, everything will be okay." I speak low, using as soothing a voice as I can manage. If she bolts or does anything to wake Queenie, there'll be hell to pay. And, quite frankly, I'm flat broke in the give-a-shit department.

"Cat still got your tongue?" I revert to my role as her pseudo-sibling, the obnoxious older brother. Maybe it will set her mind at ease in some backassward way. Of course, I wouldn't blame her if it doesn't. After all, I've just held a knife to her throat and threatened to kill her.

Hell, I don't even trust myself.

As far as I know, no one's ever figured out exactly what happened to Skylar before she came to live with us, but it was traumatic. Over the years, the docs always said there was no physical reason why Skylar couldn't speak, and they encouraged psychiatric treatment. My crazy-ass grandmother's philosophy was that Sky would speak when she damn well wanted to. I reckon she's never wanted to. Her silence used to piss me off as a kid, and I'd torment the hell out of her, but she's never uttered a word that I know of, except in her nightmares.

She bites her lip to keep from smiling and nods, looking at the floor again and curling those cute polished toes.

"Jesus. I'm such an idiot."

She snickers and nods, peeking at me through her long bangs.

"You didn't have to agree so readily," I grumble, tweaking her nose. "Forgive me?"

A hint of a smile plays at the corner of her mouth. She shrugs. I wink at her, and the corners lift more.

Desperate times call for desperate measures. It's time to lay it on thick. Dramatically, I drop to my knees and attempt a repentant look. "Please, Princess, have mercy on me. You *know* I'll never hear the end of this from Queenie. Spare me, most merciful one. My fate rests in your hands."

She's grinning now, and her shoulders shake with that eerie, silent laugh of hers.

Encouraged, I continue my over-the-top apology. "Not that I'd blame you for telling on me, but maybe we can strike a deal?"

One eyebrow shoots up, and she leans forward, looking interested.

I pull out the big gun, the one that worked when she was a kid. "I'll treat you to a hot fudge sundae at the Snack Shack. It's still there, right?"

She nods and pantomimes locking her lips and tossing the key before clasping my hand in a firm handshake. Then we fist bump and link pinkies. This routine from our childhood makes me chuckle.

I stand, and my grin fades as I stare at her, still amazed by the changes in her appearance. "My, my, when did you grow up?" *Fuck, did I just say that out loud? Get your shit together, Jedidiah Jackass.* Nervous, I run a hand through my hair, dislodging the knot I've got it in. It tumbles around my face. Running my fingers through it, I redo it into a ponytail.

Sky backs into a shadow, pretends to drive a car, and points at me.

"I ran outta gas about six miles down the road. I cut through the woods to get here. That's why I had the knife. The underbrush around here is terrible."

She motions telephoning.

"And wake the Queen? Oh hell no."

I'm rusty on finger spelling, but I'm ninety-nine percent sure she just called me a dumbass.

I follow her out the door of my bedroom, but she stops in her tracks, and I damn near run into her. She peers at me, her eyes wide. I flip off the light. Her breath hitches, and its warmth skitters across the bottom of my throat.

"I hate that room," I whisper. "I'll sleep outside."

She shakes her head and forcefully pushes me aside, flipping the light back on. With a stomp of one bare foot, she points at the bed, glaring. When I don't move, she crosses her arms again.

"I told you, I'm not sleeping in here. I'll see you in the morning." I move to exit the room but pause beside her. "I'll be on the porch. Don't sneak up on me. Make noise, okay?"

She scrunches her eyes closed, covers her ears, and pretends to scream. Of course, not a sound leaves her mouth. It never does when she's conscious.

I pull her hair, and her eyes snap open. "Funny girl." Grinning, I give her a sharp salute before heading out.

CHAPTER SEVEN

SKYLAR

I TIPTOE DOWNSTAIRS, speeding past the second-floor landing. I need caffeine and lots of it before dealing with Jed and Queenie. After he refused to sleep in the house, I stayed awake all night, fighting the memories the knife incident invoked and knowing if I slept, I'd be plagued by nightmares. Or maybe sleep eluded me because of the look on Jed's face when he stared at me, like he was ravenous for that sundae he promised.

Stopping at Queenie's room, I pause and listen. Soft, rhythmic snores filter through the closed door. With luck, I should be able to enjoy my morning coffee before helping her bathe.

"Didn't I tell you to make noise?" a deep voice rumbles behind me.

I jump, plastering myself against the door, my heart beating so fast I feel dizzy. *How does he do that? I didn't even hear him.* This isn't like me to be caught off guard. I need to cleanse my aura; obviously something has clouded my intuition.

Holding a coffee cup, Jed yawns and stretches. His long-sleeved T-shirt rises, showcasing a dark trail that disappears into his faded jeans. He's always been handsome, but now I have an awareness of him that feels primal. It's like a jump start to my system, and this powerful energy is new and exciting. My toes curl inside my slippers. He's wearing his hair pulled up in a *man bun*. I've never seen a guy wear his hair like that except on television. I find it strangely appealing, but I'll be interested in Queenie's reaction when she sees it *and* his beard.

The intensity of his gaze makes me want to squirm, but I remain still and sneak a peek at him from under my lashes. Hard lines now etch the corners of his beautiful eyes, whether from age, the elements, or a combination, I have no idea. He's always had an uncanny way of looking at me as if he knows my secrets.

"Coffee?" He raises his cup. Widdershins purrs and weaves through his legs. "A black cat. How cliché. When did you get it?"

I hold up two fingers and attempt to walk by him. His arm stretches out, blocking me. "What's the secret password?"

I look at him and mouth, *Asshole.*

He chuckles and drops his arm, allowing me to enter. "What time does Her Majesty get up?"

I hold up eight fingers.

"I hoped you'd be talking by now. Do you sign much?"

I sigh. I'm not used to so many questions, especially before my morning coffee. I shrug and hold up my finger and thumb to indicate a little. I don't do much formal sign language. There's never been a need for it since Queenie understands me. I mostly use a pad and pen to communicate with others.

He frowns. "Do you have a cell phone?"

I shake my head.

"What? You need one. What if you or Queenie needed something? At least you'd be able to text."

I roll my eyes. *Who does he think he is?* He hasn't been here for ten years, and he thinks he can just show up and boss me around like he knows what's best? Of course, he's not the first to suggest this. Caleb's been after me to get one, too. I shove away the niggling reminder that I'm the one who summoned Jed here precisely because I'm having problems dealing with Queenie. Pouring a cup of coffee, I add plenty of cream and sugar. Behind me, he laughs. I turn and raise a questioning eyebrow.

"Why don't you just drink milk or eat ice cream?" He refills his mug. He still drinks it black. I'm tall, but he makes me feel tiny in comparison. It isn't his size so much as his personality. He gulps the hot coffee as if it's a glass of water.

I put my cup down, motion eating, and point at him.

"Just coffee's fine." He pulls out a chair for me, and I sit, watching him.

He joins me and looks around the kitchen, shaking his head. "Some things never change."

I shrug and smile. He's right. The wallpaper hasn't changed since long before he and I moved here. Garish flowers are splashed across a dingy white background. The white steel cabinets are dented, and amber and cobalt liniment bottles line the counter. Darrell's offered to help me paint and put up new wallpaper, but Queenie refuses, thinking it too costly. The kitchen may be dated and cluttered, but it's full of light. The plants in the window and drying herbs are homey and comforting. Some of my happiest moments have occurred right here, helping Queenie cook or make an herbal remedy for a sick neighbor.

Jed and I sit in a companionable silence, letting the caffeine work its magic.

"Did she know I was coming?" He thumbs over the top of his mug, watching me.

I nod and motion that we read the tea leaves and the wind blew in a different direction.

It's his turn to roll his eyes.

"You know that's all crap, right? I mean, you're old enough

not to believe in fairy-tale magic anymore."

I point at him and do a wide sweep of the room with my arm. If it's crap, why is he here?

He snorts. "It's called coincidence. So, how is she?"

I motion a downward decline and then circle my temple with my index finger.

He nods. "And physically?"

I frown and signal a thumbs-down. I'm afraid he's in for quite a surprise when he sees her.

"Anyone ever check on her?"

I wrinkle my nose and shrug. People come here almost every day, but not necessarily to check on her. They come for readings, tinctures, and spells. But one regular visitor does seem to care for her, even if his wife doesn't. Folding my hands together as if praying, I stare up at the ceiling, trying to look pious.

His blank face tells me he doesn't understand. I repeat the praying sign and then tap my fingers together rapidly to signal talking.

"I don't understand."

I find a pad and pen and write, *Pastor Buzbee.*

He looks as if he smelled something bad. "Ugh. Pastor Pontificate? I hope Queenie still gives him theological hell."

My smile confirms it.

He chuckles. "Good. So, it's just you two?"

I write, *Darrell.*

"Dammit Darrell's still around?"

I nod.

"He needs to paint this house."

I nod and rub my fingers together.

"Queenie doesn't have the money to pay him?"

I shrug. She *has* the money. She doesn't want to *spend* it. Most of it is buried in the backyard under the garden bench.

To my surprise, Jed captures my hand in his. His hands are rough and work worn, unlike Caleb's. I notice the scars and dusting of fine hair across his tan knuckles. He gives my fingers a friendly squeeze. Out of habit, I try to pull away, but he holds tight.

"Hey, you." He lowers his head, attempting to make eye contact with me.

Reluctantly, because I know he won't give up, I peer at him, and he smiles. It's like the sun breaking through the clouds on a dreary winter day.

"Thank you."

I furrow my brow.

"For taking care of Queenie…" He breaks eye contact this time. Looking at the ceiling, his throat bobbles underneath the beard I wish he'd shave. "I appreciate it. If I were any kind of decent grandson, I would've been here—or at the very least checked in more often. I just…" His gaze sweeps the kitchen as he appears to struggle with his emotions. "Yet another failing," he murmurs more to himself than me.

With his shoulders sagging, he reminds me of a picture Queenie once showed me of Atlas holding the world on his back. Gone is the carefree mischief-maker I once knew. In his place is a man full of sorrow and guilt.

Jed's leg starts bouncing; he's ready to bolt. He's always been antsy, wanting more, searching for something. But this darkness I'm seeing in him is deeper, more disturbing than the restlessness he had as a teenager. Queenie used to caution him about thinking the grass is greener on the other side of the fence. He never was one to take her advice.

I've always been his complete opposite, and I sense that I still am. I'm the yin to his yang. I'm content with my life here. However lonely it's been the past few years, I can't imagine being anywhere else, even if it's confining at times.

On impulse, I bring his hand to my lips and kiss it. Embarrassed by my foolishness, I leap to my feet, using the pretense of wanting more coffee. I steal a look at him as I pour a refill. He stares at the table, looking lost in thought. Thankfully, Queenie's impatient bell ringing breaks the awkward moment.

JED

I've never been so thankful for my grandmother in my life. Sky leaves the room, and I shift, loosening my jeans, which feel a little tight at the moment. This new awareness of Princess as a woman kinda makes my skin crawl. We were raised like siblings. And yet nothing has felt more right in a long damn time. The incessant bell clanking stops, and I shake my head when Queenie berates Sky for being "slow as molasses in January."

I've missed my grandmother's bitching about as much as I miss my drill sergeant barking orders. I refill my coffee and start a fresh pot. Judging by the purple smudges under her eyes, Princess needs more than two cups. I stretch, cracking my neck and mentally preparing for the argument sure to follow when I tell Queenie I'm only here for a day or so.

It isn't just because I hate that damn turret room.

I don't like responsibility.

I don't like expectations.

I don't like surprises.

Actually, I don't like much of anything. The VA docs call it depression. I call it boredom and being fed up with life in general.

I'm not even really sure why I came back. A few days ago, I was sitting in a bar after work, nursing a beer, and that corny song about country roads taking you home started playing. The next day, I quit my job, collected my pay, and headed back to the Land of Sky. And here I am, in this run-down house, and it's like I've been whisked back ten years through a time tunnel.

Looking around at the perverse Victorian Halloween décor of the kitchen, I shudder. Pots of plants line the windowsill, but none are the recreational sort I like to use to mellow out. Witch bottles are suspended in the window, and other strange charms are nailed over the doorframe. On the wall is a cross, a medicine wheel, an om, and a star inside a crescent moon next to a Star of David. Queenie's always had a different approach to religion, a cover-all-the-bases mentality. We grew up singing gospel hymns, chanting Hindu mantras, praying the rosary, and saying the Kaddish. We've done drum circles and Samhain rituals.

It's all bullshit.

Skylar returns and gives me a tentative smile. She used to be all awkward arms and legs. Not any longer. Her coltish limbs now operate with an inherent grace. A memory of her standing on my feet as we danced in the old-fashioned parlor makes me smile.

What it would feel like to hold her in my arms, without a knife to her throat?

I give myself a mental shake. Where the hell did that come from?

Princess prepares a bowl of cereal for Queenie, her movements quiet and efficient. Watching her, a rare sense of peace settles over my restless spirit. I find myself immersed in the moment, enjoying just being here. My former therapist would shit rainbows if I told him I'd had an actual moment of tranquility.

Glancing over her shoulder, Skylar's eyes lock with mine,

and her warm smile seems to brighten the dingy, faded room. She turns back and finishes preparing the tray for Queenie.

It occurs to me that there are two things I *do* like:

Women who don't chatter.

And eyes the color of the Appalachian sky.

Skylar swings around and shoves the tray at me, ending my ridiculous musings. Like the princess I call her, she points an imperious finger toward Queenie's room. If my hands weren't full, I'd flip her one in return.

"Skylar! Where are you? Leaving me to starve to death…" The loud, clanging bell resumes, muffling Queenie's complaints.

So much for fucking peace.

"Thanks a lot," I mutter. "I guess it's true: payback's a bitch. I may have to renege on that sundae."

A careless shrug is her answer. I sidle up close and whisper, "Mmmm…hot, gooey chocolate melting over vanilla ice cream. Come on, you know you want it." I waggle my brows and thrust the tray toward her. She pushes me away and pours herself another cup of coffee. There's a definite smirk lingering on those full lips.

"Skylar!"

Resigned to my fate, I square my shoulders and make my way toward my grandmother's room, the china clinking with the silverware. I'd rather be on a ruck march into enemy territory; it'd be a hell of a lot easier.

"Good morning!" Shoving the door open with my hip, I take perverse pleasure when Queenie jumps and shrieks. Propped up against pillows in the massive four-poster bed, her lost-looking blue eyes widen in her creased, thin face. Her hair is now completely white and hangs in a messy braid over one shoulder with colorful ribbons woven in it. I'm a little taken aback. Despite Sky's warning, I wasn't expecting to find her looking so frail.

"Jumping Jehoshaphat, I know your evil plan, you scoundrel! You're trying to kill me," she gasps, clutching her chest. Her look darkens as she points a crooked, bony finger at me. "Well, it won't work, Jedidiah Lafayette Jackson. I knew you were coming. And you're not getting my money that easy. Besides, I plan to leave it all to homeless cats."

I grin. "Perfect. I can see the headline now: 'Death of the Queen Bitch Benefits Unloved Pussies.'"

The cat marches in and meows, apparently pleased by her plan. I wouldn't put it past my grandmother to have some sort of whackadoodle will that does something weird with her money. Not that I need it, being a trust-fund brat.

"Don't be impudent," Queenie mutters.

As I place the tray over her lap, she grabs my face, jerking it from side to side. A sharp tug pulls my hair out of its ponytail. "Nice. I always did want another girl. Maybe you and Skylar can share clothes. Now go shave that mess off your face. Where is she?"

I can't help but laugh. Having a beard and keeping my hair long was a fuck-you message after I parted ways with the army. Pissing off the Queen? *Bonus.*

Her brow furrows as she looks at the bowl of cereal. "What is this?"

"Cardboard and dead flies," I tease.

"Why would I eat that?" The woman before me is my grandmother. But the person in front of me looks like a lost child. My throat constricts. *She doesn't remember that's what I used to call this disgusting bran cereal with raisins?*

Princess breezes through the door and tucks a napkin under Queenie's chin like nothing is out of the ordinary. The noose of responsibility tightens around my neck, and I make myself take a deep breath. When my grandmother doesn't move, Sky places the spoon in her hand and gently guides it into the bowl.

Queenie smiles weakly.

"Thank you, dear." The fog of confusion seems to clear, and despite the tremble, she manages to get the spoon to her mouth. "After breakfast, you two go outside and play. You're not going to mess up my clean house. You can see if Caleb wants to come over. That boy needs to get outside in some fresh air, too."

Well, maybe not totally cleared. I glance at Skylar and grin. "Can we have some money to go to the Snack Shack?"

"Not if you don't learn proper English, young man."

"*May* we?"

Queenie puts her spoon down and glares. "I knew you came here after my money. No."

Skylar bites her lip and quickly turns and opens the curtains wider. The morning light reveals the long curve of her neck below her messy bun. Just above her shirt collar, there's a small freckle beckoning to be kissed...

Mentally kicking my own ass, I pull my thoughts away from that uncharted, muddy path.

"When did you arrive?" my grandmother asks.

"Last night. I didn't want to wake you."

I wait to see if Sky tattles. She never did as a little girl; that was Caleb's role. She sits and encourages Queenie to resume eating. When she steals a glance at me, she winks. I relax and collapse into the threadbare chair covered in hideous pink roses.

"How long are you staying? I trust you found your room clean." Queenie blots her mouth.

I pinch the bridge of my nose and prepare for battle. "I'm not staying in that mausoleum. I'll only be here a week at most."

The spoon slams down on the tray. "And just where do you expect to stay? You can't put Skylar out of *her* bed."

The thought of being with Skylar *in* her bed makes me shift. I glance at Sky's flushed cheeks and wonder if I'm the only one having these bizarre thoughts. *Is there some kind of weird hallucinogenic herb in the coffee?* Thankfully, the doorbell interrupts us.

Skylar leaves to answer.

"Who in the world would be calling this early?" I ask.

"We have a life. Maybe it's one of Skylar's boyfriends." Her blue eyes are now clear and full of devilment. "Or one of mine."

My eyebrows lift. I'm not sure if I'm more disturbed by the thought of Princess dating or Queenie.

"What? You don't think Skylar's pretty enough to have a boyfriend? Kip Rogers has been sniffing her skirts since she was thirteen."

I scowl and swear under my breath. I've always hated that motherfucker.

"And Caleb Buzbee's back home. He bought Guthrie's pharmacy. He's considered quite the catch these days."

I snort. Like Skylar would ever give *him* the time of day. The thought makes me laugh.

I used to like Caleb before "the misunderstanding," as it became known. He was a quiet, intense kid who always had his nose in a book—that is, when it wasn't bleeding. I swear he had more nosebleeds than Queenie had complaints. He was super smart but socially awkward, being two years younger than the rest of our class. He fit in like a hair on a biscuit. But being an outsider myself, I felt sorry for him, and we became friends. Sort of... He could rarely do the things I liked doing. Instead, he'd sit and read to Sky on the porch.

But our relationship soured the afternoon I thought he'd hurt Skylar. Full of rage, I beat the crap out of him. I was lucky I was only seventeen when it happened. Mrs. Buzbee was hellbent on pressing charges, but, surprisingly, Pastor Buzbee intervened on my behalf and suggested I needed a "structured environment." A week later, on my eighteenth birthday, I enlisted in the army. Looking back, I sometimes wonder if serving time would've been so bad…

Skylar returns and looks at Queenie and me, as if aware she was the topic of our conversation. She hands my grandmother some money.

"Is that fool girl back for another protection spell?"

Skylar nods.

"When is she going to learn to quit trying to do love spells? They always backfire, especially since she doesn't know what she's doing. You can't look that stuff up on the internet and expect it to be correct. No practitioner worth their salt is going to give away all their secrets." Queenie shakes her head and pushes her empty bowl away.

I sit up straighter. "You're joking, right? This is the twenty-first century. No one believes in that shit."

"Watch your language, young man. And, obviously, some *do* believe. If you weren't so full of your own self-importance, you might, too."

I roll my eyes. And this is only one of the reasons I couldn't wait to get the hell out of this backwoods place. I head out to see if Darrell will help me get my truck home, doubtful I'll make it a full week here.

SKYLAR

After supper, we settle in the parlor. Queenie's more with it than usual for so late in the day, which makes me happy.

Eyes closed, his long legs stretched out, Jed pats his flat stomach. "Homemade vegetable soup is my favorite. Thank you."

"It *was* good, wasn't it?" Queenie agrees. "Skylar will make someone a good wife."

I feel the heat in my cheeks, and Jed opens one eye and scowls. Of course, as if on cue, the phone rings with my nightly call from Caleb. I pick up, knowing he will do the talking.

"Hey, Skylar, how was your day? I bet it was good. Mine was the same ol', same ol', except Mrs. Langford got upset because I didn't have her prescription ready when she arrived. She'd called it in two minutes before she walked in the door. But you know how impatient she can be. She banged her walker, making the biggest ruckus. It was kind of funny.

"Darrell stopped by and said Jed was home. I, um, hope it's going well. I'll be out of town for a couple of days, getting some CEUs for my license in Asheville, which might be best, you know...with my and Jed's history. Hopefully, we can repair our friendship at some point in time. I'll miss you while I'm gone. I promise to bring you back something special. I hope you have a good night. Sweet dreams, Skylar. Bye."

I smile and hang up. He's such a thoughtful person.

"Was that some crank robo call? You shoulda just hung up," Jed comments.

"That was her boyfriend."

"Ew, Kip?" Jed makes a face and gagging noise.

"No, Caleb. Is he coming over this evening?"

I shake my head no. It feels strange talking about Caleb in front of Jed.

Jed shifts in his chair. "Why don't we turn the TV on? You know, see what's going on in the *real* world."

"No. I don't want to hear about our crooked government."

"What about the weather?"

Queenie stops knitting, pulls down her glasses, and glares. "Didn't I always tell you to be a meteorologist? You can be wrong ninety percent of the time and still keep your job. My knees are better at predicting the weather than that educated fool."

"Well, what the he—er, heck do you do for fun at night?"

"We read, and we talk. It's called broadening our minds."

"I bet Chatty Cathy over there talks ninety-to-nothing," he mutters.

I don't take his insult personally. He's just being Jed and is literally twiddling his thumbs. He's never liked being still. I walk over to the old record player and sort through the 45s until I find the one I want and drop the needle. Ben E. King starts singing "Stand By Me." The record is scratchy, but Jed looks up and smiles when I walk toward him, holding out my hands. When we were kids, this was our favorite record. It was our theme song.

We're rusty, but we somehow manage to throw in a few rumba moves like Queenie taught us, with him chuckling at our missteps. Jed's robust, booming laugh rings out when we're done. Queenie claps her hands, and her eyes are bright, her smile wide.

And for this brief moment in time, everything's perfect.

After I put her to bed, I meet Jed on the upstairs porch. He's in his hammock with one foot on the floor, pushing himself. The night air is cold, and I grab the quilt from the swing and bring it to him. I wish he'd sleep inside.

His hands are behind his head, and he's staring at the ceiling. As I tuck the quilt around him, he pulls me onto the hammock, snickering when we almost flip over. My head lies on his shoulder, and I have one leg thrown over his. He tucks the quilt around us.

"Seems like old times," he murmurs.

I nod, pushing his hair out of his eyes.

"Guess I should tell you a bedtime story."

I nod and smile.

"Once upon a time there was an angry boy. He hated his parents for dying. He hated his grandmother for being an evil witch trying to take their place…" His chest rumbles as he talks. I rub a circle around the button on his flannel shirt.

"And he hated being different from everyone around him. He didn't believe in fairy tales and magic. He didn't believe in God. No one understood his pain. No one understood the white-hot anger that simmered in his gut, ready to explode at any moment. He was trapped in a world where nothing made sense, tied to an impossible situation that he couldn't get out of."

I lie still, listening to his story.

"The angry boy did escape, but it wasn't for the right reasons. He left because he couldn't contain that anger any longer and was sent away as punishment. Free at last, he discovered he could use this anger in his new job. And he was good at his job. *Too* good. But he hated the profession because he realized nothing had really changed. His insides still burned with an icy rage that left him feeling hollow and even more unhappy…"

The hammock is no longer moving, and Jed's warm breath is slow and even on my forehead. His body heat keeps me warm, and his arm wraps tighter around me.

I now understand why he's come home. It has nothing to do with my summoning spell. He's come home to heal. I'm a healer. It's my gift, and I will take his sins from him so he can find his peace.

But the only way I know how to do this is if he were to die…

CHAPTER EIGHT

JED

THE TEEN BEHIND the counter shoves her phone in her pocket and sighs at the sight of Skylar and me. I have no idea who she is; she was probably a toddler when I left the area. Other than the personnel and the price hikes, everything in here looks the same as when I was a kid.

"Welcome to the Snack Shack. Can I help you?" Her bored look highlights her enthusiasm.

"Hold on. We're still deciding."

It's been a long, arduous week since my arrival. It wasn't my plan to stay this long, but I also wasn't expecting to find things so changed. However, I don't know how much longer I can tolerate Queenie and her craziness. Sky's a saint for putting up with her. No doubt about it. Thanks to Pastor Buzbee and his wife, we finally have an afternoon off while they visit with Queenie. When I was a kid, I loved going by Caleb's after school. Mrs. Buzbee was "normal" and a good cook. She'd fuss at me, but so did every other adult in my life except Darrell. But today, even though it's been ten years, she was downright cool and obviously not happy to be at Queenie's. I had to laugh when Sky made a gagging face behind her back over the carrot cake she'd brought.

Just before we left, the reverend mentioned Caleb was home sick with an asthma attack. He hasn't been over since I've been home, but he's called Sky every night, even when he was away. I'm not really sure what's going on between them—it's not like I can glean anything from eavesdropping.

Before we left, Queenie instructed Sky to give the Buzbees some herbal tea. Mrs. Buzbee had insisted Caleb's medications were working, but behind her back, the pastor had slipped the baggie in his pocket. To me, it looked like low-grade pot, which would probably help Caleb more than anything else.

The girl behind the counter shifts nervously and stares openly at Princess, who's wearing one of my old button-down white shirts belted with a rope over a long, colorful skirt and more jewelry than most people own. On her head is an old stovepipe hat, and she's woven ribbons through her hair. On the way here, I told her she looked like a time traveler from Woodstock.

The girl leans across the counter, cupping her mouth with her hands and enunciating loudly, "What. Do. You. Want, Skylar?"

"She isn't deaf, and, obviously, she's still deciding." I don't bother to hide my irritation.

Skylar either ignores the clerk's rudeness or is unaware how condescending her manner is. She points at the menu and holds up five ringed fingers, her bracelets clinking down her arm.

"Five *what*?" the snotty kid asks.

Skylar points down five times at the menu. Counting down five, I see it's a hot fudge sundae.

"Hot fudge sundae. Pickles on the side," I snap at the rude clerk. "I'll have a large vanilla with a bag of barbecue potato chips."

Princess flashes a wide grin, letting me know I got it right. We always did like weird ice cream combos. We settle in a booth, and Sky takes her first bite, closes her eyes, and smiles. The look of pure, unadulterated joy makes me happy we came. God knows she needs a break.

I get busy with my own ice cream, scooping it with a chip. The tang and salt mixed with the soft-serve vanilla is heaven on earth. Dipping another chip, I offer it to Sky. Her cold lips brush my finger, and it suddenly feels kinda warm in here. Good thing this isn't a glass tabletop between us. *Jesus H. Christ, I need to get laid.*

I concentrate on eating my ice cream until Sky's fist pounds the table three times, bracelets tinkling as she gets my full attention. I look up, now aware everyone is watching us. And by everyone, I mean the snotty clerk and the elderly couple sitting behind Skylar.

"What the fuck are you looking at?" I growl at the nosy couple, anger blurring my peripheral vision. "Quit looking at us!"

"Watch your language, Jedidiah Jackson." The old man's eyes dart nervously toward Skylar. I glare at him, and he looks away. His wife turns back around with a disgusted harrumph. I don't remember who they are, nor do I care.

With her back to the couple, Sky didn't see their judgmental looks. She's stock-still, her spoon suspended midair as chocolate fudge drips onto the table. The look on her face reminds me of a wild, trapped animal.

Or a child holding a live grenade...

I rub the heels of my palms into my eyes, trying to banish the image. I feel myself falling down the well-traveled pit of PTSD flashbacks. With my world spiraling out of control, my vision tunnels, and all I can see is the melting bowl of ice cream. It feels like I'm being sucked into a vacuum, and I can't breathe as sweat trickles down my back.

"Let's go." I throw my spoon down and nod toward the

door.

Sky shakes her head.

"Fine. Walk home." I hurl myself from the booth. If I don't get out of here, I'm going to implode or explode. And neither one will be pretty nor productive.

These episodes started after I returned stateside. They're violent, and sometimes I don't even remember the damage I've inflicted. I've been known to smash things and break people. The worst one earned me a trip to a VA psych ward. I slam the door so hard the bell clanks against the glass. The bright sun does nothing to alleviate the darkness hijacking my tormented mind.

I can't do this. I've been home one week and already my skin crawls. My heart races so fast it's a wonder I don't have a heart attack. I lean against the building as stars burst like a kaleidoscope behind my eyelids. I take slow, deep breaths like the head doc taught me, and gradually the sense of impending doom starts to recede. I turn to leave, ready to hit the gas and never look back, but a plucking at my sleeve stops me.

"What? What do you want?" My voice ricochets like sniper bullets bouncing across the alley.

Skylar stomps her foot and swirls a finger next to her temple. The sun hits her bracelets, and I squint.

"Hell yeah, I'm crazy. Don't you ever forget it!"

She taps her ear, and I immediately regret my outburst. This overwhelming feeling of not being in control is *my* problem, not hers. And she doesn't deserve my irrational anger.

"I know. I know you're not deaf," I mutter, pulling on my beard. A woman walks by holding a little boy's hand, giving us a wide berth and a furtive glance. She kind of looks familiar. I think we were in school together.

"Take a picture; it lasts longer," I snarl, not caring if I scare her or the kid. I bend over, hands on knees, taking deep breaths.

Climbing off my emotional ledge, I'm embarrassed, which doesn't help my agitation. I look up when I realize Skylar's "talking" to me.

She points at me, snaps her fists as if breaking a stick, and finishes with a pantomime of taking a picture. *Funny girl.* I relax and reluctantly grin. "If my face breaks a camera, it's only because it can't take in all this handsomeness."

Princess rolls her eyes and dances around, making faces. Her silliness works; I no longer feel like I'm going to crash and burn. I chuckle and hang my head a moment longer as my heart rate slows to normal. Looking around, I notice no one is staring. No one gives a damn. It's all in my fucked-up head. *PTSD sucks.* Skylar spins on her heels and marches down the street. *Where is she going?*

"Hey, Princess, the truck's the other way."

To my surprise, she keeps going, raises a bracelet-clad arm behind her, and gives me the universal one-finger salute.

I jog to catch up with her. "Get in the truck."

Staring straight ahead, she continues marching down the street, ignoring me.

"We've already established you're not deaf. Now get in the goddamn truck."

She stops and spins to face me, blowing out a deep breath. *Now what?* That stubborn chin lifts, and her eyes narrow. Pointing at my mouth, she then makes her fingers do the walking.

I find myself mirroring her motions as I speak. "I *know* I told you to walk. You *know* I didn't mean it. Don't play dumb with me." Immediately I want to kick myself and apologize. "Sorry. I'm not a PC kind of guy. Just get in the truck."

Finger spelling *PC*, she looks adorably puzzled.

"Politically correct—saying and doing the right thing. It was my attempt at a lame joke on the double meaning of the word *dumb.* It seems all I do is ask for your forgiveness. Cut me some slack. I'm a guy—*we don't do that.* You're going to get my Asshole Manhood card revoked."

The corner of her mouth twitches. She crosses her arms and waits.

I pinch her nose. "Fine. *I'm sorry.* Forgive me?"

The wind blows a strand of hair across her full, provocative lower lip. I tuck it behind her ear, knocking her ridiculous hat off in the process. We found that hat years ago in a trunk full of old, musty clothes. I catch it before it falls and shove it back on her head. "Please?"

Like the princess I call her, a casual shrug is all she deigns to give me. She walks toward the truck without a backward glance, so I figure all is forgiven. And damn, if that girl isn't a sight to behold. The gentle sway of her hips flips a switch straight to my cock.

I really need to get laid.

SKYLAR

I sweep the breakfast crumbs into a dustpan and think about Jed's episode yesterday. Coupled with the memory of him holding the knife to my throat, I'm realizing he needs more healing than I thought. *How has he withstood all this mental pain?*

In the other room, Queenie's seated in her wheelchair, watching some morning talk show. Growing up, Jed and I weren't allowed to watch television, but now it keeps Queenie

WHAT THE TREES KNOW

occupied when I'm cooking or doing housework.

"You know, it would make more sense to just sweep the dirt out the back door," Jed comments. He's freshly showered and wearing a gray army sweatshirt and jeans. Instead of helping, he leans against the kitchen counter and folds his arms.

I shake my head. I'm not about to invite bad luck into the house or risk Queenie's wrath. She taught me long ago to sweep it into a pile and *then* remove it from the house.

"At the very least, open the door and let some fresh air into this crypt."

"Why don't you get off your lazy butt and do something to earn your keep, young man?" Queenie offers from the doorway, stuck on the door facing. Her wheelchair steering is almost as bad as her car driving. "Don't you have papers to deliver?"

Jed sighs. "I'm a grown-ass man, not eleven. I don't deliver papers anymore."

His growing annoyance with Queenie's fading memory is frustrating all of us. I thought he'd be able to help and give me a break in the day-to-day dealing with her. But he doesn't seem to understand this dementia isn't her choice and, for the most part, is harmless; it's just tiring for the caregiver. I've found it's easier if I placate her. But no, he insists on trying to badger her back to reality.

"Just what *do* you do, Jedidiah?" Queenie snaps, drumming her fingers.

"Not a damn thing, usually. I'm a trust-fund baby, remember? When I'm bored, I do construction."

"Then do something constructive instead of picking on Skylar," she barks. "There's no such thing as a free ride around this house."

He gives her a smart-ass salute and pushes away from the counter. Opening the back door, he jolts backward when a sparrow flies in.

Queenie's eyes widen, and she covers her mouth. My heart lurches as we both turn to stare at Jed. *Death is near.*

Either unaware or not remembering a bird in the house is a bad omen, Jed grabs the broom from me and manages to shoo it back outside before slamming the back door. The phone rings, and Queenie and I stare at one another, knowing we're about to hear bad news.

"Hello?" Jed frowns and hands the phone to Queenie. "Here, I can't understand a word she's saying around her caterwauling. Someone's upset."

Finished with the sweeping, I take the dirt outside, my heart heavy with the impending news. Someone has died. When I return, Queenie is assuring the distraught woman everything will be okay and her son, Gary, will now be at peace.

I sigh, knowing what lies in store for me. And with the veil between the worlds thinning this time of year, it's going to be harder than usual. *Will I be able to come back this time?* Going to my sewing basket, I take out three lengths of black cloth and embroider Gary's name on each. Jed and Queenie are talking in the other room as he tries to remember who the deceased is. Once I finish the three funeral cloths, I walk back into the kitchen and grab the sugar bowl.

"Where are you going?" Jed asks.

"She's going to tell the bees about Gary's death. It's called respect."

I don't wait for Jed's response and head out the back door toward the three beehives that sit between our property and Darrell's. He's sitting on his porch, cleaning his gun and watching me. As I approach the boxes, he takes off his cap and bows his head.

After draping the boxes with the black cloths and sprinkling the tops with sugar as an offering, I drop to my knees and stretch out on the cool, damp grass, grounding myself in preparation for the wake. I hate performing this ritual, but, as Queenie has explained, it's my gift. I just hope Jed stays home. The bees hum, spreading the word. The wind has a strange feel to it, and the trees shiver. They know, too. They always do.

Change is in the air.

CHAPTER NINE

SKYLAR

"MAKE WAY; THEY'RE here," Mrs. Langford says in a quiet but authoritative voice, rapping her knuckles on the overloaded dining room table three times.

The crowd shuffles and parts as skittish mourners move to the front porch or leave. The room goes eerily silent as I push Queenie's wheelchair through the open front door toward the casket. The grandfather clock has been stopped and the mirrors covered to prevent further death. A low murmur once again sifts through the group as we approach. The dead man's mother sits beside his expensive coffin—one that's rumored to have taken most of her savings. Her muffled sobs mingle with the low voices of those paying their respects and those who are here out of morbid curiosity.

It's always more personal when the wake is in the home. A cloying essence of sweat and perfume mixes with the smell of the funeral sprays. The heavy air snaps and crackles with energy like a brewing storm. I force myself to take slow, deep breaths. With this many people packed into the small house, it's hot despite the open door.

Jed walks behind me, and I hear several people greet him. No one speaks to me or Queenie. He hasn't a clue that we're not just here to pay our respects. He insisted on driving, which is a good thing. But I'd hoped he would just drop us off and pick us up later.

"Why are you here?" Pastor Buzbee's tired voice cuts through the hushed whispers and weeping.

Ignoring the judgmental frown of his sanctimonious wife, Queenie motions for me to stop in front of him. "Same reason you are, preacher. For Gary." She nods toward the coffin. She doesn't like to be questioned. Although her mind slips more often than not into her own little world, tonight she's clear and present and has arrived with a purpose. God or Goddess help anyone who tries to stop her.

"I'm not here for the dead, Guinevere. Funerals are to comfort the living." Speaking in a low voice, he places his hand on the bereaved mother's shoulder. "Your son's fate has been decided, and God is merciful. It's out of our hands. You know this. We pray we'll meet him again in heaven."

His voice isn't unkind, but he speaks with a dignified, quiet authority. He always has.

Several people shift uneasily, and three slip out the front door. His wife nods, a gleam of fanaticism in her piercing gaze. Unkindly, I wish someone would wipe the smug smile off her face, and then immediately regret the negative thought. I need to channel love, not hate, tonight.

Someone from the kitchen is making his way through the crowd. "Sorry, sir. 'Scuse me. Didn't mean to step on your foot, ma'am." As Caleb approaches, he accidentally knocks off the black cloth covering the mirror, and his eyes meet mine in the reflection. His face mimics his father's apprehension. "Oops, sorry. I've always been clumsy." He quickly re-covers the mirror.

An uneasy whispering, like the sound of birds taking flight, rustles through the house, and two more people scurry from the room. It's bad luck to look in a mirror after a death has occurred. Presumably the person in the mirror will die next. I grab Caleb's hand and trace the number seven on his palm with my thumb.

"That tickles," he says, grinning. He motions to an empty chair. "Would you like to sit over here with me?"

He looks nice tonight in his black suit, starched white shirt, and subdued gray-patterned tie. His brown eyes are kind and full of concern as he awaits my answer.

I shake my head and look at the floor. Thankfully, he doesn't argue and takes a seat. Standing behind Queenie, I prepare myself for what's to come. I look over at the dining table. The lace tablecloth is barely visible underneath all the dishes. It's tradition for neighbors and loved ones to cook copious amounts of food, each trying to outdo the other, even though the bereaved couldn't care less about eating. God help the woman who uses dark meat in her chicken salad. She'll be shunned and whispered about for years. Casserole dishes are neatly labeled so they can be returned later. It's considered bad form to bring it in a disposable container.

Queenie didn't bring food. There's no need.

I'm her offering.

Dabbing at her eyes with a soggy tissue, the dead man's mother motions for her youngest daughter, Ginny, to come over. Stella, her oldest, isn't here. Yesterday afternoon, Queenie read her cards and cautioned her not to come. Unbeknownst to her mother—or boyfriend—Stella's pregnant. She heeded Queenie's warning that if she were to see a corpse, her baby could be marked for life.

I've known Ginny for years; we're the same age. For the one and only disastrous year I attended public school, we were inseparable. She blanches and shoots a desperate look toward her mother. She's terrified of me now, but her mother nods toward the table. Head down, she plods over and picks up an overloaded plate. A huge cupcake of Mrs. Buzbee's prize-winning carrot cake sits prominently on top. I sigh. Carrot cake is disgusting. The way Ginny's hands are shaking, it's a wonder she doesn't drop the plate. Solemnly, biting her lip, she approaches her dead brother and places the offering on his chest.

"What the hell?" Jed whispers behind me.

"Shhh," someone hisses. The room buzzes with silent anticipation, and goose bumps skitter across my arms. I always wonder if this will be the last time… With the thinning of the veil between this life and the afterlife as Halloween approaches, I'm afraid it's a real possibility.

"Witch." The whispered allegation is hurled from the back of the room, the accuser too cowardly to reveal her face.

Jed jerks around, scanning the crowd. His bewilderment is quickly replaced by anger. "Who said that?"

I grab his hand and give it a reassuring squeeze. Queenie and I have heard this before. In this county, folks both fear us and revere us.

"She isn't a witch," Caleb asserts, standing. He glares at those gathered. I appreciate his misguided support.

"'Thou shalt not suffer a witch to live,'" Mrs. Buzbee stage whispers, closing her eyes and raising her hands as if casting out demons.

"Mom!" Caleb rebukes.

Her aura burns as black as cast iron. I shudder. She might give verbal credence to love, but hate binds her heart. I'm thankful Caleb is more like his father.

"'A fool's mouth is his destruction, and his lips are the snare of his soul,'" Queenie responds.

I bite my tongue to keep from laughing. *Queenie knows her Bible.* Even Jed grins, and a few mourners nod.

"This isn't witchcraft," the good reverend asserts, shooting his wife a warning look. "This is superstition carried down from people who couldn't read nor write. They had no understanding of Christian theology. It's an archaic, ridiculous practice. Everyone should leave and not give credence to this nonsensical ritual. Jedidiah, please take Queenie and Skylar home. This is turning into a spectacle."

"I never thought I'd agree with *him*," Jed mutters.

Four more people mumble their goodbyes and hurry out the front door. The rest stay, eager to see what comes next. I stand in front of the grieving mother and bow my head, silently asking her permission.

"Do it," she whispers, followed by a choked sob.

"Skylar, let me take you home," Caleb urges, taking my hand in his.

"Sky, what are you doing? What's this about?" Jed asks. He jerks me closer to him, one arm wrapping around my shoulder. This tug-of-war, one-upmanship between the two men isn't helping my concentration.

Queenie grabs his other arm and hisses, "Hush, Jedidiah. Sit down."

Mrs. Buzbee wraps her arm around the grieving mother's shoulder but speaks to her son. "Go home, Caleb. You don't need to worry about *her*." Hate narrows her gaze, and muddy colors swirl around her like a kaleidoscope.

The preacher's wife is hard for me to read and always has been. Her aura is now a pale pink, showing true feeling for the grieving parishioner and her son. All eyes focus on me as I shake off Jed and Caleb. The only sounds are my footsteps as I approach the coffin. I'm here for a purpose. My bracelets jingle together, breaking the eerie silence. Without the unnatural light of a funeral home, the corpse's face appears orange with a touch of gray; the funeral home makeup was unable to completely hide the violence of his self-inflicted death.

What kind of self-hatred pushes someone to hang himself?

Without touching the cold, silent corpse, I can feel his pain.

Gary isn't in heaven, nor is he in hell. His soul remains here, clinging to the fevered, unconditional love of his mama. Lingering between the worlds, he's lost, and the agony he suffered on earth continues. With my touch, his pain will become my pain. I dread it, but this is my calling—to ease his transition to the other side.

"What the hell is going on here?" Jed bellows behind me.

Interrupted, I glance over my shoulder to see several mourners pulling him away. They either don't want to risk me not doing my job or they don't want to interrupt the show.

Using my eyes, I plead with Jed, begging him to let it go.

Beside him, Caleb bows his head. The light on his sandy blond hair shines like a halo. I know he's praying for me, and I appreciate it. His heart is in the right place, but I need to focus on the task at hand. I turn to face the dead man once again.

My fingers tremble as I touch the cold, lifeless hands folded below the laden plate of offerings. Closing my eyes, I see myself leaving my bedroom, walking down the stairs into Queenie's kitchen. I hear the squeak of the steps, smell the herbs drying in the window. I walk out the back door to the edge of the woods. The pine trees sway above me, and a crow caws in the branches. Beneath my bare feet, the ground is cool and prickly as I make my way to the swing that hangs from an ancient oak tree. The tree welcomes me, knowing I seek safety. I sit and pump my legs, going higher and higher…

The temperature in the room rises, but my blood runs ice cold as energy moves from me into the corpse. It always starts the same, a sense of buoyancy. I feel as if I could raise my arms and float to the ceiling. Silently, I implore his God to have mercy on his lost soul and welcome him home. The next step is the one I fear most. The despondency of the deceased engulfs me, and my body now feels leaden. It's that sinking feeling in the pit of my stomach, only a thousand times worse. I'm drained, hollow, lost in a sea of emptiness.

But that's okay.

I'm not supposed to be here anyway.

I'm the girl who walks between the worlds. Each time I journey into the hereafter, I move closer to the edge of darkness, and it's harder to come back. Someday, I'm afraid I won't return. I don't want to go, but if it happens, I know I'll be reunited with my mama.

My vision tunnels as I spiral away from this cramped, run-down home toward the pits of the unknown. The luminosity of love and peace is now a mere pinhole in my inky surroundings. The dead man's emptiness and fear engulf me as I take on his uncertainties. Pressure builds within my chest as he slowly journeys toward enlightenment.

The energy shifts with a jolt akin to a lightning strike, and I struggle to breathe. It's as scary as drowning, only this time I don't fight it. I'm not a victim; I'm a conduit. Just when I think I'll never be free of death, the weight lifts, and air fills my lungs. The deceased no longer walks this world, lost and unattached. He's reunited with eternal love. Struggling through the murkiness of this physical plane, I sort through my vault of memories, looking for Jed. He's what grounds me; he's my reason for returning.

If this were a B-flick horror movie, a wild storm would occur, thunder would boom, and lightning would rip through the sky.

None of this happens, because this is real.

However, the front door *does* slam shut. A woman screams.

"It worked," someone gasps.

"He's gone," Queenie affirms.

"It was merely a gust of wind," Pastor Buzbee counters.

These differing opinions don't distress me. I'm exhausted and just want to resurface from the dead.

"Skylar!" Jed's concern speeds my ascent back toward light. Relief floods my soul. He's my anchor. I wonder if I would've returned this time without him.

A scraping noise pulls me closer to the here and now. Someone has moved a chair behind me. I sink into it, my legs no longer able to bear my weight. I'm drenched in sweat, and despite the stuffiness in the room, I'm freezing.

Jed kneels beside me, brushing my damp hair off my face. "Dear God, what are they doing to you?" He pulls me into his arms and holds me, snarling like a rabid dog when Caleb tries to intervene.

My body shudders convulsively. I have nothing left, but my job isn't over. Reluctantly, I pull away and pat his hand.

"Jedidiah! Let her finish," Queenie commands.

"Let her finish what? This is superstitious bullshit!"

He doesn't go without a fight, pushing and shoving against those trying to remove him. Much as I want to help him, I'm too weak to protest. And I have a job to complete. Closing my eyes, I focus my energy on the dead man before me. Behind me, Jed's shouted curses fill the air, combined with the sounds of him wrestling to be free. A woman behind me starts keening, and Ginny and her mother quietly weep while someone else begins to pray. The cacophony of noises is disruptive.

Above the din, Queenie yells, "Hush."

The room instantly quiets, except for Jed's cursing.

Caleb rubs my hands and whispers, "Take some deep breaths."

Pastor Buzbee says, "Caleb, stay with Skylar. Jedidiah, let it go. Step out on the porch with me."

I hear them leave, and it's as if a part of me has flown away. Jed's presence made this journey easier. Caleb shrugs out of his jacket and wraps it around my shoulders. He strokes my hair, murmuring quiet reassurances. I'm grateful for his concern.

Him being here is as comforting as one of Queenie's old quilts.

Now able to concentrate, I grab the plate of food and pull it to my lap. Under different circumstances, everything would be delicious except that awful carrot cake. The food burns my parched, raw throat. Despite the discomfort each bite brings, and my intense dislike of the overly sweet cake, I'll eat everything on the plate. As I consume the sins of the dead man, masked in the guise of food, my insides boil like a cauldron. The room swirls, and I feel sick to my stomach. Fire surges through my veins. It's hot in here. *So hot.* My heart beats so fast it's hard to catch my breath. Everything around me seems exaggerated somehow. People are talking slower, colors are brighter, the air is thinner. *Is this how it will end?* I've never had this intense of an experience before, and I can feel myself slipping closer and closer to the other side.

But I don't fight it.

This is my purpose in life.

I'm a sin eater.

I consume your soul.

Because I don't have one.

JED

My gut reaction is to march back in there, grab Skylar, and get the hell outta this place. But I get the distinct impression I wouldn't get far. These crazy, superstitious hillbillies would probably lynch me for interrupting their circus. It's like we've been thrown back in time a hundred years.

Reluctantly, I follow Pastor Buzbee to the front porch. Peering into the house, I watch as Caleb squats next to Skylar, holding a bottle of water and talking to her. Her eyes appear glassy, but she takes the bottle and chugs it. He strokes her long blond hair off her face, cupping her flushed cheek. For whatever reason, this interaction between the two of them irritates me. I vaguely recognize a few folks standing around smoking and gossiping, but I'm not interested. I'm still trying to process just how whackadoodle my grandmother has become and what she's done to Skylar in the process.

"Let's walk and talk," Pastor Buzbee says.

I nod and follow him into the yard. "This is crazy." I look to the reverend for validation that it isn't *me* losing my mind. I'm almost hoping this is a weird flashback from some drugs I shouldn't have done when I was overseas…

He chuckles and squeezes my shoulder. "This might be the first time we've ever been on the same side of an issue. It's an ancient belief that if someone takes his or her own life, his or her soul resides in limbo. The locals believe Skylar has the gift to walk between the worlds. What you just witnessed is called *sin eating.*"

"Surely you don't believe this crap. And what's Caleb's role in all of this?"

"Caleb cares about Skylar. They've rekindled their friendship since he's moved back to the area. Neither of us believes this superstition. But what can I do except live my truth, educate, and love my neighbor? I try to lead through love and by my actions."

I roll my eyes. *I need a stiff drink.* "What Queenie's done to Skylar is criminal."

"I wouldn't say 'criminal'; Guinevere loves Skylar. We both know she's always been eccentric. But I won't lie to you—I'm concerned. Her forgetfulness has gotten worse, especially the last few weeks. Eleanor has noticed it, too. You need to step up to the plate and be the man of the house. They need you, Jed. Now, stay here out of trouble, and I'll go check on Skylar." He gives me a final pat on the shoulder and heads back inside.

Oh hell no. I tug at my shirt collar. Responsibility constricts my throat before settling square on my shoulders. The weight of it damn near suffocates me. Strangely, the old R.E.M. song about the end of the world as we know it begins looping through my mind. I pace off some of my nervous energy, considering my future. I never planned to stay. I'm not even sure why I came. A strange feeling pulled me back home, and now I can't wait to leave.

Some things never change.

There's a commotion from inside the house. People are shouting. I race to the porch and run right into Skylar, who falls into my arms. She's stark naked, wild-eyed, and making unintelligible, guttural sounds.

CHAPTER TEN

SKYLAR

SOMETHING NUDGES ME awake. My head pounds with a staccato rhythm that's incongruent with Widdershins' purrs. I shove my cat off the bed, only to have him jump back up. Cracking open my eyes, I groan at the clock, wondering if it's seven in the morning or at night. I sit up, startled to find I'm naked. Hands over my face, I rub my aching head, trying to remember what happened. The last memory I can recall is the plate of food in my lap at Gary's wake…

Gingerly, I get up and shower and brush my teeth, trying not to jolt my throbbing head. Downstairs, I run into Jed. He frowns and pours me a cup of coffee, sliding it across the table. I add my cream and sugar as he walks back and forth like a caged lion. There's something different in the air today—a restlessness mirrored by his pacing. As sure as my name *isn't* Skylar, something big is going to happen. I can feel it. Jed's green plaid flannel shirt bunches, defining his cut biceps with his movements. I focus on the rip at the knee in his old frayed jeans.

"Look at me," he bellows.

With a sigh, I do as he commands and immediately regret it. *Why is he looking at me like that?*

Later I need to throw some cards to see if I can gain any insight, without Jed interfering. His negativity could skew the reading. On the table are three of Mrs. Buzbee's carrot cupcakes. *Yuck.* She must've sent them home with Queenie last night. *If she only knew how many I throw out every week...*

"We need to talk about last night. What Queenie's done to you with her cockamamie bibbidi-bobbidi bullshit is wrong. I've a good mind to declare her mentally incompetent. It shouldn't be hard after all those damn witnesses saw that craziness in action. That was insane. What the hell got into you?"

I'm not up to arguing, so I opt to ignore him. Just because he doesn't believe doesn't mean others don't. Queenie and I helped that family yesterday...

I need some quiet time to think and process last night, but this pounding headache makes it difficult to focus. Jed continues muttering under his breath as I relish my coffee and worry. I've never had a blackout after a sin eating before.

Jed stops in front of me and glares. "I'm too upset to talk about this right now. I'm going to go for a walk to cool off and pretend like I'm a rational man. Drink your coffee and be ready to explain this nonsense when I return." He slams out of the house. The potted plants in the windowsill quiver in his wake.

I decide on homemade biscuits for breakfast, enjoying the mundane ritual. Queenie always says preparing food is the best kind of spell when done with love. Jed just needs to unwind and realize we can either go with the flow of life or rail against it. I choose the path of least resistance, something Jed has always had difficulty doing.

A little while later, the timer dings. I open the oven and, without thinking, grab the pan with my bare hand. I jump back and drop it, berating myself for being an idiot and not paying attention. Good grief, I've got to pull myself together. A biscuit falls to the floor. *Great, unwanted company is bound to show up*

WHAT THE TREES KNOW

today.

Sure enough, someone knocks at the back door. I look up and, through my tears, see Caleb peering in the window. Seeing I'm hurt, he hurries in the back door.

"Skylar?"

I'm shaking my red, burned hand. He grabs it to take a look.

"Ouch, that has to hurt, sweetheart."

He's never used a term of endearment before. I'm not sure which burns hotter, my palm or my cheeks, as he stares at me. I lower my eyes.

He cuts a leaf off the aloe vera plant and rubs the goo on my burn. "Accidents happen. I'm sure after last night you're, uh, tired…" Without asking, he pours me a cup of coffee. "Butter and jelly on your biscuit? Or honey?"

This is what I love about Caleb. He treats me like a normal girl.

He nudges my arm. "Honey for my honey?"

I nod and smile. Flustered, I get the butter out of the refrigerator. I'm the hostess. It isn't right that he should be waiting on me. I motion that I'll take over.

"No, I've got this. Besides, this way I can have a cup of coffee and a biscuit with your honey. It's good for my immune system. Did you tell the bees about the death in the community?" he teases gently.

I nod. Some don't believe in telling the bees, but Queenie taught me long ago that unlike trees—*which know everything*—bees must be *told* if something out of the ordinary occurs.

Caleb pulls out my chair for me.

"You're adorable." He grins. "I love your whimsical nature."

I return his smile, wishing he understood this isn't whimsy. It's real.

He's wearing a white dress shirt, navy pants, and his tie is a lovely paisley pattern. His hair is still damp from what I presume was his morning shower. He must be on his way to work. After graduating college, Caleb worked in Asheville, but he moved back home after buying the one and only pharmacy in town. Lately he's been very interested in Queenie's herbal remedies. Of course, with her paranoia, sometimes she thinks it's because he wants to steal her grimoire. At other times, when she's more her old self, she shares her knowledge of the local plants and how she uses them in her remedies.

"Are you okay?" Caleb places a pad and pencil on the table. "I mean, last night was, er…intense. You were pretty out of it there at the end."

I nod and cross my fingers under the table for the small fib. I'm *not* okay. Something is definitely off.

He places our breakfast on the table and brings the cream and sugar for the coffee. "May I?" he asks before sitting.

Such a gentleman. Caleb's demeanor is like steadfast granite, in direct contrast to Jed's kinetic, burning energy.

"I'm worried about you. I'm sure there will be plenty of talk after what happened last night." His tone isn't judgmental, and his aura is a beautiful shade of aquamarine.

I sign that I'm okay.

"You know I don't believe in that stuff—"

I straighten in my chair and pull the pad and pen toward me. Stopping me, he places his hand over them.

"Let me finish, please."

I cross my arms, waiting for yet another diatribe about how crazy Queenie and I are.

"In my psychology class, I learned just how powerful the mind is. And while I may not agree with the method, the comfort you brought to Gary's family was a magnificent demonstration of compassion. And humbling. What you did was beyond the clichéd platitudes most folks—me included— offer in times of grief."

Shocked, I stare into his eyes and relax. He shrugs as if he hasn't just said one of the nicest things I've ever heard. Buttering his biscuit, he slathers on the honey. I need to give him a jar of it to take home.

"Mmm, good." He refills his coffee and sits back, talking about mundane things like the weather and the locals without actually gossiping.

I relax and enjoy my coffee, but I get the sense he wants to talk more about the sin eating.

"I don't know how to say this, so I'll just come out and tell you. My mother was quite shocked by what went down last night. But I don't care what she thinks. I'm an adult who can make up my own mind. I want to assure you, I'll do my best to stop any talk buzzing around town... I mean, obviously you weren't aware of things when you—"

The back door opens, and Jed strides in looking mildly surprised. "What are you doing here?" His tone isn't exactly warm and inviting.

Caleb offers his hand, which Jed ignores, instead folding his arms, waiting.

"I stopped by to check on Skylar. I'm headed to work. And, uh, I was going to remind her about the Fall Festival at church on Sunday."

Jed snorts. "Sky would be more inclined to attend a black Sabbath after last night's spectacle." He throws a coat at Caleb. "Here's your jacket."

Why did Jed borrow Caleb's jacket? It had to have been too small for him.

"I don't believe that to be true," Caleb replies calmly, but his neck is bright red. "She couldn't help it. She wasn't herself—"

"Sure, you do. You believe she's going to end up a toasty critter in the pits of hell. Remember the time you tried to baptize her in the kitchen sink? Now I'm sure everyone who witnessed the show last night will believe the same thing."

"For crying out loud, that was *years* ago. We were just *kids!*" Caleb turns toward me. "Ignore him. You weren't yourself last night; everyone knows that. The gossip will die down. If you'd still like to go with me, I can pick you up at four. Dinner will be after the service, and there's the hayride and usual games."

I'd forgotten about the festival. The hayride will be a disaster for his allergies. I hesitate, wondering what gossip he's talking about.

"What? Just a boring hayride? No doomsday house to frighten everyone into heaven?" Jed goads.

I glare at him and shake my head. I don't know why he's so antagonistic. Jed used to be the one who would take up for Caleb when Kip was bullying him. I turn to Caleb and nod that I'll go.

Looking at these two different men, I realize Caleb is like the sunshine peeking through the canopy of the tall trees, whereas Jed is the earthy darkness of the forest floor. Me? I'm the sacred space of silence separating the two.

Caleb stands a little taller, and his smile widens. "Great. See you then." He gives Jed a curt nod and leaves.

Jed leans against the counter, staring at me yet again. "Has Queenie had the *talk* with you?"

My mouth drops, and heat spreads from my chest to my cheeks. I wonder if he's joking, but his face says he's dead serious.

I sign that I'm almost twenty-four and roll my eyes.

He shrugs. "As backwards as everything else is around here, I just wanted to make sure. Now what the hell happened last night?" He frowns. "What did you do to your hand?"

I point at the pan of biscuits and oven.

"Learn to think!" He breaks off a piece of aloe and rubs the juice on the burn. I bite my lip to keep from snickering over the fact he's practicing folk medicine. I also don't mention that Caleb's already done this. My hand looks tiny in his, and his calloused fingers are surprisingly warm and gentle. I wonder what they'd feel like on other parts of my body…

"Skylar!" Queenie's insistent bell ringing interrupts us.

Jed pulls away, looking annoyed, and scratches his beard.

I wish he'd shave. I miss seeing his dimples and the smell of his woodsy cologne. For months after he'd enlisted, I slept on his pillow just for that scent. The day Queenie washed that pillowcase, I sobbed for hours. My eyes focus and linger on his thinning mouth. *Does his beard tickle?* He once again starts pacing, muttering under his breath.

I push him out of my way and motion for him to get out and go smoke.

"She can't be hungry. I gave her some coffee and a cupcake earlier. And haven't you noticed I don't smoke anymore? I quit. Over two years ago."

I make a slashing motion across my throat.

His brow furrows. "You want to slit my throat because I quit smoking? You used to beg me to quit."

Grabbing a pen and paper, I write, *YOU'RE DRIVING ME CRAZY.* Again I motion for him to leave and get out of my way.

"You know, I don't do a lot of texting, but I'm pretty sure using all caps is considered rude and shouting. And I still have a lot of damn questions about last night."

The bell begins again with renewed force.

"Jesus H. Christ, I'd love to throw that damn thing away. I can't take it. I'm leaving today."

I shake my head, not believing him. My intuition doesn't see him leaving. He really needs to either take up smoking again or get laid. You'd think having served in the army he'd be used to demanding people.

"Stop ringing that goddamn bell. We're not your servants!"

he shouts, heading toward Queenie's room.

I wish he wouldn't yell at her like that; it only aggravates her.

"No, you're thieves, both of you. All you want is my money!" Queenie shrieks. "Help me! Somebody, help me!"

Today isn't going to be a good day. I hurry to intervene. Arguing doesn't help her fading grip on reality. When will Jed realize she has good days and bad days? It's best to ignore her ranting. She's always worse after going out or having company, anything that upsets her routine.

"Stop ringing that damn bell and acting crazy, old woman."

"I'm not the one who's crazy, you are! Killer! Murderer!" The ringing stops, and the bell soars out the door, hitting the wall, barely missing me.

"Help! He's killing me!"

Skidding to a stop, I see Jed blocking her flailing fist and wrestling her for the phone. He grabs it and slams the receiver down. The energy in the room sizzles and snaps as Queenie screeches nonsensical sounds, throwing things within her reach like a toddler having a temper tantrum. She's never been this bad before.

Jed runs his hands through his unruly hair, and it tumbles loose. He scans the room, as if searching for a hidden enemy. I find the wary look in his eyes more unnerving than Queenie's inane cries for help. It's like he's here in body only, much like his grandmother. Queenie continues fussing, fiddling with her lap blanket as she attempts to stand.

"I come from a long line of fighters," she wails, pointing her finger at Jed. "I'll put you in your place. No one gets the best of a Lafayette."

Fearful she's going to fall, I rush toward her but freeze when I see the gun pointed at me.

"You two won't get my money!"

Rationally, I know the gun isn't loaded. But my past surfaces from its shadowy depth, hijacking my brain.

I hear my mother screaming as the gun empties in sharp blasts.

Blood, so much blood.

"Don't look at me. She deserved it."

I cover my face, trying to block the memories. Knocked from behind, I hit the floor, which jars me back to the present. I look up to see Jed diving for Queenie, wrestling the gun from her hand. He tosses a pill bottle at me, but I can't move; my body feels like lead. The medication bounces and rolls under her chair.

"Open it and give her one."

Do what? I freeze, unsure what he plans to do. The pills he threw are her sleeping medication.

"Ow!" he yelps as Queenie pulls his hair. "Goddammit, Skylar! Pull your shit together. I can't deal with you freaking out and her craziness at the same time." He releases Queenie and, finding the pill bottle, pops it open. As she screeches, he drops a pill in her mouth. Horrified, I rush to help her, pulling on his arm to make him stop.

"Swallow it. Now," he demands, shoving me away.

"Poison! You're poisoning me," she splutters when he moves his hand.

"I'm not poisoning you. Calm down. You tried to kill Skylar, you crazy old bat."

Oh no! He doesn't know the gun is empty; he thinks he's protecting me. I try to push him away, but it's like butting against a cement wall. Finally, I worm myself between them and take a hard hit to my chest. My breath escapes with a whoosh— Queenie's stronger than she looks. Wrapping my arms around her, I wait her out. Her flailing slows, her aim becomes less direct, and her eyes roll back as she now fights sleep, not me. I hug her tight, rubbing her back to reassure her everything will be all right. *Or am I comforting myself?*

"Neil?" she whispers, looking over at Jed but seeing her dead husband.

"Shh. It's time to go to bed, Queenie. That's it…just relax." He speaks in a soothing voice as he picks her up, placing her in bed. Tucked in tight, some of her fight returns. She manages to work her hands out from under the covers. Grunting, she strains, pressing on Jed's chest. He doesn't budge, caging her with his arms, their faces almost touching.

He kisses her cheek and softly sings "Across the Universe," an old Beatles song she used to play for us when we were kids. It works like magic. Her eyes drift closed, and she relaxes, stroking his hand as the medication takes hold.

"I love you, goddammit," he chokes.

The room is a disaster, and angry purple bruises mar Queenie's paper-thin skin.

"Shit. This looks like elder abuse. They're going to put me away for this," Jed mutters.

I shake my head. Everyone knows her mind isn't what it used to be. And she's old; she's always running into things with her walker or wheelchair and tearing or bruising her skin.

He jumps up, clearly agitated. "Who the hell do you suppose she called? Does she have caller ID? I don't know if the call actually went through… This is the last thing we need after you ran around that wake last night butt-ass naked. What has become of this family? Am I the only sane one?"

I shrug and pick up the overturned table. Queenie thinks caller ID is the government spying on her and refuses to have it. And he's joking about last night…*isn't he?*

"I have to get you out of here."

What? I stop straightening the room and stare at him.

"Pack your shit, and pack light. We're leaving. That crazy

old woman is going to kill us in our sleep. And you don't need to be here. This isn't *normal*, Skylar."

I shake my head and resume picking up the room, amused by his exaggeration. Queenie wouldn't hurt a fly. And aside from her fading cognition, everything is perfectly normal... I stop as a memory of Jed carrying me upstairs teases the corner of my mind. And Caleb spoke of gossip. *I was naked when I woke up.* No wonder Jed's upset. *What happened?*

"Do it!" he roars.

I take a step back, now less sure of myself. According to Queenie, he's the one who went crazy when he got out of the army. She's just confused. Maybe it's time for *him* to go. I motion for him to leave.

"I'm not leaving you here. She's lost her ever-lovin' mind, and she has a gun. If she spouts off that we're after her money and trying to kill her, it's gonna look bad on us. And after last night, this family is already in the crosshairs of the county gossips."

Good grief. I pick up the gun and open it, showing him it's empty. His paranoia parallels hers. Last night couldn't have been that bad... *You were naked, silly girl, of course it was bad!*

He grabs my hand, pulling me behind him up the stairs. I tug to break free. Precariously balanced on the staircase, Jed grabs the handrail and manages to catch us before we both tumble down the steps. His breathing saws harshly in the silent house. He lets go of my arm but traps me against the wall. Pulling my pad from my pocket, I scribble, *You're crazy.*

"True, but Queenie's a danger to herself and you. That trumps my craziness. As paranoid as she is, I bet she has bullets hidden all over the place."

I roll my eyes and write, *Pot calling the kettle black.*

"I'm not arguing with you. I should've gotten you out of here years ago. You need a normal life, not this magical, mumbo-jumbo shit." He tosses the pen and pad over the banister but freezes when the doorbell rings.

"Don't answer it," he whispers, wild-eyed.

He reaches for me, but I dodge under his arm and race down the stairs. He stomps down behind me, yet I manage to slip out of his grasp. Yanking open the door, relief overcomes me.

A voice of reason stands on the doorstep, and I've never been so happy to see Pastor Buzbee.

CHAPTER ELEVEN

JED

I WATCH SKYLAR collapse into the startled preacher's arms. Her bright blue eyes look wild, but at least they aren't unfocused and glassy like they were last night. If I hadn't known better, I would've sworn she was high. Even Queenie was worried, so I ruled out her giving Princess some peyote or other hallucinogenic for the show.

"What's going on here?" The preacher's sharp gaze zooms in on me as he comforts Skylar.

Caleb bounces up the steps behind him.

I thought that fucker had to go to work. The changes in Caleb hit me all over again. They're even more profound than in Princess. No pimples, no glasses—he still looks conservative in a missionary kind of way, but definitely not nerdy. For some reason, this pisses me off. He glares at me after he takes in Sky's disheveled state. I realize my shirt's untucked, and my hair is all over the place. Part of me wants to make him jealous; the other part of me is creeped out since Sky's like family.

Skylar pulls away and makes the *crazy* motion with her finger, but instead of pointing at me, she points toward Queenie's room. I'm grateful for that, at least.

"Guinevere? That's why we're here. She called and seemed a

bit hysterical. I knew Caleb had just left your house, so I phoned him to meet me back here. Are you okay?" Pastor Buzbee holds Sky by the shoulders and peers at her face.

She drops her gaze, looking uncomfortable. Her hair's a mess, her white peasant blouse shows cleavage, and she's obviously unsettled.

"Jedidiah?" Pastor Buzbee has always been the master of open-ended questions. The man should've been an attorney.

I'd lay money down that he still hasn't forgiven me for the Sunday I brought a copperhead into his church service and asked him to prove his faith by snake handling. Or the time I substituted real wine for the grape juice. I bet he's now mentally adding *virgin defiler* to my list of sins. *Surely he doesn't think I took advantage of her last night...*

Sky nods, stepping back and straightening her blouse. To my surprise, she reaches for my hand. Lingering suspicion remains on his face, but Pastor Buzbee brushes past us into the house, with Caleb following. I let out the breath I've been holding. It hits me just how woefully unprepared Skylar is for emergencies. This is Queenie's fault. She's kept Skylar entirely too sheltered and disengaged from the real world. Princess needs more than basic sign language and pen and paper to communicate. I'm taking her to get a cell phone today, and I'll add her to my plan. I hurry toward Queenie's room, hoping it doesn't look as bad as I think.

Nope, it's worse.

"Good Lord! Guinevere, are you okay? What happened?" Pastor Buzbee's head spins toward me like he's being exorcised. He steps over the mess toward my unconscious grandmother. Meanwhile, Caleb hovers over Sky. I feel an irrational urge to punch the concern right off his face.

Skylar's fiercely scribbling on a piece of paper at Queenie's desk. *Great.* She's probably writing about what a shit grandson I am for manhandling and drugging an old woman. Maybe I should just sneak out and hit the trail. I need outta here. At a minimum, I need to calm the fuck down and breathe. I need the grounding that comes from the woods.

Pastor Buzbee clears his throat, a vocal reminder of my responsibility. I redo my hair in a tight ponytail, hoping the restriction will help suppress the mental refrain: *get out, get out, get out...*

"Well. This has been an upsetting twenty-four hours," he notes. "Tell me what happened this morning."

Caleb is still hovering over Skylar. I don't like it. Not one bit. Damn, I wish I had a cigarette. I miss smoking most when I'm stressed. Since my return to retro America, this seems to be pretty much all of the time. Given the state of the room and number of people here, escape would be tricky. I'm trapped in this damn time warp.

I dive in with my explanation before the reverend calls the law. "Queenie's gone over the edge. She's even worse than last night. She's totally lost it—"

The curious curate lifts one eyebrow. No doubt he's thinking I look like the crazy one in the room. Before yesterday, I'd have agreed with him because of my PTSD, but now I seem like the most rational one in the bunch.

"Queenie pulled a *gun* on Skylar. I didn't know it was unloaded. I simply reacted. We wrestled over it, and she fought me like a wildcat." I look over at my bruised grandmother and add, "I didn't mean to hurt her."

I don't volunteer the fact I forced her to take her sleeping pill. Not with Mr. Professional Pharmacist here.

Sky shows the note she's written to the minister and Caleb, who both look sharply at me.

"You gave her a sleeping pill?" Caleb asks.

When did she become a tattler?

I shrug. "To calm her down. I didn't know what else to do."

Pastor Buzbee removes his glasses and cleans them. Some things never change; it's always been his tell when delivering bad news. I brace myself, wondering how many years I'll have to serve in the state pen. I'll die if I'm locked up. *I need to go.* Why didn't I leave last night?

Skylar brushes past me. *She's the reason I'm still here.* I need to save her from this looney bin.

"Son, I know you haven't been back long, but we touched on this last night. Your grandmother has good days and bad days. She's always been eccentric, but the past few weeks, she's been more irrational and paranoid than usual." The pastor's harsh truth is spoken with kindness. "And last night couldn't have been easy for her. After what happened with Skylar, she seemed very confused and upset." His cheeks are red as he glances over at Skylar, who still appears to be clueless.

Caleb takes Sky's hand in his and squeezes it. *Just how close are they?* I look away, surprised by the protective jealousy surging through me like an electrical current. I want to snatch her hand out of his and hold it myself. And the fact that he saw her naked makes my blood boil.

Pastor Buzbee turns his attention to Skylar. "We've talked about this, and I know you've been resistant in the past. But now that Jed's here, it's time to have Guinevere assessed somewhere like an Alzheimer's unit, where trained staff have the ability to do what's best for her."

I'm both surprised and relieved by his support. Maybe I need to rethink my opinion of the man.

"He's right, Skylar. She needs more help than you can provide. I'm worried about you." Caleb's gazing at her like a lovesick pup.

I stuff my hands in my pockets to keep from dragging him out of the house by his ear.

Skylar shakes her head, crossing her arms in front of her chest.

My stubborn girl.

"I know this is hard, and I'm not saying this would be a permanent placement. Maybe Guinevere just needs her medication adjusted. At the very least, she needs to be evaluated. Let me call an ambulance to take her to the hospital. No one is saying you've done a bad job, Skylar. But you want what's best for her, don't you?"

Glancing at Queenie and then the floor, Skylar nods. Pastor Buzbee and I have butted heads plenty of times over the years. As a teenager, whenever I bucked Queenie's authority too much, he'd step in as a father figure. I resented the hell out of his interference until he offered me the alternative to jail after I'd beaten Caleb. Looking back now, I realize he was always a fair man and not prone to rash decisions. Seeing him deal with this situation, my respect for him grows. I like the fact he's talking to Skylar. She's the one who's been here for Queenie, not me. She's the caregiver. I don't want her feeling like this decision is being made without her input. Truthfully, I've been gone for so long, I have no idea who Queenie has named to handle her affairs or if she's had the foresight to name anyone.

Moving like a ghost, Sky smooths Queenie's blanket before leaning over and kissing her cheek. In a rare occurrence, Princess looks me in the eye and nods. Despair shimmers in her blue eyes, and guilt slams my conscience like a round from an M2010.

Who's gonna take care of Sky?

Caleb wraps an arm around her shoulder, whispering in her ear.

Son of a bitch.

"Good. I'll make some phone calls. You should pack a few things for her. I know they'll need a list of her medications."

The reverend walks out, dialing his phone.

Skylar stares at the floor, looking lost.

"I'm sorry. It's for the best," I offer, trying to be reassuring.

Ignoring me, she busies herself with packing a small overnight case. When finished, she crawls on top of the duvet and lies next to Queenie, silently crying. Her pain is raw and palpable. And I feel responsible. Without waking, my grandmother reaches out and holds Sky's hand. I'm lost on how to comfort her, and, truth be told, my first instinct is still to take off. Caleb sits on the side of the bed, his head bowed, hands clasped.

I doubt his prayers will help.

Pastor Buzbee motions to me. Reluctantly, I follow him to the front porch.

"They need you." His soft voice lacks admonishment. It's a simple statement of fact.

I rub the back of my neck. "I didn't plan on staying. Can't Sky make the decisions?"

"Is that what you really want to do?"

Yes. My conscience nudges me. *No... Maybe.* "I want what's best for everyone. I haven't been here. Who am I to come in and make these decisions?"

"You're her grandson and next of kin. In her desk, you'll find the legal documents to manage her money and healthcare." Pastor Buzbee hesitates, as if weighing his words. "I know you didn't plan on staying, and Skylar's a sweet girl, but Queenie kept her much too sheltered. After last night, I fear the talk around here will be bad. She and your grandmother are *different.* You know what folks around here think..." He shifts and once again starts cleaning his glasses. "And communication with Skylar is an issue."

Through the window, I see Caleb giving Skylar a hug. *Caleb seems to have no problem communicating with her.* I plunge ahead and mention what we've all been dancing around.

"I haven't had a chance to talk to Sky about last night. She was out of it and slept most of the way home. That was just nuts. What do you suppose triggered it?"

"I asked Caleb what happened while we were outside talking. He said she ate and kept motioning for water. Her skin was flushed, and she didn't look well. She jumped to her feet and ran around the coffin, making inarticulate noises, which in and of itself was alarming since she never speaks. When Caleb tried to assist her, she became almost violent and stripped off her clothes before running outside and into your arms. Personally, I think it was some sort of delusional episode brought on by that ridiculous ritual."

"I believe you, except her skin was hot to touch, and her pupils were huge. Maybe it was a fever? Or food poisoning?" I'm grasping at straws, not wanting to think my family is *that* whackadoodle but fearing it's true.

"No one else got sick. Maybe it was psychosomatic. The mind is a powerful thing. Jed, what I'm trying to say is, I don't know that Skylar is capable of taking care of your grandmother or herself. The gossip going around—"

Even though I've been thinking something similar, I automatically get defensive. "Skylar's very self-sufficient, and we've never given a damn about what others think of us. Sky's like another grandchild to Queenie. She's been here…" The tightening in my throat feels like a noose. All I want is to get out of here, free and unshackled, with no responsibility to anyone but myself.

"Are you trying to convince me or yourself? Do the right thing, son. Guinevere took you and Skylar in when you needed her most. It's a natural cycle. The child becomes the parent."

"It's not fair," I blurt, feeling trapped.

He sighs. "With your military background, you've witnessed

more than most young men your age. Answer me this—is life ever fair?" He puts a hand on my shoulder. "Man up. Do what's right."

Tough love. He's taking a page from Queenie's philosophy. I'm a selfish bastard and freely own it, but I'll meet him halfway. "I'll stay until Queenie's settled and things are squared away. Then I'm out of here. And *I'll* take care of Skylar." I glare through the window at Caleb and Princess.

"Fair enough. Another thing: this is a small town. And after what happened at the wake, it might look better if Skylar came to stay with Eleanor and me until you leave—"

A siren sounds, interrupting him before he can finish. I watch the ambulance approach and wonder how long before nosy neighbors line up to see what's going on. His unspoken rebuke lingers as I recall the feel of Skylar's warm, naked body against mine. *He's probably right.*

"What about *Caleb*?" I ask, not hiding my curiosity.

"Caleb moved into his own home. He's renovated the room above the pharmacy to be a studio apartment."

"We'll see." It's all I'll concede. My fight-or-flight response is leaning heavily toward flight. I give him a curt nod, and he guides me back inside, a hand on my shoulder. I wonder if it's because he can feel how strong my urge to bolt is.

Skylar sits on the bed, holding Queenie's hand. Tears linger on her long lashes, and she refuses to look at me.

Within twenty minutes, we're following the ambulance to the hospital. With my blinkers flashing, I drive over the speed limit. I resist the urge to flip off Kip Rogers as I pass his patrol car. I never did like that cocky little bastard or his daddy, the sheriff. Skylar stares out the window, shredding a tissue in her hands.

"I know with everything going on with Queenie we haven't had time to talk about last night."

If she weren't already nonverbal, she'd be giving me the silent treatment.

"What happened? I mean, I know when you were a little kid you used to like to strip naked, but something was wrong. Were you sick?"

She continues staring out the window, and it pisses me off.

"You made sound. I know you can talk. You've always had the ability; you talk in your nightmares, dammit. Now's a good time to open up and tell me what happened. I have enough on my plate dealing with Queenie."

That stubborn chin lifts, and she motions for me to leave.

I sigh. "I'm not leaving. And we *will* talk about this, I guarandamntee it."

The huffed rebuke and her sharp look tell me she has no plans to talk about anything. We arrive at the hospital, and she hops out, slamming the door, further punctuating her feelings.

Whatever.

I watch her sprint toward the ER entrance. Taking my time, I grab the sweater she left behind and slowly emerge from the truck. Running a hand through my hair, I rework it into a knot and re-tuck my shirt into my jeans. I have enough self-awareness to know I'm stalling. I hate hospitals and their myriad of questions and paperwork. A semicomatose, repressed sense of duty keeps me from dashing through the woods surrounding the edge of the parking lot.

I grab Queenie's suitcase, check a tire that doesn't need checking, and stop to admire the shrubbery before heading inside. As soon as the hospital's automatic doors open, it's instantaneous sensory overload. The pungent smell of disinfectant assaults my nose. From behind a set of closed metal doors, a child's terrified screams make me wince. The desk phone rings nonstop, and the television blares bad news. No one in the waiting room is even watching it. My skin crawls, and sweat trickles down my back. *Focus.*

I find Skylar at the admissions desk, gesturing.

The clerk does what most people do when dealing with Sky. She raises her voice. "Hon, I don't understand. Are you here to be admitted or to see someone?" Not only has she shouted, she's enunciated each word.

Skylar stomps her foot and slams her clenched fist on the desk. Her bracelets clank together, and her breasts heave inside her peasant blouse. I steady her, tucking my finger in her jeans loop. Today, instead of a hat, she's wearing a scarf and big hoop earrings. Her dominatrix-style boots make us almost even in height.

"She's nonverbal, not deaf. We're here to admit Guinevere Jackson. She's just arrived by ambulance." I pull out Queenie's information and wait. The admissions clerk hands me a buzzer like we're waiting for a table at a restaurant. We sit and wait to be called. Sky's knee bounces the entire time, and she shivers. I drape her sweater over her shoulders.

Ten minutes later, the buzzer lights up, and we're ushered into a cubicle to fill out the admission forms.

Sky grips the back of my T-shirt. Without thinking, I plant a quick kiss on her temple. She gasps, and her lashes sweep her pink-tinged cheeks for a second. When those amazing blue eyes peer at me, it's like being caught in a whirlpool, and I'm momentarily mesmerized. A clearing throat reminds me we're not alone.

But I'll be damned…

I wish we were.

And that's more confusing than this shitload of paperwork.

SKYLAR

Jed hasn't said one word since we left the hospital.

I like that about him. He doesn't feel the need to compensate for my silence with inane conversation. Caleb's the same way since he came back home. They accept me for who I am. Silence tends to make most people uncomfortable. For me, it provides a protective barrier. I'm safe in my silence.

He parks the truck, and we sit for a moment, staring at the dark house. It looms before us like a monster in the shadows. I wanted to stay with Queenie, but the staff wouldn't allow it. I even offered to stay in the waiting room, but Jed refused. None of this makes sense to me. If Queenie's lost touch with reality, how will placing her in a strange place, isolating her from those who love her, help?

As we were leaving, Pastor Buzbee and his wife stopped by the hospital. Caleb was still at work, but his father said he'd check on me tomorrow. Mrs. Buzbee cried and offered to help, but her aura was murky. Considering we were on a geriatric psych floor, everyone's aura was off, the colors muddled. I don't know whether to trust my gut instinct about the preacher's wife being disingenuous or feel bad for judging her unfairly. She and Pastor Buzbee invited us to supper, but I'm glad Jed declined. I'm not the least bit hungry and still not feeling right after last night's sin eating.

Widdershins crosses the driveway in front of us, probably looking for his food. I reach up and make an *X* on the windshield.

"Superstitious bullcrap," Jed mutters, parking the truck.

I cross my arms and glare. *You're the one full of crap.*

Jed exhales and pulls at his beard. "You okay?" he asks softly.

I start to nod but end up shaking my head. I'm *not* okay, far from it.

"Come on, I'll walk you to the door."

What? Is he leaving me? Alone? I fumble with the door latch, my heart racing. The last quarter of the waning moon provides very little light, and I trip on the uneven sidewalk. His warm hands catch me.

"Careful." He steadies me, standing so close his breath fans my cheek. I wonder if he's warning me against the dangers of the uneven cement or the perilous relationship terrain we've been tiptoeing around since his return. An air of danger surrounds us, and it's tantalizing.

The night breeze whispers through the trees, reminding us that autumn is here. I shiver, pulling my sweater tighter. He pulls me to his chest, wrapping his arms around me. Clinging to him, I pray he won't leave. Although I'm a loner, I haven't truly been alone since the night my world turned upside down.

"Skylar." His voice sounds strained, and he moves me an arm's length away. "I think you need to go pack a bag. It would be best if you stayed with the Buzbees—"

I shake my head and slap his arm. Patting my chest, I point toward the house. *This is my home; I'm not leaving.* I silently beseech him not to send me away, clasping his hand with both of mine.

"But Queenie isn't here. Even though I'm sleeping on the porch, it won't look good. We're not actually related, and this is a small, gossipy county. After your streaking episode last night, there's already talk…"

Streaking? I throw my hands up. And since when has he ever cared what others think? *Fine.* I stomp onto the porch, find the hidden key above the doorframe, and throw the door open with every intention of slamming it in his face.

No such luck. His hand catches it.

"Whoa. What's up with the attitude?" He pushes his way

into the house and slams the door for me. Before I can reach the light switch, he has me pinned against the wall. Our ragged breaths compete with the ticking grandfather clock.

I stare in the vicinity of his face even though I can't see a thing. He's so close I can smell the peppermint he just ate. *Do his lips taste minty?* Blindly, I grip his biceps and move closer. His beard tickles my nose. My breasts ache as I press myself into his immovable chest. It only takes a few seconds for our harsh breaths to sync. The darkness sharpens my other senses; I feel almost preternatural. He catches me by the waist but doesn't push me away, as if waiting on my next move. Boldly, I lace my fingers behind his neck, tangling them in the few loose strands of his hair.

"We can't do this," he whispers.

I see no reason why we can't.

He presses against me. "Is this what you want? Because if I stay, this is what *I* want." His voice is laced with unfulfilled promises.

Is it? Tension radiates from his body, and danger hangs heavy in the air. If we go down this road, there's no turning back. *But was there ever a choice?* This is our fate; I know it as surely as I know my real name…

A whisper of a kiss brushes my forehead. His hands cup my face. I turn slightly and kiss his palm, urging him to continue.

"I—" It's as if the word's stuck in his throat. Taking a deep breath, he whispers hoarsely, "Skylar…"

My own breathing stutters, and I grip him tighter, afraid he'll leave. I've fantasized about this moment, alone in my bed. Now that it's reality, I'm scared and nervous, but I refuse to let go. This is my dream. This is my chance. More importantly, this is our *destiny*.

His beard tickles my jaw, and I jump. Soft kisses trail toward my mouth.

"Last night, holding you naked…" he whispers as he nibbles and teases my lips to part. While I've been kissed before, it's only been twice—two stolen kisses with Caleb. The first time was an awkward occasion when we were teenagers. The second time occurred at dusk a few weeks ago. It was definitely better than the first and left both of us smiling. Caleb told me the stars were reflected in my eyes. But that sweet, tender kiss was nothing like this.

Jed's mouth is demanding, and his teeth nip my lower lip. He growls, "I want you."

His words throw gasoline on my burning desire.

There are no stars in my eyes tonight—flames, perhaps.

I swallow, hesitating. Fear of doing something wrong mixes with my intense curiosity.

Timidly, I open my mouth, and his tongue dances with mine as he deepens the kiss. One hand makes its way beneath my blouse, settling on my lower back, and he presses harder against me. Sexual awakening flows through my body like molten lava. His lips travel across my jaw toward my neck. I roll my head back, granting him better access, and his beard tickles, heightening the sensation. An incredible longing for something more takes over any rational reasoning. It's like I'm Sleeping Beauty and his kiss has brought me to life. My scarf flutters to the floor. I'm thankful his hands hold me up because my legs feel wobbly, and it has nothing to do with my boots.

As if he somehow knows I'm about to fold beneath him, he backs me against the wall again. He nibbles my earlobe, and a jolt of liquid need rushes through my bloodstream. It warms me more than one of Queenie's medicinal toddies. Every place Jed's lips and hands touch, my nerves light up like a switchboard on overload. Desire builds deep within, simmering toward a slow, steady boil.

"Sky," he whispers into my neck as his tongue teases my

pounding pulse. He presses his forehead to mine, and although it's so dark I can't see his eyes, I know he's searching for answers. Answers I can't speak. Unnerved by his intensity, I close my eyes, afraid that even though it's dark, he'll somehow see my secrets. I press myself closer, signaling I want more.

"When I was in that land of hell, I'd look up and think of you…" He kisses me and whispers, "I was so damn homesick…"

I know exactly how he felt. After he left us, I'd sometimes go with Queenie to the river while she and Darrell fished. I'd sit several feet from the shore, terrified of the water yet drawn there by the moss-covered rocks that reminded me of Jed's eyes.

Tugging on his hand, I pull him toward the stairs. To my surprise and delight, he tosses me over his shoulder and takes the stairs two at a time. I silently giggle and smack his back when my head hits the doorjamb. He spanks my butt in return. The resulting hotness spreading across my bottom is a much different reaction than when Queenie used to tear it up. We hardly make it past my door before we're shedding our clothes. I toss my jewelry on the dresser, and for the first time ever, I hate my boots as I struggle with the laces. The darkness provides a sense of urgency and, strangely, safety.

Once I'm naked, I jump into his arms, and we tumble together onto my bed. He's here, and he's mine. I've only dreamed of this.

"Whoa, Princess," he murmurs, laughing. "You still love being naked, don't you?"

I smile against his neck and nod. As a child, I'd run around the backyard unencumbered by clothes, feeling at one with nature. Once, I had my legs switched by Queenie when I convinced Caleb to get naked with me. I was six, and he was eight; Jed was ten and off fishing at the time. Caleb had come to visit with his parents. As they sat on the front porch, drinking sweet tea and discussing theology, we ran around the backyard playing tag, naked as the day we were born.

It was Darrell who told on us. Mrs. Buzbee called me a heathen and didn't allow Caleb to visit for a long time after that. His father was more forgiving and had brought him to visit behind her back. After that day, Mrs. Buzbee quit pretending to like me.

Lying on top of Jed, I clasp his hands in mine. I know he could easily overpower me and stop this, but I pray he doesn't. My dreams mix with reality. The coarse hair on his chest tickles my breasts. He shifts his hips, and I gasp and clench his hands tighter at the welcome sensation.

"Nice, huh?" He groans as his mouth finds mine, tempting me with his skill.

It's more than nice. Instinctively, I rub against him in a steady motion, faster and faster. Tension builds until I can't contain it. I shatter, catapulting into the uncharted territory of fulfillment with another person. I grip his hands, riding my release, shuddering uncontrollably. It's different and better than anything I've ever experienced on my own. He frees his hands from mine and caresses my back, my sides, exploring my body by stroking, pinching, and rubbing in delicious circles. The sensations are new and exhilarating.

This is heaven. I'm sure of it.

I find myself flipped onto my back, and he gasps. "I want you…"

He hovers above me, using his mouth to explore spots that make my toes curl. One hand strokes my neck to my throat, and I freeze; my breathing hitches. In a panic, I grab his arm, and, thankfully, he picks up on my discomfort. He moves his hand, nuzzling my neck.

"You okay?" he whispers.

I nod. And I am.

Grinning, he blows a raspberry on my collarbone, making me smile.

"Dammit, you've never been ticklish."

I grin and shake my head. After I moved here, he'd try to torment me to get me to laugh. But I never did. He licks my skin like I'm an ice cream cone on a hot summer day.

"I need you," he whispers between kisses. His hands are everywhere, and then he softly rubs me…and a sense of urgency has me needing more. I want him to devour me, to become my own personal sin eater—except there's no way something as beautiful as this could be wrong or sinful. It's as natural as when the sun sets or the moon rises.

His hands and lips trace over my body, and his deep growl blends into a divine sensory overload.

"More?" he gasps, positioning himself over me. "Tell me to stop and I'll stop."

I playfully slap his shoulder.

He laughs. "Fine. Never mind the *telling*… Kiss me to go on. Bite me to stop."

Kissing him with everything I've got, I wrap my legs around his waist and draw him in. My breath catches at the intrusion. I urge him deeper, wanting him and needing him as much as I need air to breathe.

He sinks deeper, and I gasp, not expecting the pain. His harsh breathing stills, and he kisses my forehead, pausing as I adjust to the new sensation. "Princess, I'm sorry. I didn't think—I should've known… Did I hurt you?"

Shaking my head, I grasp his face in my hands, my thumb skimming over his lips. His hair has fallen loose, and I run my fingers through it, using it to pull him closer. Capturing his mouth, I try to kiss his fears away. All my life I've felt lost, but with Jed my soul—which I wasn't even sure existed—locks with its missing piece. I'm so aware of him I'm not even sure where my body ends and his begins. We're melded together in the fabric of the universe in this sacred space.

"This is wrong…"

I shake my head, silently pleading for him to stop talking, to stop thinking, and to just feel.

To feel me, feel us.

Grabbing his face, I kiss him deeply, thoroughly and completely.

He pulls back, and my heart plummets, only to rejoice when he pushes back in, deeper this time. I feel full, not altogether uncomfortable, and the pain is gone.

"You sure you're okay?"

I nod, and he resumes, soon establishing a steady rhythm. For the first time in my existence, I feel truly connected, at one with both worlds. It's so much more than just a physical act. It's two bodies, one shared experience, but it's also a *spiritual connection*—whether Jed acknowledges it or not. We're bound together for eternity. He's my first, and in this moment I know he will be my last, my alpha and omega. Jed shifts, and using his thumb, he coaxes me closer to the edge of fulfillment. When it occurs, I breathe his name into his sweat-drenched hair.

"Fuck!" Clenching his teeth, his arms lock, and his entire body shudders.

He collapses on top of me. Our bodies are slick from the exertion.

I can't move.

I *don't want* to move.

Jed holds me, lazily stroking my arm. I realize too late the possibility we've formed a new life. We've used no protection. *So be it. If it's meant to be, it will be.* I smile against his soft hair, knowing I'll remember this perfect moment to my dying day. There are no words adequate to describe the love I feel for this man. Jed rises, bracing himself on his arms.

"Shit," he hisses.

And with that expletive, the bliss is broken.

Even before he pulls out, I feel him slipping away from me. Desperate, I grip his arms, but he disentangles himself from me, refusing to make eye contact. He sits on the side of the bed and snaps on the bedside lamp. I blink as the harsh light of reality reveals a man in torment.

"What have I done?" He buries his face in his hands.

What has he done? What does he mean? He's made me the happiest girl on earth! Because of him, I realize I *do* have a soul. I want to hold him and revel in the newness of our deeper connection. I wrap my arms around him, resting my cheek against his back, and rub my hand up and down his arm. To me, this experience simply solidifies what deep down I've always known. We were meant to be. Our fragmented souls are now whole.

Jed straightens his shoulders, and I cling to him a little tighter. But my tenuous grasp on his body and, more importantly, his heart, slips as he shrugs away. His aura has gone from passionate red to a depressing gray.

Please don't leave me.

Gently but firmly, he unwraps my arms and gets dressed. The tension between us builds, and air hisses between his teeth like steam from a kettle. For the first time, I notice the scar on his right hip. I'd forgotten he had to have a hip replacement after he was injured overseas.

With awkward, jerky movements, he shrugs into his jeans as I lie there, confused and hurt.

"I'm sorry. Look, we'll go tomorrow and at least prevent any further mistakes."

Mistake?

The word reverberates in the silent room, ripping a hole through my happiness. Tears threaten, but somehow I manage to hold them in check.

"Don't look at me like that," he snaps, now pacing.

Immediately I lower my eyes. *Stupid girl.* How could I forget? I'm not worthy of love. I'm the throwaway girl. *The mistake.* Fear grips my throat, and I'm projected back in time—submerged under water, fighting for a breath of air, terrified.

"I told you to quit looking at me! You were a mistake from the get-go. I never wanted you. I'll make sure you never look at me again, and you damn sure won't talk." Breaking free and surfacing, I sucked in a breath and cried out, *"Daddy, stop! I won't tell, I won't tell, I won't tell—"*

But my father didn't listen, and the darkness silenced me.

My jewelry rattles with the impact of Jed's fist on my dresser, jolting me back to the present.

"I gotta get out of here. I need some time alone, to get my mind straight."

I sneak a peek at him from under my lashes.

Hands on his hips, he hangs his head, looking lost. "Or as straight as it can fuckin' get. Dammit, I've fucked this up beyond any other fuckup in my history of fuckups."

If I weren't so terrified and angered by the thought of him leaving, I'd laugh at the ridiculous number of f-bombs he just dropped. In her prime, Queenie would've washed his mouth out with soap, switched his legs, and made him write lines.

I watch him finish dressing, silently willing him to stay, to no avail. Heading out the door, he stops, bracing himself on the doorframe. In some weird way, his stance reminds me of Jesus on the cross.

I take a deep breath, attempting to shore up my courage. I've never been alone. Not since I was left for dead in that godforsaken lake.

Please don't leave me; please don't leave me.

As if he's heard my silent plea, he spins and faces me, his

face softening. "I'm sorry, Princess. This is *my* fault. It's not *you*..." He shrugs, looking as confused as I feel. "I don't know what to do." He squats before me, cupping my cheek in his hand, and he leans in and kisses me. It has the bitter taste of goodbye. "I'm not good for you. We're total opposites. You're light and love, fairies and unicorns. I'm dark, broken and dead inside. I've done despicable things, things that can never be forgiven. I don't deserve—"

I place my hand over his mouth, silencing him. *Doesn't he realize we're just different sides of the same coin? I'm dead inside, too.* Taking my pinky, I hook it with his the way we used to, swearing our loyalty to each other. It's the only way I know to explain that we're linked and have been forever.

I don't know if he understands, but he hooks my finger and gives me a quick kiss. Sighing, he sits on the bed, pulling me into his lap. With his strong arms around me, my world settles back on its axis. My eyes grow heavy. Jed kisses my forehead, lays me down, and spoons me from behind. I'm still naked; he's dressed. I want to face him, but I'm afraid to move, not wanting to scare him off. He hasn't said another word.

And the silence is no longer comforting.

CHAPTER TWELVE

JED

I STARE AT the ceiling, hating myself, wishing I'd hit the road two days ago and never looked back. What have I done? Isn't it enough that I've killed people because it was my job? Or that I physically fought with my grandmother, which resulted in her being hospitalized? Apparently not, because tonight I took advantage of the best friend I've ever had, an innocent girl. I didn't even use a damn condom.

And I was her first.

Shamefully, I experience a perverse satisfaction knowing Caleb hasn't known Sky in the Biblical sense, so to speak. But guilt makes me wonder what he means to her. Have I just complicated her relationship with a man she cares for?

Sound asleep, she pins me with her warm, naked body. The trapped feeling that results is irony at its best. Or is it karma? *Whatever.* I can't breathe, much less think, with the swelling bubble of panic rising within me. My heart races, my throat constricts, and the urge to run becomes overwhelming. Carefully, I slip out from underneath her, thankful she doesn't stir. Like a thief in the night, I slip into my shoes and sneak down the stairs. By the time I barrel through the back door, I'm at a full run.

The forest behind the house beckons. It's always been my refuge. Leaves crunch underfoot as I head deeper into the woods. As if the trees are working against me, branches slap my face; thorns grip my clothes and tear my skin. I don't care.

The babble of the river lets me know I'm close to my destination. Above me an owl hoots its displeasure, and something scampers past me, snapping twigs, but I'm not afraid. The sounds of the woods are comforting compared to the dissonant noises of that hospital.

Or Skylar's unsettling silence.

Although I'd almost swear she whispered my name...

I look back, but the house has disappeared behind the trees. Guilt slows my pace, and I listen to the owl still screeching from the treetops. I can't help but feel like it's warning me not to go down this dark path, both literally and figuratively.

"Too late," I bark, instantly feeling foolish for talking to myself. My head doc would have a field day with this entire incident and probably cite Freud.

I shouldn't have been with her.

I shouldn't have left her.

Well, crap. When did I develop a conscience?

Certainly not in the army.

Certainly not in the three years since I got out on an honorable discharge after being wounded overseas.

Not a few hours ago, when I made love to Sky and didn't even use a damn condom.

I charge down the path, running from my demons until oxygen deprivation gets the best of me. Hands on knees, I try to suck some air into my lungs. The guilt I'm carrying is too much to bear. I fall to the ground and cover my face, filled with remorse and shame. This beautiful, sweet girl was raised on fairy-tale stories of happily-ever-afters. Her first time shouldn't have been with a morally bankrupt asshole. She deserves better.

I've had my share of sexual encounters, but I've never been anyone's first. For the most part, I've chosen my women carefully. I never wanted to be tied down or invest the time and energy needed to sustain a relationship. My therapist said I was emotionally blocked and cited childhood trauma, PTSD, *blah, blah, blah.*

I disagree. The fact is—I'm lazy. Women are complicated creatures, and I like things simple and easy. Relationships require too much hard work. Aside from when she first came to live with us, being with Sky has always been easy—until now. By overstepping this boundary, I've propelled us into a complicated and confusing place.

I let out a deep breath. But tonight was different from any other time I've been with a woman. I've had screamers, filthy talkers, or the absolute worst, the clingers—those who wanted to talk afterward about feelings and expected roses and chocolates and a future.

With Skylar, it was more than sex. It was—dare I say it? It was a spiritual experience...

Did she really whisper my name? Or did I imagine it?

I know she talks in her nightmares. And during that religious ecstasy or whatever it was at the wake, she'd made sounds.

The trees whisper above me, as if they're trying to tell me something.

I close my eyes. *Jesus H. Christ.* I can still smell her skin and her hair, feel her soft lips on my body, the erotic tug of her fingers tangled in my hair.

I want to taste her mouth again.

I want to make her scream my name.

What the hell am I doing?

I'm running away.

It's what I do when I can't deal. After my parents died, I

took off to escape the pain. I didn't get far before I was found, but a pattern began. I used to run to these woods when I was upset with Queenie and her eccentricity. I joined the army to circumvent getting into trouble with the law. After my discharge and a brief stint in the nuthouse, I fled the head docs and stayed away from home to avoid Queenie's lectures.

I'm constantly running, yet I can't seem to get away from my demons.

The bitter truth stabs me in the gut. *I'm a coward.* It's my biggest shame.

Sky deserves better than me—someone like Caleb.

Disgusted by my weakness, I let loose with a primal scream, releasing my guilt, frustration, and self-hatred. The woods fall as silent as the girl I left behind. My impulse is to get up and run farther, but something prevents me from rising. Rolling to my back, I stare up at the trees, searching for the sky, but all I see is darkness. No stars, no moon, no glimmer of hope.

I know why.

My Sky is back in that damn house

SKYLAR

It's him. He's laid out for a wake; his dark eyes are empty, black holes, his ugly, horrible mouth frozen in a sneer. On his chest is the plate of food.

"*You need to eat it, Skylar,*" *Queenie instructs.*

I shake my head. I don't want to consume his sins. They're too vile. I'm naked and start dancing around his coffin. He's dead and can't hurt me or my mama ever again. I feel free and alive. I'm happy.

He reaches up and grabs my arm—and twists. It hurts, and I cry out.

"Don't say a thing," he growls. He's the devil, he's evil incarnate, and I can't escape...

Startled awake by my nightmare, I sit up, clawing at my neck, trying to breathe.

Frantic, I look around for Jed, but he's not here. Was being with him a dream, too? The lingering scent of him and the ache between my legs says it wasn't. I wrap my arms around my knees and listen, knowing it's useless. I can't feel his energy.

He's gone.

The grandfather clock downstairs tolls its gloomy quarter-hour chime. Just to be sure, I scramble from the bed and check the roof, the porches, and every room in the house. The back door is unlocked. My disappointment borders on devastation. *Why am I surprised?* This is what Jed does. He's been running as long as I've known him.

I lock the back door. If the jerk returns, he can darn well climb the trellis again. Weary and heartbroken, I creep back upstairs, pausing every other step to listen. The old house has always creaked and groaned, but being alone, the sounds seem amplified and spookier.

All of this has a dreamlike quality to it, yet the physical reminder assures me it isn't. I ache in places I've never hurt before. I have no doubt tonight will haunt and tease me forever. But hopefully not the way my nightmares do.

I shower, scrubbing all traces of my foolishness away, my tears mixing with the soapy water swirling down the drain. These few minutes of self-pity are all I'm going to allow myself. After all, I've survived worse. When the water turns tepid, I turn it off and haul myself from the shower. Taking a deep breath, I look in the mirror, taking in my flushed face, swollen lips, and red-rimmed eyes. For the first time in the last twenty-four hours, I'm thankful Queenie isn't here. She'd take one look at me and *know* I've crossed the threshold from a girl with dreams to a foolish woman. I cup my flat stomach and wonder if a life has been made. I don't think so; I feel too empty.

Wearing my oldest, comfiest nightgown, I strip the bed and replace them with clean sheets, kicking the dirty ones to the side. I don't have the energy to take them to the washing machine right now. Emotionally spent, I crawl in bed, not wanting to think about him.

Hands behind my head, I stare at the ceiling, missing Queenie. *Is she frightened? Are they being kind to her?* I've never considered what would happen to me if she wasn't here. Even with her decaying mind, she's been a permanent fixture in my life, securing me to the here and now. In the hospital, when I hung suspended between the worlds, she took my hand and willed me to live, refusing to let go as the ultimate final peace beckoned. Now I feel adrift, lost in a sea of uncertainty with no anchor. And an overpowering sense of doom hangs heavy in the air.

It's been years since I slept with the dragonfly night-light on, but I'm tempted to do so tonight. I pull the sheet over my head and drift into a fitful sleep. Horrendous nightmares wake me not once, but twice. In the first one, Jed was trying to drown me. I woke up gasping for breath. In the second, he'd left me, and I was mired in blood. It was thick like quicksand, and the harder I tried to escape, the deeper I sank.

Feeling silly when I wake, I snap the bedside light on, too scared for just a night-light, and pull the covers over my head. I silently repeat the twenty-third Psalm, which Caleb taught me a long time ago.

Once again, something startles me awake. It takes me a

second to realize it's the ringing phone downstairs. I glance at my bedside clock. It's five in the morning. Queenie isn't here. *Who's calling so early?* Jed? The hospital? I rush out of my room and race down the stairs to pick up the phone, terrified.

"Are you okay?" a voice whispers.

It's still dark outside, and I've watched too many scary movies. The pounding in my ears rises in direct correlation to my panic. The hair on my arms stands on end, and I slam the receiver down. I instantly regret doing so. What if that *was* Jed calling from the hospital about Queenie, and he was whispering so he wouldn't wake her?

No… She didn't have a phone in her room.

Is this him playing a prank?

I peer out the window. His truck remains where we left it last night.

The phone rings again, echoing in the still house. In between rings, the ticking grandfather clock seems to get louder and more ominous. Hesitant, I once again pick up the phone. Even if I wanted to speak, my mouth would be too dry.

"…you scared? I'm here…get you—"

My pounding heartbeat drowns about every third word, but I've heard enough. I hang up and leave the phone off the hook. *He's coming to get me?* This time, I'm taking action.

Darting to the kitchen, I snap on the light and drag the chair across the floor to the pantry. Fear makes me clumsy, and in my haste it tips over. I grab a shelf, but my grasp doesn't hold—it collapses. Landing with a thud on my knees, boxes and canned goods rain down on me, one hitting me on the forehead. Undeterred, I scramble back to my feet. *I have to find those bullets.* Righting the chair, I try again, reaching frantically for the top shelf.

Even on my tiptoes, I'm still unable to see, and in my desperation, I knock more things to the floor. Something sticky is oozing down my cheek. Whether it's blood or something I've spilled, I have no idea, nor do I care. My hands finally find the cardboard box I've been searching for. The back screen door slams against the house. I jump off the chair, shaking so hard the box slips, and bullets scatter like marbles across the kitchen floor. Adrenaline surges through me, and in a panic, I grab as many as I can. A box of salt lies overturned on the floor. I pick it up and pour it across thresholds and windowsills. A protection spell can't hurt, but I'm pragmatic. At the moment, I have more faith in Queenie's gun stopping him.

Throwing things willy-nilly in Queenie's room, I make an even bigger mess than the one left earlier by Jed. Good thing she's in the hospital; she'd have a hissy fit. Finally, I find the pistol under her wheelchair. Shaking like an old woman with palsy, it takes me five tries to get the bullets loaded. I race up the stairs, slamming my bedroom door. Using all my strength, I shove my dresser in front of it. Something pounds the back door. I have no idea if it's the wind or an intruder.

He may try to kill me again, but this time I won't go down without a fight. Jumping at every little noise, I back into my closet and close the door to wait, praying to whoever is listening.

JED

The sun is just rising as I trudge up the back steps. A surprise pop-up storm drove me to shelter in the old cabin for the night. *Is this what it feels like to walk the green mile?* I'm tired, hungry, and more than a little uneasy at how I'll be received. If I'm lucky, Sky will still be asleep, and I can just slip back in bed. Or maybe I should play the considerate lover/friend role and bring her breakfast in bed? At the very least coffee.

Yep, sounds like a plan.

While hunkered down in the cabin, I took a hard look at myself. What I found wasn't that great. But I vowed to try to change and be here for Sky. With her I don't feel so disconnected. She's the bright, full moon shining on my dark soul. I can't promise I won't say *fuck it* and disappear at some point in time. *But not today.* Today I'm gonna do that one-day-at-a-time psychobabble bullshit and try to make amends. I'll man up to my responsibilities and be there for my family.

First on the agenda, offer my apology and sort things out with Sky. Even if she doesn't forgive me, she's got to get the morning-after pill. Neither of us is equipped to handle being parents.

The back door's locked. *What the hell?* Being the mature adult that I am, I beat on it and swear profusely. Sky doesn't hear me, so I kick it before marching around to the front door. Widdershins is lying on the rocking chair, glaring at me with typical cat disdain. He flicks his tail with smug satisfaction when I can't get in. My exasperation glides straight into worry. I don't remember locking the doors. *Calm down.* I search for the key Sky used earlier, but it isn't there. Things escalated so fast last night, replacing the key wasn't even a thought.

The trellis remains an option, but it damn near collapsed on me the other night. I don't need to end up with a broken leg. Returning to the back door, I use my driver's license to pop the lock. Widdershins darts in ahead of me. He's a spooky little shit. Queenie needs some deadbolts. Even though this is an isolated area, there are risks, maybe more because it *is* so far off the beaten path. My to-do list is growing and will keep me busy for at least a couple of weeks. *Fuck, I hate responsibility.*

Opening the door, I freeze in my tracks. Cans and boxed goods are scattered across the kitchen floor, along with an overturned chair and a broken shelf from the pantry. Did Sky hurt herself? Before I can call her name, I slip on something and almost hit the floor. My gut clenches into a tight knot.

It's a bullet.

My senses now on high alert, I grab a butcher knife and silently make my way toward the stairs, scanning my surroundings for any movement. Fear permeates the air; I can practically smell it. Not knowing what's happened, I cautiously creep up the right side of the stairs, pausing to listen every third step.

Putting my ear to Skylar's closed door, I hear nothing. Is she in there? Should I wake her? Or just peek in and check on her? I take a deep breath, pulling the brake on my growing paranoia. Nothing goes on in this sleepy area; it's just my overactive imagination, and we'll have a good laugh—after I wring her neck for scaring me like this. She probably went looking for something and was too exhausted to clean up her mess. When she was a kid, Queenie used to fuss at her all the time for not picking up her toys.

Quietly I turn the knob, but the door doesn't budge. Concern overrules rational thinking. Stepping back, I kick the door open and barrel through, tripping over some piece of furniture in the process. As I'm trying to push it out of the way, a deafening blast of gunfire splinters through the closet door.

Fuck, that burns!

My army training kicks in, and I duck for cover and assess my situation. Thanks to my wallet, the bullet has only grazed my ass. I crawl to the closet door, yank it open, and crouch out of the way.

I find Skylar hunkered down like she's prepared for a disaster drill with Queenie's gun dangling from her shaking hands. Angry and scared, I stand and grab her ice-cold fingers, pulling her from the closet. Unfocused, haunted eyes stare at me, and beneath the purple bruising on her forehead, she's as white as a ghost. Dried blood mats her tangled hair. I know the signs well; she's going into shock.

"Skylar, you're okay," I assure her, using as calm a voice as I can muster. I pry the gun from her trembling fingers, more than a little concerned she might shoot again, either accidentally or—given my behavior last night—on purpose. Moving slowly to keep from frightening her any further, I place it on the dresser, which is now located in the middle of the room. Her teeth chatter like Spanish castanets. I wrap a blanket around her, checking her for other injuries. Her pounding pulse matches mine.

"Tell me what happened. Was someone here?" I'm torn between checking her out and searching for what has spooked her bad enough to hide in a closet with a gun.

She doesn't respond, as if she didn't hear me.

"You're okay. I'm here." Helping her lie down, I tuck pillows under her feet to get some blood back into her pale face. Her rapid, shallow panting is like that of a trapped animal. I rub her icy hands to get some circulation.

"Breathe nice and deep for me, Princess." She appears unharmed except for the purple goose egg on her forehead. The blood in her hair is only a surface scalp injury. In a few minutes, her ragged breathing slows, and color returns to her pallid cheeks. Scrambling to sit up, she attempts to shove me out of the way.

"What's going on?" Fear for her safety makes my tone sharper than I intended.

She slaps me across the face, not holding back.

Startled, and now pissed, I snap, "Tell me what happened. Do we need to go to the police? Did someone break in? Are you

151

hurt?"

She shakes her head, shrugging out of my grasp. To my surprise, she hops up and shoves her feet in her tennis shoes. She reaches for the gun, but I get to it first.

"Oh hell no. Are you insane? I'm in charge of the weapon." I check and, sure enough, there are still two bullets in it. "What the hell are you doing? I'm calling the police." I shove the dresser back where it belongs, but Skylar runs past me, blocking the door. Eyes wide, she shakes her head.

"What? Why not? Tell me what happened."

She signs, *No police. I didn't tell.* And before I can respond, she races down the stairs. I follow as fast as I can, wincing with every step, my ass throbbing like a motherfucker.

"Skylar, stop." Her air of desperation is more frightening than her bruised, bloody face. "You're hurt, and this place is wrecked."

She stomps her foot and writes on a pad she finds on the counter. Scribbling furiously, she shoves it in my face.

You LEFT me. You're a JERK!

"I know, but that's no reason to kill me. Well, maybe it is, but not much of one. I guess idiots have been killed for less."

She shakes her head and pantomimes a phone call. Spinning on her heels, she races out the back door.

She's this upset because I didn't call? Or did someone else call? And if so, who was it? I need more information. Running after her, I trip on a can of green beans, and my already aching ass slams against the floor. My string of expletives would've made my drill sergeant blush.

CHAPTER THIRTEEN

SKYLAR

WHAT HAVE I done? Growing up, I wanted to believe Queenie when she said I was a good person. What happened today proves otherwise. *I'm my father's daughter.* No amount of spell casting, aura cleansing, chants, or prayer can change that. My ability to consume the sins of others stems from the magnitude of my own. I simply absorb the evil, melding it with my inherent nature.

Despite Queenie's teachings and nurturing to do no harm, I shot with the intention to kill. I'm the lost girl, the girl with no soul who has hate in her blood. Me thinking Jed's soul was part of mine was just the ridiculous wish of a stupid girl. This incident has unleashed the full potential of my black energy, and it will affect those I love. I can't let this happen. I've already injured Jed. The only way to stop providence and protect my family is to leave.

The early morning sun tints the sky pink. The ground is slick from the rain last night. Some unseen force drives me to the river. I slip on pine needles but catch myself and keep going. *What if I'd actually killed Jed?* A sob chokes my throat as thorny branches snag my nightgown. It rips, but I keep going. Above me the trees whisper, but I can't understand what they're saying.

I'm out of balance with my surroundings because of the hate within me.

The babbling water draws me despite my fear. If only it could cleanse my sins… Maybe I should've let Pastor Buzbee baptize me years ago. I want to drown my shame, but, instead, fear forces me to my knees. No longer able to contain my self-loathing, I vomit until the dry heaves take over. Jed comes barreling up behind me, and I hide my face in my hands.

"Princess?" He approaches slowly, as if I'm a rabid dog.

I'm worse. I hold my hand up, beseeching him to stay away.

Typical of Jed, he ignores me. Without saying a word, he sits beside me and covers my emesis with dirt and leaves. My emotions swing like a pendulum. Part of me wants him to take me in his arms and forgive me; the other part wants to throw him in the river for leaving me alone last night. In the end, my love for him overpowers all other feelings.

"Talk to me, Princess. Tell me what happened last night. I know I'm the worst kind of ass for leaving you by yourself, and I'm sorry. Trust me, you didn't do anything wrong. It wasn't you; it was *me.*"

Through my lashes, I watch him snap a twig and send it sailing into the stream.

It brings back a memory from years ago. Jed and I were burdened by survivor's guilt and moping. One afternoon Queenie marched us to this very spot. I was terrified and crying, trying to get away from her like a wild animal on a leash. But she held tight and assured me nothing bad was going to happen. When we arrived at the edge the river, she sat on a huge flat rock and held me, rocking and singing about a moon river. I don't know how many times she sang the song over and over, but I finally calmed down. While I was having my meltdown, Jed somberly skimmed rocks. She called Jed back over to where we were sitting and gave us each a stick, instructing us to pour all our fears, anger, and frustrations into them. Jed rolled his eyes and said it was stupid, but when she insisted, he sighed and closed his eyes. His knuckles turned white as he gripped his stick, and a lone tear slipped down his cheek. I cried watching him, but when Queenie gave me *the look,* I closed my eyes and concentrated on my own stick. After a few moments, she had us open our eyes, break our sticks, and throw them in the river.

Shaking her finger and narrowing her eyes, she said, *"Now quit brooding and start acting like kids. The past is the past. Just like those sticks floating downstream, you need to move on with your lives."*

Without another word, she walked away, leaving us alone. Jed held my hand as we watched our sticks drift away. When they floated out of sight, we hooked our pinkies, spit on the ground, and bumped fists in silent camaraderie.

And from that day forward, we smiled more often.

He rubs the back of my head, petting me like a cat, pulling me from the past. "All I can say is I'm sorry. Forgive me?"

I sit up and nod. He pulls a leaf from my hair. His smile grounds me, and my anxiety starts to dissipate. Sniffling, I point at him, circle my heart with my fist, and point my finger like a gun to relate how sorry I am for trying to kill him.

"Of course. I forgive you. I know you were scared. Start over?"

I nod.

"I'm going to wash your face, okay? No baptism, I promise." He winks, and I smile in spite of my trepidation. He scoops some water and cleans my face and lets me rinse out my mouth. "Tell me what happened. What spooked you?"

Hanging my head, I use a stick to write in the dirt: *I'm evil, no soul.*

"You're so far from evil that's almost funny. You're good through and through. And for what it's worth—since you've

WHAT THE TREES KNOW

been hanging with the Buzbees—there ain't no heaven, and there ain't no hell. All we've got is what's right here. We're just bodies on this earth. When we die, we'll be nothing but the damn dirt you're writing in, so don't worry about whether or not you have a soul."

He pauses, taking a breath. "Sky, I'm worried about you—not about where you'll end up but what's going on in the present, especially after that crazy so-called sin eating. I dunno whose influence is worse, the Buzbees' or Queenie's, to be honest."

I watch his broken stick drifting with the current. He's wrong; there *is* more. As an emissary between the worlds, I've seen the place that is neither here nor there—it just *is*. I've witnessed the color of joy and the darkness of despair. And I've experienced the fear of being caught in between.

He starts humming *The Twilight Zone* theme song and snaps his fingers in front of my face.

I glare at him and finger spell, *Jerk*. However, his spreading grin is contagious. I never could stay mad at him.

"You got that right. Jerk shoulda been my name instead of Jed. So, we're good?"

I write, *Why did you leave? Where did you go?*

"I came out here and got caught in the storm, so I crashed at the cabin for a couple of hours. I was scared, confused. What we did seemed *wrong*, yet at the same time was *so right*. Sex changes things, Princess. We have to figure it out together, where we go from here..."

Heat infuses my cheeks.

"Look at me, Sky."

I stare into his stormy eyes. *Does he love me?* They soften, and for one brief second, I see my feelings reflected in their fathomless depths. It's enough to offer me hope.

"Again, I'm sorry. I can't promise I'm not going to leave

again, but I *can* promise I'll make sure to tell you first..." He stares at the river. "And I'll always take care of you and Queenie, no matter what."

I reach out and give his hand a squeeze. What he doesn't know is that all of this is my fault for interfering with his free will and bringing him back here with a spell. But I've learned my lesson. We lock pinkies, spit, and fist bump. He forgives me, and I forgive him. As if mirroring my waning inner torment, the sun breaks through the trees.

"Now, when will you learn to wait to pull the trigger until you see the whites of their eyes? You've always been a lousy shot." Jed nudges my shoulder.

I stick my tongue out at him, and he laughs, pulling me to my feet. The cold, damp earth has seeped through my thin gown. I shiver and rub my arms. His eyes darken as they zero in on my hard nipples. Cupping my face, he pulls his gaze to my eyes, then concentrates on my mouth. The look on his face has shifted from amusement to something more intense, more personal. I'm firmly in the present and hyperaware of everything about Jed: his scent, the roughness of his thumbs grazing my cheeks, the sound of his ragged breathing, and the conflicted emotions crossing his handsome face.

And in this moment, I have an epiphany. The whole reason he's here was mapped out long before I did that spell. It's divine intervention. My world melds with his. Last night we were physically joined as one. As I gaze into his eyes, I realize this is beyond that experience. It's a *deeper* level of intimacy. He may not believe we are more than flesh and blood, but I *know* differently. What's that old hymn? *I was blind but now I see...* The light of knowledge has removed my doubts, and everything has become crystal clear. We are nothing without each other. Apart we are broken pieces, but together we are whole. We are meant to be together, to save one another.

I feel hope growing inside me like a seed watered by a spring rain. Soon, it may very well break through the dirt of my past. Jed stares at me, worry creasing his brow.

I smile, wondering if he feels this too. Does he know he'll never be free of me?

"What kind of spell have you cast on me?" he murmurs.

Hooking my fingers through his belt loops, I pull him to me and close my eyes. I kiss his chest where his heart beats. The power of female energy blooms within me. *Silly boy, it isn't a spell. It's fate.*

His hands bunch my gown and creep underneath, and, despite the chill from the morning air, my skin feels like a burning furnace. In one fell swoop, my gown is off and floats to the ground. He brushes my breasts, and my toes curl. Trailing kisses down my neck, he tickles me with his beard, and I squirm, making him chuckle.

"You should tell me to stop," he whispers, continuing his teasing descent.

I shake my head and tug him closer. He sinks to his knees in front of me and presses a kiss to my stomach.

"We're friends..." His tongue dips into my belly button as his hands grasp my breasts and squeeze.

Using both hands, I tug his face upward. Hooded with desire, his eyes twinkle with devilment. I raise one eyebrow and grin back at him.

"I should treat you like a sister..."

I roll my eyes and shove his shoulder before stomping away. A hand snakes out, catching my ankle and tumbling me to the ground. He has me flipped and underneath him before I can get away, caging my body with his. The leaves beneath are damp, cold, and prickly, but I couldn't care less.

"Say uncle." He waggles his eyebrows. "Or finger spell it," he amends with a chuckle. Then he wrinkles his nose and makes a face.

I frown.

"You're a stinker. Literally."

Heat rises in my cheeks, and the vile taste in my mouth gives credence to his words. I move to get up, but he traps me and grins. "Just no kissing, okay, vomit breath?" he teases.

Mortified, I try to roll away, but he settles on top of me, his head resting over my heart. Pinned, I give in and wrap my arms around him, my fingers combing through his hair. His body and the lazy circles he's tracing across my goosebumps warm my skin. Even with twigs and leaves digging into my back, a sense of peace surrounds us. We are exactly where we are meant to be. It's a perfect moment in time. Squirrels jump from tree to tree, chattering; behind us the river flows effortlessly. I smile, realizing the sound doesn't invoke my usual fear. With Jed, I have nothing to be afraid of. Through the changing leaves, birds serenade us with a happy tune. The forest is alive, and so are we. The dark terrors of the night recede with the light of hope.

As if Jed can read my mind, he whispers, "I don't want to go back and face the real world. Why can't this be real? I feel…" His voice trails off, and his smile spreads as he plants a kiss over my heart. "I feel—I'm fuckin' *feeling!* It's strange, like I've been dead before…" Full of raw emotion and wonder, his words choke.

I shiver, and he snuggles in tighter, sharing his body heat.

I hold him close, stroking his back, absorbing his past pain. Together, we can do anything. This man has saved me. I will do the same for him. He's been dying ever since he left this mountain, running from his past. I will consume his sins. I will teach him to live. Looking up at the treetops and the rising sun, I smile and silently chant my new mantra.

I am not my father's daughter.

I am Jed's lover.

JED

I've never believed in heaven, but lying here in Sky's arms, I'm as close as I'll ever get. The awakening woods seem to welcome us, and nearby an animal crashes through the trees. I don't care. We belong here. This sanctuary is home. I shift and cover her more completely. I know she must be cold, but I just can't bring myself to move yet. The moment is too perfect. Skylar brushes a kiss on top of my head and wraps her arms a little tighter around me. I sigh, perfectly content being in the moment.

Eventually I roll off of her and wince. I really need to tend to my ass, but I don't want to return to reality. The fall leaves seem brighter, the sky bluer. I hate to admit it, but maybe Queenie was right. Life isn't a spiral or descent out of control, or at least it doesn't have to be. Life and death are natural. You can flow with the movement or fight it and lose. *Shit*. What has this girl done to me? My sappy musings sound like some damn Disney cartoon.

We lie side by side for a moment, staring at the canopy of stately pines and oaks rustling above us. Sky points, signing that the trees are talking.

"I guess you could say they're whispering," I concede. It does sound like that.

She smiles and nods.

Maybe this living-in-the-moment shit isn't so bad. If only we could freeze time and stay here forever. I guess that's what memories are for. Pull on the good ones to sustain you through whatever shit life hands you.

Sky sits up, shivering. Even though it's been unseasonably warm, it's still early, and she's soaked.

The distant sound of a siren breaks the peaceful reverie, reminding me I have responsibilities. First on the list, taking care of Princess, then check on Queenie. I help Sky to her feet and look around for her gown. Her pale skin is a stark contrast with the colorful woods around us. Her wistful look reflects my reluctance to return.

"You okay to go back?" I still don't know what scared her. But I can sort it out later. She looks down, and I follow her gaze to my bloody jeans. Suddenly she drops to her knees, her hands tugging at my pants. I pull her back to her feet.

"It's fine. You just grazed me. And it proves my point."

Her lower lip trembles, and she makes rare, uninitiated eye contact.

I chuckle and pull a lock of her tangled hair. "You're a pain in my ass."

She rolls her eyes and grins but again circles her chest with her fist.

"I know you're sorry. Will you tell me what happened?"

She shakes her head and scampers down the mountain, butt-ass naked. Grabbing her gown, I follow, enjoying the view. As we near the back of the house from over the hill, there are more sirens, the sound of two-way radios, and the crunch of gravel breaking the serenity we've just experienced.

Something's not right. I hurry forward and grab her hand, stopping her at the edge of the woods. *What the hell's going on?*

I motion for her to be quiet and push her behind me as I peer through the dense undergrowth to assess the situation. Three squad cars, an ambulance, and at least seven other cars are parked in the yard and driveway. Armed officers are milling around the yard, poking in the shrubbery, taking notes. One has a camera, taking pictures. Nosy bystanders contained behind yellow police tape are laughing and carrying on like it's a goddamned church picnic.

Off to the side, I spy Dammit Darrell talking with Pastor Buzbee, Caleb, and Sheriff Rogers. The poor man looks like he's about to have a stroke, pointing at the cars parked haphazardly on the meticulous grass he keeps mowed like a football field. Caleb pulls out his inhaler and uses it. Before we can duck back under the cover of the woods, Kip Rogers yells and points at us. Half the damn county turns its attention our way, most with phones held high.

Behind me, Sky scampers back into the forest. I wheel around to toss her the gown, but she's already halfway up the hill.

"Shit!" I know from experience running from the law is never advised. But when have I ever taken advice? I take off after her. "Sky, wait!" I wave her gown at her, but she's not looking back.

She darts through the dense forest, veering off the path away from the river. I slip, barely managing to keep from busting my ass.

"Stop. Hands up!" Kip yells from behind me.

I've been hunting with the dumbass before, so I'm ninety percent sure he has his gun pulled and trained on my back. He's a twitchy, inept little bastard who one time tripped, shooting himself in the foot. Better to be safe than dead or maimed. I stop and raise my hands. Today is not the day to play hero. My priority is to take care of Sky.

"On the ground."

I drop to my knees and lie prone. He has me cuffed in no time, his heavy breathing sawing like a dying accordion.

"Maybe you should cut back on your donut consumption," I scoff. He responds by jerking my arms harder than necessary.

Several officers storm past us in pursuit of Sky. "Don't hurt her. She's scared!" I yell. "Quit trying to act tough, you son of a bitch."

Kip yanks me to my feet and pushes me toward the backyard.

"What the hell's going on? Shouldn't you be reading me my rights or something?"

"Why don't you tell *me* what's going on? You're the one with blood all over your clothes." Keeping a beefy hand on my arm, he propels me toward his father, Caleb, and the good reverend. When we're within earshot, Kip starts reading me my Miranda rights. It's probably the first time the idiot has ever had to use them.

"What the hell is going on?" I repeat.

Sheriff Rogers glares at me, and unease creases Pastor Buzbee's face. Caleb takes off running after the officers who are chasing Skylar, grabbing her gown on his way. I'm relieved. At least I know he won't hurt her.

Dammit Darrell's bushy brows pull together, and his mouth thins. I can feel the anger emanating from him. Noise from the woods pull our collective attention. Three deputies are roughly escorting Sky into the opening. Hands secured behind her back, she keeps her head down. *Oh shit.* She's naked, bruised, and scratched. Blood mats her tangled hair. She looks like a victim of domestic violence. Caleb blocks them from coming into the yard, arguing with the officers.

"Sky!" I struggle to go to her, but Kip yanks me back. *If I ever get loose, I'll stomp his motherfuckin' ass into the ground.*

She doesn't look up and shivers.

Aware of the nosy neighbors with cell phones pointed at us, I snarl, "Geezus, one of you get her a coat. She's cold and scared."

"The witch is naked again," someone in the crowd shouts.

Caleb attempts to drape her gown over her, but the officers refuse to uncuff her. Pastor Buzbee shrugs out of his coat and, with the sheriff's permission, covers Sky. "Skylar, are you okay? Who hurt you?" Pastor Buzbee asks gently as he buttons the coat.

It barely covers her, but at least it's something.

With a sinking heart, I realize what everyone must be thinking given the state of the house and Sky's appearance and my bloody ass. This scenario's going downhill fast. It won't be easy to talk my way out of it, but I'm damn well going to give it a go.

"Can we take this inside, away from the prying neighbors over there?" I ask, nodding toward the zillion phone cameras aimed at us.

"What the hell, Kip? Get those idiots off the damn property," Sheriff Rogers barks.

My opinion of Kip's daddy rises a notch.

Two officers escort Skylar to the back porch and uncuff her, handing her a pad and paper. Dammit Darrell wraps a quilt around her, still glaring at me. Caleb bounds after her, his cell phone to his ear. My heart lurches. I should be the one comforting her, taking care of her…

A deputy moves to block my view and starts the questions.

CHAPTER FOURTEEN

JED

THE SMELL OF cheap hamburgers permeates the truck. Skylar's asleep and didn't even stir when I ordered at the drive-thru. It's been a long damn day, and I'm tired and starving. It took us hours to convince the cops there was no domestic violence. Caleb even went so far as to call a lawyer—for Sky.

I finally learned the part of the story that had been missing. While I was AWOL, Skylar received a mysterious phone call and made the mess looking for the bullets to Queenie's gun. Turns out it was just Darrell calling to check on us when he saw her light on, but Sky hung up on him—twice. When he heard the gunshot, he came over. Finding the kitchen destroyed and us gone, he called the police.

A trip to the ER assured everyone Skylar was fine, just a bump on her head, some bruising, and scratches. After they released her, she seemed shaken and distant. She's refused to communicate what happened.

The ER took care of my injured ass cheek, but my pride is another matter. The detectives kept questioning me about the shooting and implying I'd hurt Sky and she'd shot me in self-defense. I told them the truth each time they asked. Tired of them rephrasing the same questions to see if I would change my story, I asked for a lawyer and started answering with my name, rank, service number, and birth date. The lawyer they'd called for Skylar arrived, and they either finally believed us or got tired of asking the same thing over and over.

After being checked out at the ER, we tried to see Queenie, but it wasn't visiting hours. The nurse had looked at me like I was a deranged lunatic who belonged in the same lockdown unit, which, while true, didn't improve my mood. It took me over an hour to convince Sky we'd come back tomorrow. We both need some downtime, sleep, and food. And I need some answers.

"Son of a bitch." I slow the truck, mystified by the number of parked vehicles. There are two media vans from television stations sixty miles away. I barely have enough room to turn into the driveway.

Sky stirs, yawning and stretching.

"Get down," I hiss.

The crowd swarms toward us, but I don't stop. Instead, I gun the engine and flip them all off. Sky ducks as cameras snap pictures. Parking the truck, I urge her to run as we hurry to the back door amid shouted questions.

Sky races through the house to the front window and points outside, questioning me with her wide eyes.

"I don't know." I'm just as confused as she is. As I'm pulling the drapes, the doorbell rings. We both jump. We're as twitchy as Kip Rogers' trigger finger.

"I'll take care of this." I throw open the door to find a film crew and reporter. Some nosy locals scurry closer. "Get off my property."

A woman shoves a microphone in my face. "Is it true the girl's a witch?"

"Does she hold naked rituals in the woods?"

"Was the house wrecked by some sort of paranormal

activity?"

"Is this some sort of Halloween prank?"

"Tell us about this sin-eating ritual. Is it part of a satanic cult?"

"How much money will you two inherit?" a man asks, recording me with his phone.

"What exactly is your relationship with the girl? Is it true she never speaks? And if so, why not?"

The asshole that asked the last question is trying to peer around me. I know Fred. We grew up together. I blink and hold my hand up to shield my eyes from the glare of the lights. The rapid-fire questions and camera flashes make my skin crawl. These people are lunatics.

"No comment. I'm telling you one more time to get off my property. I'm calling the law." I slam the door and lock it. Sky looks to me for answers, but I have none and shrug. She wanders to the kitchen and starts picking up the canned goods strewn across the floor. The phone rings. Without caller ID, I don't know whether to answer it or not. Sky covers her ears against the incessant ringing, so I grab the receiver.

"Hello?"

"Bring Skylar to me." Pastor Buzbee hasn't asked, he's demanded.

My immediate instinct is to buck his authority. "Excuse me?"

"The local newspaper has turned the sin eating and what went down this morning into a media frenzy. Caleb says it's all over social media, and the local television news stations have picked it up. I wouldn't be surprised if it lands on the national news since it's almost Halloween."

"What? Are you kidding me? This entire thing is going viral because superstitious, bored people are grabbing their fifteen minutes of fame?"

"Apparently. I've done my best to diffuse the situation, but people love scandal. Eleanor and I want to protect Skylar."

"Scandal? There *is* no scandal. This morning was all a misunderstanding. This is crazy. And it's up to Sky if she wants to come to your house."

She shakes her head and crosses her arms. Opening the fast-food bag, she nibbles on a cold fry and wrinkles her nose.

"Jedidiah."

His serious tone catches my attention, and instead of hanging up, I listen. "Some locals are questioning Queenie's rapid mental decline and insinuating things that make me uneasy. If either of you has done anything, I'm here to help…"

"Has the entire world gone mad?" A knock sounds at the back door. "Don't answer that," I bark.

Pastor Buzbee sighs. "I'm sorry. Maybe I shouldn't have said anything. I'm just worried. Like I said, this is a remote area; people have nothing better to do than gossip. Caleb has offered to take Skylar out of town if need be…"

"I wasn't talking to you. Someone's at the back door. I gotta go." I slam the receiver down.

Years ago, miscommunication made me lose my cool, and trouble followed. That same explosive anger is simmering once again, threatening to consume me. Somehow, we've become involved in an actual, modern-day witch hunt. I look around for Skylar and hear someone talking to her.

Christ on a crutch… I march back to the kitchen.

"Thank you for the tea. It helps me sleep better." Mrs. Langford's eyes widen when she sees me. My hair is loose and tangled, and I'm still wearing my blood-splattered jeans. I probably look like a madman or a serial killer. It doesn't help that she and I share an unpleasant history. When I was eleven, I picked some of her zinnias to make a bouquet for Queenie. Instead of appreciating the gesture, much less thanking me, my grandmother whipped my ass and had Dammit Darrell supervise the replanting of her damn flower garden. I also had to mow the old bat's lawn for the rest of the summer for free. And she was hypercritical, pointing out every blade of grass I missed.

She steps toward the back door, holding a cheesecloth bundle and her walker. Skylar holds her elbow, guiding the elderly woman around the spilled pantry items littering the floor.

"Thank you, my dear. I thought you two would be exhausted and hungry. I hope Guinevere feels better soon. I'll check in later this week. Perhaps you could read my cards then?"

A humongous picnic basket sits on the table. Skylar nods and motions, *Thank you*. After another inquisitive look around the trashed kitchen, the busybody leaves.

I growl, frustrated. "This is all Queenie's fault, always talking that mumbo-jumbo crap and luring you into her insanity—"

A can of green beans sails past my ear. Judging by Sky's scowl, if she were truly a conduit of the supernatural, I'd be keeling over dead.

"You missed because you never follow through when you throw. If you're going to kill me, you'll have to learn to aim first. I'm here to *help* you. According to Pastor Buzbee, people think you're a witch and one or both of us is plotting to kill Queenie."

She responds by rolling her eyes.

Grabbing her by the arms, I give her a shake. "This isn't a joke."

The phone rings again. This time I pick it up, break the connection, and immediately call the sheriff's department. I inform them that if they don't keep the inquisitive bastards off my property, I'm liable to do something I'll regret.

I leave the phone off the hook. "Those idiots aren't going to stop. Our best bet is to go and let the gossip die down. Grab your purse and a jacket, and pack."

She shakes her head. There's another knock at the back door—this time three short raps followed by two. I try to prevent her from answering, but she manages to squirm out of my grasp.

Caleb enters.

Great. Super Nerd to the rescue.

"You okay?" he asks Skylar while shooting me a death stare.

Color blooms in her cheeks as she nods, staring at the floor.

"She's fine. I'm handling this."

"Yeah, I can tell," he scoffs. "Sky, we have a couple of options. I can take you to my mom and dad's, or I can get you out of town. I have friends in Asheville, where you can stay."

Even though I just voiced a similar thought, I yell, "She isn't going anywhere. We're standing our ground because we didn't do anything wrong." I refrain from adding that it would be a cold day in hell before I'd let him take her anywhere. Silently, I pat myself on the back for adulting.

Skylar shrugs, looking confused and exhausted.

Caleb crosses his arms and glares at me.

I sigh. "Look, your dad insinuated there are rumors we hurt Queenie. If we leave, it will look like we're guilty." I'll be damned if we're going anywhere.

She signs, *That's crazy.*

"I *know.* You're preachin' to the choir, Princess. Do you want to go to jail? Do you want *me* to go to jail? Because I think some of those idiots are itching to make me pay for my teenaged pranks."

Again, she twirls her finger next to her temple. She goes about cleaning up the kitchen as if the entire world hasn't gone mad.

Caleb reaches out and gently stops her. "Sky, can we talk?"

He looks at me and adds, "Alone?"

My patience is done, and I don't hold back on the sarcasm. "Sure, she'll tell you all about her spectacular day. She doesn't talk, moron."

This time it's Sky who glares at me. She nods, takes his hand, and heads to the parlor, where she shuts the door.

To keep from throwing Caleb out on his ass, I start picking up the kitchen with a vengeance. I want to rage and make noise and slam shit around, but I don't. Because I'm too busy trying to eavesdrop...

SKYLAR

I just want to be left alone.

I shut the door behind me and lean against it, waiting to hear what Caleb has to say. I know he's worried about me. Earlier today, his help with the lawyer was kind. He paces, and I watch his polished brown shoes tread back and forth across the faded rug.

"I wanted to get you alone, just for a moment, to check on you. I've been worried sick."

I'm spent and only halfway paying attention. He moves to stand in front of me; his white oxford shirt has a sharp crease down the sleeves and is neatly tucked in. He always looks so put together. *Does he do his own ironing?*

"What's between you and Jed is your business, but dammit..."

I look up, startled. Caleb *never* swears.

"I want to protect you, take care of you. Did he hurt you? In any way?" His eyes search my face, and I shake my head and look away. I'm not stupid. I know Caleb has more questions than these benign ones...and I'm not ready to answer them yet.

"Skylar, please let me take you away from here. I'll find another job; I have savings. You need to get away from this circus. They're calling you a witch, for God's sake."

To my surprise, he pulls me close, and his lips mold to mine.

"Hey, Sky, I could use some help in here. This mess is yours, remember?" Jed shouts from the kitchen.

Caleb pulls away, looking flustered. I try not to show my relief at the interruption.

"Sorry," he whispers. "I overstepped. You're tired, and your bodyguard is liable to come barreling though the door. I know my limitations, and he'd beat the crap out of me."

I smile at his attempt at a joke. He's right; physically, he's no match for Jed. Taking Caleb's hand in mine, I give it a squeeze. Part of me longs for the steadfast love and security he can offer. For a brief second I wonder if it could ever be enough.

I don't think so.

Caleb smiles in return. To circumvent a confrontation with Jed, I walk him to the front door. He pauses and moves to give me a kiss goodbye. I turn my cheek to meet his lips. He slips out and runs to his car. Thankfully most of the crowd has dispersed.

After Caleb leaves, I go to help Jed finish picking up the kitchen.

"Are you going with Saint Caleb the Rescuer?" he asks, slamming a can of green beans on the counter.

I'm in no mood to fight; I just want order back in my life, not this chaos. I shake my head no and press my fingers to my throbbing head. The last twenty-four hours have been both a dream and a nightmare. The questions from the police were nothing compared to the invasive exam at the hospital. I feel violated and somehow shamed. No one wanted to believe me when I told them what Jed and I had shared was special, that the bruises and blood in my hair weren't his fault. I finally took the pill they said would prevent pregnancy, even though I could've made a tea to do the same thing. Now I'm regretting it, feeling queasy and exhausted. I toss the cold fast food into the garbage.

All I want is a shower, a hot cup of chamomile tea, and to crawl into bed, preferably with Jed. I need him to hold me.

"I'll have to cut a new shelf tomorrow," he mutters, more to himself than me. "Let's call it a night."

I'm in total agreement, wishing we could turn back time.

JED

My ass hurts, I have a pounding headache, and I need peace and quiet to decompress. Caleb left in the nick of time—just before I threw him out. Possessive jealousy made me see red when he asked to speak to her alone.

Purple smudges circle her eyes, and her movements are slow and deliberate as she tosses the cold hamburgers and fries in the garbage. I still have some unanswered questions, and I hate to press her, but I need to know the answer to at least one.

"Skylar?"

She looks up, making eye contact for a change.

"Did they, uh, take care of—you know...something to

prevent pregnancy?"

She nods but turns so her hair covers her face.

Guilt floods me, and I step behind her, wrapping my arms around her chest. "I'm sorry, Princess," I mumble into her hair.

I don't know what else to say. She turns and buries her face in my neck, gripping my shirt. Her cheek is damp, and I hold her tighter, kissing her forehead.

"I'm sorry this is such a mess," I offer again, sounding like an idiot. Dammit, I should never have come home. I'm not good for her. She needs someone who's rock solid and sound in mind. *Someone like Caleb.* The thought makes my chest feel like it's caught in a vise.

Our stomachs grumble at the same time in a strange symphony. We need to eat. I peek in the basket of goodies the old biddy dropped off and find homemade brownies, fried chicken, and potato salad. Another knock sounds at the back door, and before I can stop her, Skylar opens it.

Has she no sense of self-preservation?

"Evenin', Skylar. I just wanted to let y'all know I told everyone out front to go on home. I'm pulling some overtime, and Daddy told me to drive by every couple of hours on my patrol. You can rest easy tonight." Kip Rogers is talking to Sky and looking at her breasts.

"Oh, I'm sure we'll be fine with *you* on the job. Did your daddy let you have a bullet for your gun, Barney?"

Kip puffs up like a rooster. "I don't find your humor particularly funny. You better talk to me with respect. I *am* the law, after all."

I snort and give him a smart-ass salute. Before he can react, Sky intervenes by escorting him outside, signing, *Thank you.* She shuts the door, and her shoulders sag.

"What a jerk. Like Deputy Do-Right is going to scare anyone. Let's eat and get some sleep. We can finish cleaning up in the morning before we go see Queenie. Go get your shower. I'll bring supper upstairs."

Rising on her tiptoes, she plants a sweet kiss on my cheek before scurrying away. She's hurting, and I need to get her settled down. Tomorrow, I'll get answers.

Grabbing a couple of colas, two forks, and the picnic basket, I head upstairs. I pause at my bedroom and sigh, defeated. As much as I hate this room, the porch doesn't sound very comfortable right now. I peer out the window, and, thankfully, the television van is gone. Kip's out there talking to a few of the busybodies, but at least they aren't on the damn property. I kick off my socks and shoes, not wanting to sit and put pressure on my throbbing ass. I need to eat before taking the painkiller and antibiotic they gave me, so I don't hurl.

A shower helps, but, damn, I don't remember the last time I felt this exhausted. I'm ready to eat and collapse. Pulling the shower curtain back, I jump, yelping like a little girl. Skylar's sitting on the closed seat of the toilet holding a pair of scissors. She snickers and makes a slashing movement like Norman Bates in *Psycho*.

"I didn't hear you. You're too damn quiet," I joke, drying off. Before I can wrap the towel around my waist, she stops me, turns me around, and starts bandaging my butt. I glance behind me. Her damp hair is haphazardly braided, and she's wearing a modest white nightgown. I stroke the top of her hair and attempt to make her look up at me. I need to know she's okay.

She shrugs away and slaps my leg for me to be still. When my butt is bandaged, she helps me step into my pajama pants before handing me the pain pill and antibiotic with a glass of water.

"I need to eat, and you must be starving, too."

She nods, and I follow her to the upstairs porch, where I threatened her less than two weeks ago. It seems like a lifetime has passed since then. Peering through the window first, I make sure the coast is clear. The noose of responsibility tightens, and I silently wish for the oblivion the pain pill offers. Sky hands me a quilt, and I gingerly lower myself onto the porch swing. She cuddles in beside me, wrapped in her own quilt. Silently I wolf down a piece of chicken and a brownie. Skylar picks at her food, her mood pensive.

With the curiosity-seekers gone, the only sounds are those of the night creatures, the squeak of the swing, and the purring cat who's somehow magically appeared at our feet. Sky shivers, and I uncurl her quilt and pull her in closer to me. This feels so right, having her by my side. I know I'm not good for her, but at the moment, I just don't care. I wrap my arm around her shoulder and keep a steady push on the swing.

SKYLAR

The gentle movement of the swing is a direct contrast to my racing thoughts. I'm feeling discombobulated. Part of me wants to snuggle with Jed, but part of me wants to be alone. Reluctantly, I stand and brush a kiss to his temple. His anxiety is unsettling, his aura a swirl of red and black.

He follows me inside. At the stairway toward my room, he pauses. But after last night, I think we both need to be alone, to process what happened. I know if I push, he'll run. I squeeze his hand and head upstairs.

Sleep eludes me. My room is still in disarray, which doesn't help. *Is Jed asleep, or is he trying to figure us out, too?* Did last night mean as much to him as it did to me? Or will I simply be another on his list of however many women he's had? My stomach is still crampy and queasy from the pill they gave me to prevent pregnancy. I took it, knowing a pregnancy would've pushed Jed even further away. Even if he stayed because of duty, he'd have felt trapped, and he's too wild to be bound by physical or emotional tethers.

After tossing and turning for an hour, I give up and tiptoe downstairs to Jed's room. He's asleep but fitful, muttering incoherently about what I presume is stuff from his past. How I wish I could slay the demons that possess him. It isn't that much different than sin eating; it's simply offering comfort. I slip into bed and softly stroke his back the way Queenie used to do when we were kids. Tomorrow, I'll make him a dream catcher. And I'll see if Darrell will help me repaint the walls to make it more like Jed's room.

Without waking, he calms down and rolls to his side. I snuggle in against his back and wrap my arm around his waist. My eyes drift closed, and my own fears slip away.

SKYLAR

"No! It's an ambush," Jed yells.

I jerk awake and find him thrashing about, arms flailing. Glancing at the clock, I realize I've only been asleep about an hour. I stroke his arm, trying to wake him gently from his nightmare. He grabs me and rolls on top, trapping me. Finger combing his hair out of his eyes, I gently kiss his face.

The sound of his erratic, labored breathing fills the room. "Jesus H. Christ," he mumbles, hanging his head. He sits up and rubs his face, his body still shaking with the aftermath of his night terror. "Shit, my ass is sore," he mutters.

After we visit Queenie, I'm making him that dream catcher. For now, I'll perform a quick nightmare spell. Leaving the warmth of his bed, I run to my room and grab a white candle, a hand mirror, and my sewing scissors. I don't have time to properly dress the candle with oils and herbs, but mentally I do a quick spell and light it. I return to bed and place the small mirror and scissors under Jed's pillow.

"What the hell are you doing?" he mumbles, sounding tired. Cradling his head, he sits hunched over on the side of the bed, elbows on his knees.

I pat the bed, beckoning him to lie down. He shakes his head. "No, I can't sleep after a nightmare. I'm sorry you've had to witness my craziness again. I swear, being back here has unhinged what little mental health I have left."

Climbing behind him, I press my body to his, draping my hair over his shoulder and holding him. If he'll let me, I'll keep him safe. I'll consume his demons. Rubbing the tension from his neck and back, I feel his muscles slowly relax. His body is drenched with sweat, and he shivers. With my encouragement, he finally lies back down. Facing him, our foreheads touching, I press myself close and hold him tight. In response, his fingers trail up and down my spine.

"Thank you," he whispers. His eyes drift closed, and his breathing slows to soft, easy breaths.

I know he's faking being asleep, but he's calmed down, so I leave him alone. The candle burns brightly, lighting the way for his demons to leave. I'm here, and I refuse to let the darkness claim him. After all, I'm a sin eater.

JED

I will my pounding heart to slow through conscious breathing, which is hard to do with Princess's soft body curved into mine. I stay still for an hour until, at last, her body relaxes. I think she's asleep, but I'm not sure with my paranoia on high alert. I haven't been this bad in a long time. *What's wrong with me?* It's this place. I've never fit in here.

She shifts, and her breasts press into me; her arms tighten around my waist. I feel terrible. *I* should be taking care of *her*. But how? Our relationship has changed, roles have blurred, and I have no idea who we are anymore. We were friends, raised almost like siblings. Now what? Are we lovers? Friends with benefits? Or, worse, deviants?

Regardless, we're doomed to be fodder for the rumor mill in this narrow-minded place.

She isn't going to like it, but we need to move. I'll show Skylar there's life beyond this mountain, that we're not the goddamned Wiccan Waltons.

I'll talk to the docs and find out what my grandmother's prognosis is for the long term. I think it's obvious that Queenie's deterioration has put her beyond the scope of being cared for at home. She's gone from eccentric to demented, and her physical ailments only make it worse.

My decision isn't going to get me nominated for grandson

of the year, but it's the only logical answer. Plus, it will give Skylar a chance to live her own life, away from this superstitious, backward place.

Caleb offered the same thing...

I push that thought away and continue rationalizing.

There's help for people with disabilities in a bigger city. Sky's bright, and I have no doubt she could find a job. I fault Queenie for not pushing her to live up to her potential. The more I think about it, my resolve grows to take charge and start the relocation process. I'll have Queenie moved to a nursing home in the city. Skylar can move in with me, and I'll help her adapt to the real world, a world where *Hocus Pocus* is a movie, not reality.

I relax, solid in the knowledge that I now have a working plan to take care of those I love. The sooner I can get away from this place, the better.

My last thought before I drift back to sleep is that I should blow out the candle.

But the light is strangely comforting.

CHAPTER FIFTEEN

SKYLAR

"Morning."

I open my eyes and find Jed facing me, the furrow between his brows deep. He brushes a loose strand of hair off my face. "You make this hideous room almost tolerable." He rolls to his back, winces, and returns to his side. "You sleep okay?"

I yawn and shrug. He asks too many questions before coffee. But I smile, happy to be here with him. I take his hand and kiss it.

He swallows, looking uncomfortable. "I've been lying here thinking This thing—whatever it is between us—others may think it's wrong."

I disagree, but I remain still. *How can love be wrong?*

He starts ticking off reasons with his hand. "I took advantage of you the other night. We were raised almost like siblings. I'm damaged—"

I sign, *I love you.*

He sighs. "I love you, too. I always have, but…I dunno if it's enough, you know what I mean?"

Of course it isn't enough. I'm not worthy of love… I lower my eyes to hide my disappointment.

"The fact is, I'm not sure what this is between us anymore.

The one thing I *am* sure of is that you've been brainwashed into Queenie's weird, witchy, whackadoodle ways. There's a world away from this mountain—"

Annoyed, I cover my ears.

"Fine, don't listen to reason. I'm going back to sleep. But my mind's made up. I'm gonna do what's best for everyone." He rolls back over, putting distance between us, and it's more than the physical six inches of bed. He's distancing himself emotionally from me and shutting down.

I'm afraid to find out what he thinks is "best for everyone." I wait a few minutes, until I'm sure he's slipped back to sleep, and get dressed.

I'll banish his negativity. He doesn't realize how powerful words are. You should only put out into the universe what you want to reap in your life. What this house needs is a good cleansing after all the turmoil that's occurred.

I understand his ambivalent feelings regarding us. I'm confused, too. What I don't understand is how he can be so ungrateful and blind to everything Queenie has done for us. For a smart man, he's pretty stupid about some things. How can he not see that magic is everywhere? He just needs to open his eyes.

After putting my sheets in the wash, I start the coffee. Lighting a smudge stick, I walk through the house, opening the doors and windows. I wave the smoldering sage in a circular motion, combining the scent with the crisp morning air. Widdershins weaves in and out of my feet. The smoke curls and drifts, and I visualize the black energy lifting and leaving.

In this darkest hour, I use my greatest power.
Negativity be on your way; in this place you shall not stay.

Feeling Queenie's approval, tears blur my vision. I miss her and need her. And she needs us; we're her family. She has to be scared, being alone and in an unfamiliar place with no one she knows. Despite the cleansing, a strange uneasiness hovers over me. What more can I do?

I decide to also strip Queenie's bed and wash her linens. It doesn't take long to put her room back to right. While I'm in a cleaning mode, I dust, vacuum, scrub the kitchen counters, and get everything lined up, ready to go back in the pantry once Jed replaces the broken shelf.

Two hours later, I'm finishing one last smudging with the sage when Jed comes downstairs, looking as nervous as I feel. His aura is murky as he looks around the kitchen. He shivers and wrinkles his nose as he closes the windows and doors.

"Oh, for God's sake. It smells like Thanksgiving with that stuff burning." He glances at his watch. "I didn't realize I slept that late. What's for breakfast?"

Irritated by his mood, I stamp out the stick. Slamming a bowl on the table, I hand Jed the cereal and milk. He picks at his breakfast as I sip a cup of coffee. The silence between us is a strained, growing chasm.

The phone rings, and I pick it up and smile when I hear Caleb's cheerful "Good morning." He tells me he'll be busy all day but will do his best to stop by and see Queenie on his way home from work. I hang up and find Jed glaring at me.

"I'm going to go cut a board for the shelf and talk to Dammit Darrell," he says, shrugging into his jacket. "Before we go see Queenie, I'm getting you a cell phone. You'll be able to communicate with *your boyfriend* through texting." The sarcasm in his voice is unmistakable.

Is he jealous? Strangely, the thought is empowering. But at the same time, his statement is ridiculous. *He's* talking about *communicating?* This man is the *king* of no communication. I pick up a pad and pen and write, *Don't waste your money. I want to go see Queenie.*

"I have plenty of money to waste, and I never want to lose touch with you again. We'll pick one up on our way to see

Queenie." His tone of voice conveys that it would be useless to argue with him. He pulls on his beard. "*Is* Caleb your boyfriend?" He sounds uncharacteristically vulnerable.

He's jealous and doesn't want to lose touch with me...

A tiny seed of hope takes root. Silly, stubborn man. I shake my head no, kiss him, and sign, *Thank you*, turning around to hide my happy smile.

SKYLAR

While we wait for afternoon visiting hours, Jed shows me how to work my new phone. I couldn't care less. I'm anxious to see Queenie, and I'm praying she's better than the way we left her.

This morning when we arrived, the Buzbees were already there visiting. Queenie was happily eating a slice of carrot cake. Thirty minutes later, she became agitated and belligerent. She even threw the cake at Mrs. Buzbee, which I secretly found amusing. I've wanted to do that every time she's brought us one.

Hearing the commotion, the nurse came in and said there were too many people in her room and asked us all to leave. Jed coaxed the nurse into letting me stay and left with the Buzbees. I tried to keep the nurse from giving her more medicine, but she insisted on giving her a shot. Queenie fell asleep within ten minutes. She looked so old and frail with her mouth open and cracked, dry lips. I sat by her bedside and cried until Jed returned and took me to lunch.

I can't shake the feeling that something isn't right. To me,

Queenie appears to be getting worse, not better.

"You're not paying attention," Jed says, nudging my arm.

I shrug, having little interest in the phone. A ding sounds.

"See? You have a text from me." Jed points. "You can change the ringtone, too. I have the flying-monkey music from *The Wizard of Oz* set on mine for when Queenie calls from the house."

I roll my eyes and open my message. I see a picture of a princess, what looks like confetti, and a pile of poop with eyes. I have no idea what it means and look at him for clarification.

"Princess Party Pooper. Those are called emojis. Send me one." He laughs and shows me where to find them.

Scrolling the emojis, I find a donkey and what looks like a middle finger and send them to him, which makes him laugh.

"You've got a full charge now. But you need to keep an eye on the percentage and recharge every so often, okay?"

I nod, unplug it, and tuck the phone in my purse. *Who's going to text me anyway? It's not like Jed ever phones. Caleb might.*

Jed's leg bounces, and he keeps looking toward the door. I *know* he's hiding something from me. I can feel it.

After he left me alone with Queenie for a couple of hours, I asked where he'd gone. He retorted sharply, "Taking care of business."

The doors to the geri-psych ward open, signaling the start of visiting hours. We approach a second set of doors, and Jed buzzes the intercom, telling them we're here to visit Guinevere Jackson. The doors open, but before we get to her room, Jed stops.

"Uh, you go on. I'm going to check in with the nurses."

Anxious to see Queenie, I nod and hurry to her room.

My heart plummets when I find her in a wheelchair, still wearing her stained gown. She's meticulously shredding a paper napkin. Her hair remains uncombed, and her lips are still dry and cracked. Beside her, the bed hasn't been made. I squat beside her chair, and her face brightens with a smile. She squeezes my hand.

"There's my girl. I'm hungry and thirsty."

I smile and hug her gently. I'm almost scared to let her go, afraid she'll slip away. I pour her a cup of water, which she drains.

"Skylar, will you help me clean up?"

Swallowing my tears, I move her closer to the sink and fill it with warm, soapy water. This is no way to get a decent bath. *I need to get her home!*

"That feels so good," she murmurs after her sponge bath. "I'll be glad when I can get my hair washed." She closes her eyes and hums while I comb through the snarls and plait her hair. I wish I had some colorful ribbons to put in the braids. Thirty minutes later, the door opens. Jed remains standing in the doorway, looking like a whipped dog, his hands jammed in his pockets. Queenie opens her eyes.

"What are you doing here?" she snaps. "Charlotte's here. Go away. When will I get to eat?"

Jed sighs. "That's *Skylar*, not Charlotte. How do you feel? The doctor's been adjusting your medicine and says you need to get that knee replaced and then have some rehab."

"I don't need to be here. I'm not crazy; you are. That doctor just wants my money. Doesn't he?" She looks to me for affirmation.

I shake my head no. Finding my pad and paper, I write, *You need to work hard so you can come home.*

"No. It's the government wanting to butt into my business and take my money. And I'm not a drunk. A hot toddy every now and then never hurt anybody."

Jed sighs. "Not that kind of rehab. Look, tomorrow—"

A nurse interrupts when she enters with some pills. "Hi, Ms.

Guinevere. Let's take your medicine like a good girl. Tomorrow's the big day!"

Big day? Does that mean she's coming home?

Queenie glares. "What's this 'let's'? You want *me* to take it. I don't see you wanting to be poisoned. And in case you haven't noticed, I'm a grown woman, not a little girl." She pushes the nurse's hand away. "Skylar, take me home."

I want nothing more. At this very moment, she sounds as sane and ornery as she's always been. I look to Jed, hoping he sees she's back to normal. Instead, he stands with his arms crossed, pulling on his lower lip. A prickling fear slithers up my spine. *He's done something...*

"Take your medicine, Queenie. No one wants to hurt you," he commands.

"When did you go to medical school? You never went further than high school. You should've gone to school when you got out of the military. Such a waste of a fine mind. Just what did you do with all the money in your trust fund since you didn't spend it on an education?"

"I blew it on whores and weed. Do you want to die? Just take your damn medicine and quit being so cantankerous."

I wonder if he's joking. *I hope so.*

"Do you want me to wash out that smart-alecky mouth?"

Here we go. When will Jed learn not to provoke her?

"I'm not going to argue with crazy," he mutters, placing his hands on his hips.

"Get thee behind me, Satan," Queenie commands, pointing her bony finger at Jed. "Karma will get you if you're not careful."

The confused look on the nurse's face makes me smile. This mixture of theology is the norm for Queenie.

Jed stops pacing and blows a loose strand of his hair out of his eyes, looking at the ceiling.

"Go ahead. Look to heaven for the answer, you little heathen. It's about time."

Jed sighs and pinches the bridge of his nose. Knowing he's about to come unglued, I escort him from the room and toward the waiting area, leaving the nurse to deal with Queenie. The geriatric psych floor is a terribly sad place; I don't see how anyone gets better here. We walk past several older people unaware of their surroundings, sitting and staring off into space. Seeing these lost souls confirms my belief that Queenie doesn't belong here. I need to convince Jed to bring her home. With both of us there to help her, she'll be fine.

Taking my pad, I write, *Let's take her home. She'll be better in familiar surroundings.*

He sighs. "Use your phone. That's what I bought it for. The doctors have redone some of her meds and say she's doing much better cognitively. But she needs a knee replacement followed by some therapy, which will hopefully give her some relief and make her more mobile. The constant pain and meds she was taking were contributing to her declining mental status. They're going to do the surgery in the morning."

Was that what Jed was arranging? This is good news! Grinning, I fish in my purse for the dumb phone and text, *Why didn't you tell me? After her surgery we can bring her home. This is great!*

"We'll see," he replies cryptically.

I jump when, over Jed's shoulder, Darrell appears as if out of nowhere. He glares at Jed, and his knuckles whiten around the flowers he's brought for Queenie. Jed gives him a nod. He walks past without saying a word, headed toward her room.

I sign, *Does Darrell know about her surgery?*

"Yep. *Flowers?* You don't think Dammit Darrell has the hots for Queenie, do you?"

I shake my head at his silliness. Although Queenie likes

Darrell and has repeatedly urged me to do the same, I'm positive there's no romance involved. He's young enough to be her son. This is just Jed's way of deflecting and not telling me something. It's starting to make me mad. I write, *What's really going on?*

"I don't know what you're talking about." His eyes shift right.

I'm tired of his untruthfulness, so I walk away, finding his negativity toxic. When I enter Queenie's room, Darrell whips around, wide-eyed, and the hair on my arms stands on end. *Why is everyone acting funny?* He pats Queenie's hand and leaves with a simple nod acknowledging my presence. He doesn't say a word to me.

A couple of minutes later, the nurse and Jed arrive. To my surprise, Queenie demurely agrees to have the procedure done. After a fairly lucid visit with her, we get up to leave after she eats her supper.

Jed leans in and kisses her cheek. "You know I love you, right?"

"I'm not dying. You're not getting my money."

He chuckles. "I don't want your money. I want you to get better."

Queenie takes our hands in hers. "You two run along and get in bed. It's late." Squeezing our hands, she recites, "'Day is over; night has come. Today is gone; what's done is done. Embrace your dreams, through the night; tomorrow comes with a whole new light.'"

When I was little, she'd say this to me each night when she tucked me in bed. It makes me feel a little better.

As we head to the parking garage, a concrete pole is in the way. I tug Jed to walk with me around it. It's bad luck for the pole to separate us.

"Oh brother. You know that's just plain silly, right?" he

grumbles as he swerves with me.

I shrug. *Why tempt fate?*

JED

After a quick sandwich supper, I go upstairs to whittle on the porch swing. Whittling and swinging help me focus and think. I need to tell Skylar I've got a job lined up in Asheville and that I'm taking her with me, at least while Queenie's getting rehab on her knee.

Four weeks ago, I probably would've been in a bar—drowning my problems in cheap beer and looking for a one-night stand. Goodness, how things have changed. Now I'm looking after my family, trying to do what's best for all of us. I sigh. Responsibility's turning me into an old man, and I'm not even thirty yet.

Skylar slips outside and sits on the swing next to me. She smells of lavender and patchouli and is bundled in her fuzzy blue bathrobe. Her blond hair is still damp after her shower and curling around her shoulders. Widdershins jumps on the railing, staring into the yard toward Dammit Darrell's house. Shit, I forgot about the cat. I'll see if Darrell or Caleb will look after him.

Skylar wraps her arms around mine and rests her head on my shoulder. I pull the quilt around her and put down the dragonfly I've been whittling. With my foot, I push the swing, searching for the words to break the news to her.

"You know nothing stays the same, right? I mean, you and I are proof of that. Things change, sometimes for the good, sometimes not. It's life."

She nods.

"You saw how Queenie acted this morning. While she seems a little better, I'm afraid it isn't enough. I spoke to her doctor—"

Her finger traces out *J-E-D* and then draws a square around it on my leg. She's doing a spell to box in what she perceives as my negativity. I stop swinging and try to get her to realize this is reality, and impractical magic isn't going to help.

"I know you're trying to rebuke me with a spell or some such nonsense. Like it or not, I'm doing what's best for all of us. Do you think this is easy? Do you think I want Queenie locked away? You saw her this morning. The medications don't seem to be working as well as we'd hoped. Throwing that cake at Mrs. Buzbee was the act of someone who's regressing."

She pulls her phone from her robe pocket and texts, *Or someone who hates that awful cake.*

I laugh and put the swing back in motion. "I *like* her cake. It's one of the things I've always liked about her. She's a good cook." I sigh, suddenly feeling very alone and unsure about my decision. "Everything about this situation sucks… I'm doing the best I can for everyone."

Standing up, Sky gives me a peck on the lips and points inside, pulling my hand. A brave man would explain the plan right now. Instead, I follow her to my room, where she's already lit a candle underneath a new dream catcher.

I may be living in a nightmare, but she's my dream.

CHAPTER SIXTEEN

SKYLAR

THE NURSE WHEELS in a stretcher, and I kiss Queenie goodbye. She smiles and tells me everything will be fine, and she'll be dancing a jig within a couple of days. Next, she turns to Jed.

"Don't be planning my funeral. I plan to live long enough to make you pay for your raisin'."

His laugh sounds strained. "I'm countin' on it."

I smile and wave as she's wheeled out the door, but the knots in my stomach tighten. Jed and I walk to the waiting room and sit in silence for thirty minutes. He shifts and sighs and finally gets up and walks around. I try playing the bubble game on my phone, but after losing fifteen times, I read a three-year-old magazine. Jed goes from pacing to pretending to nap to back to pacing.

Two and a half hours later, the doctor arrives and tells us Queenie did well. After three weeks of therapy, he's hopeful she'll be walking with just a cane. As the doc leaves, I'm so relieved I burst into tears.

Jed holds me, patting my back. "See? I told you so. When have I ever been wrong?"

I shove his shoulder, and we head to the cafeteria for something to eat. The food is bland. I pick at it while Jed inhales his and then finishes mine, too.

It's after lunch when they finally bring Queenie back to her new room, which isn't on the depressing psych floor. Visiting is more relaxed here, and the nurse allows me to stay with her. She's groggy and looks so old and fragile, but I'm thankful she's okay. Jed leaves to go ask the staff about something.

There's a knock on the door, and Caleb peeks in.

"May I come in?" he asks softly. He still has on his tie and the white coat he wears at the pharmacy.

The nurse taking Queenie's blood pressure looks up and smiles, eyeing him like he's a big piece of chocolate cake. "Sure!" she says.

She's batting her eyes and not paying the least bit of attention to Queenie or my side-eyed glares.

Oblivious to the flirtation, Caleb enters the room with a wide smile.

Queenie pushes at the poor girl who's trying to do her job. "Leave me alone," she slurs. This is followed by a sharp slap to her arm.

Caleb walks over and takes Queenie's hand. "Hey, Queenie. How's my favorite poker player?"

She quits hitting the nurse and stares at him.

One time when we were kids, he had an asthma attack over at our house, and he didn't have his inhaler. It was scary how glassy his eyes became and how his lips turned blue. He was frantic, knowing his mother would be angry he'd forgotten his inhaler, which made his breathing even more labored. Remaining calm, Queenie gave him an herbal tea and instructed him to take slow, deep breaths over a pan of hot, steamy water with his head covered by a towel. After he could breathe easier, color returned to his face and lips. While he sipped the tea, she taught him to play poker. They pinky swore she wouldn't tell his mother about the attack, and he wouldn't tell his mama about the poker. After that, whenever Caleb came over, he'd ask to play cards. But he was never very good at it.

"Who are you?" she croaks. Her eyes are vacant and hooded.

"Caleb Buzbee. Will you allow me to check your blood pressure so you can get out of here? We need to get you better. I want you to come home so I can beat you at five-card stud."

Queenie cackles and pats his cheek. "You *are* a stud. If I were younger, we'd make it strip poker and I'd beat your pants off." She nods her okay for him to check her blood pressure.

"You wish." Caleb laughs. "Now, this might pinch a bit, but only for a minute." He carefully places the cuff on her arm and holds her hand while it takes the reading.

"As long as you don't pinch my bottom, we're good, young man."

He and the nurse laugh while I grin.

The nurse leaves, closing the door. If Jed would learn to humor her like Caleb does, it would make everything so much easier. Queenie dozes off, and Caleb motions for me to follow him, but I don't want to leave. A nagging fear keeps me rooted by her bedside, holding her hand.

Instead, Caleb pulls a chair close to mine. "How are you?" he whispers. "I took a late lunch and have to get back to work, but I wanted to check on you and Queenie."

I shrug. He holds his hand out, palm up, allowing me to decide if I want to take it. I do, and his fingers clasp mine. They're smooth, unlike Jed's callused fingers. I lean against him. His quiet strength comforts me like the old oak tree in our backyard.

"Is there anything I can do to help you or Queenie?" His thumb rubs circles on the back of my hand.

I shake my head, not wanting to be a bother. I show him my new phone. He smiles, types his number into my contacts, and sends me a text from his phone.

I smile when I see the smiley face with heart eyes. I text back, *Thank you.*

"This is great, Sky. You needed this. I'll tell you a secret."

I look up, and his warm brown eyes crinkle. "I'm learning how to play poker better so I can beat Queenie. There's an app. Look—"

A knock interrupts us, and the energy in the room shifts. I shiver. Something bad is about to happen. Jed enters, looking like a whipped mongrel. Laughter from the nurse's desk mixes with an agonizing cry of "Help me, help me!" from another room. The dissonance reminds me of crows cawing to one another, warning of danger.

I stand and face Jed, swallowing nervously as I prepare for the bad news he's about to deliver. Caleb joins me and takes my hand in his, giving it a reassuring squeeze.

Jed's look darkens when he sees Caleb. He leans in, speaking low into my ear. "I've made arrangements. In two days, Queenie will be released and transferred to a rehab facility. By then she should be walking with assistance. At the nursing home, they'll regulate her medicine and make sure she gets up and moving with rehab. It's halfway between here and Asheville, close enough her friends can visit."

My mouth drops, and I push against his chest. *A nursing home?* I thought he wanted her to come *home.* I shake my head and sign that I can take care of her at home. I can help with her therapy.

"No. I've been offered a job in Asheville. Right now, it's a single project, but it has the potential to turn into a long-term job. We'll stay in one of those suites you can rent by the week. You need to see there's more to life than this godforsaken place."

I stomp my foot and shake my head. *How dare he make these decisions without me!*

"I'm not arguing with you over this. You've never been more than fifty miles from home. *You* need to live your life, Skylar, away from the superstitious bullshit. *We* need to live our lives. This backwoods area has nothing to offer us. *Queenie* will be fine. We won't be too far and can check on her weekly. If she's able to come home after rehab, great. If not, she'll already have her foot in the door for permanent residency at the nursing home."

I'm so angry I see red and clench my fists.

"What about a home health service?" Caleb whispers.

"No horseplay in the house!" Queenie barks, now wide awake. "I've told you kids to go outside and play. Take Caleb with you. That boy needs some fresh air. His mama keeps him inside the house too much."

I shove Jed out the door, and Caleb follows, closing it behind us.

Why did I ever think summoning Jed home would help? Everything has gotten a hundred times worse, and it's my fault. I shake my head, begging him to change his mind.

"Look, we'll talk about this tonight when we get home. Tomorrow we have to start packing her things for the move. Who knows, she might like the place and want to stay."

Caleb frowns. "Skylar, did you know about any of this?"

I shake my head.

"I think you're being a little high-handed here, Jed—"

"Shut up, Caleb. This doesn't involve you."

While Jed's right, he's rude. Caleb's *my friend* and looking out for me. The tension between the two of them is palpable. Something bad is bound to happen if they don't separate. I pat Caleb's arm and walk him toward the elevator. The last thing we need is a scene in the hospital corridor.

"Don't let him do something you don't want, Skylar. While I agree you shouldn't be solely burdened with Queenie's care, he's bullying you. You're the one who should be making these decisions. You've been here, not him. I can look into home health options if you'd like."

I pull out my phone and text, *Let me talk to Jed first. I'll let you know. Thank you.*

He reads the message. "Okay. But know you're not alone. I'll help however I can."

I punch the button for the elevator, wanting Caleb to leave so I can deal with Jed alone.

Reluctantly, he gives me a kiss on the temple and steps in. Jed crosses his arms, his face stormy. It's like being between two snarling dogs wanting to claim their territory. Caleb gives me a wave as the elevator doors close.

"Good riddance. Just what the hell is going on between you two?" Jed mutters.

Taking out my phone, I ignore the question and text, *You aren't giving her a chance to even try to come home. I'm not moving. Queenie will die locked away in a nursing home.*

"I'm her next of kin and responsible for her. It's why I okayed the surgery to begin with. And FYI, no one does complete sentences when they text. It's dorky. Look, if she can come home after rehab, great. But if Queenie likes the facility, do you really think I'm leaving you alone to stay in that mausoleum by yourself? How well did that work out the other night? No. I'm here, and I'm shouldering the responsibility that has been foisted upon me. This is my final decision. No discussion."

I sign, *You're an ass!*

"I know. But I'm her durable power of attorney for all legal and medical issues. Pastor Buzbee told me she'd signed the papers years ago, and I found them in her desk. My decision is final. You may not believe this, but I'm doing it for you *and* Queenie," he whispers harshly. "Arguing about it won't change my mind. This is in everyone's best interest, as hard as it is."

I'm so angry I'm afraid I might do something I regret. I turn my back to him, wondering what to do. Queenie's going to feel betrayed. She'll never understand...

He grabs my hand and spins me around. His voice gentles, and I see the conflict in his face. "Sky, please don't be upset with me. This wasn't an easy decision, but everything will be all right. We'll have each other, and Queenie will either get better or get used to the place. She's a tough old lady."

I bite my lip, trying to keep my emotions in check.

"Maybe she'll get to come home. Stranger things have happened. I'm sorry, Sky." Gently, he pulls me to his chest, and I clutch his shirt.

This is all my fault. I didn't take good enough care of Queenie. I should've made her go to the doctor more often. And made her drink more water and get her knee fixed... And I never should've summoned Jed home against his will.

As if sensing my feelings, he kisses the top of my head. "There's no blame to be had here."

Queenie once told me, *"Nothing is permanent in this life; you just have to roll with the punches."* I'll accept Jed's decision *for now.* I square my shoulders and walk back to Queenie's bedside.

Immediately, her eyes narrow and dart between Jed, the nurse, and me. "What's wrong? What's that brat grandson of mine done to upset you?"

Forcing a smile, I shake my head and sit on the edge of her bed. I tuck in the blanket and straighten her gown.

Queenie places a finger under my chin. "Look at me," she commands.

I swallow and look up. A smile graces her lined face, and although her eyelids are heavy, no confusion clouds her eyes. She cups my cheek and, using her thumb, wipes away the tear escaping down my cheek. "Everything will be all right.

Sometimes we can't foresee why things happen the way they do. Trust your instinct, girl. You're smarter than most and gifted. *Believe in yourself.*"

Softly she warbles Billy Joel's "Lullabye," and her heavy eyes close. It's the song she sang to me whenever I had a nightmare. I dry my face and give her soft cheek a kiss. She's right. I have to believe everything will work out for the best. She'll be home soon. I'm saying goodnight, not goodbye.

Jed shifts his weight and stuffs his hands in his pockets, looking at the ceiling. His eyes are bright with unshed tears. I realize I haven't given him enough credit. As much as he and Queenie clash, he *does* love her. I cling to that thought.

"You ready, Sky? We, uh, have a lot to do and need to get going." Jed walks over and sits on the other side of her bed. He kisses his grandmother's knuckles, like a knight kissing the hand of his queen. "You know I love you, right?"

Without opening her eyes, she replies, "I know. Now get a haircut. And watch out for Sky."

"Will do."

"Liar. You never do what you're supposed to. And you two better not mess up my clean house. The Buzbees will be stopping by later. No doubt Eleanor will have on her white gloves so she can report my housekeeping infractions to those old biddies in her Bible group. I wish I had the ability to turn her into a toad. Maybe I'll let her think I can. It might be fun…" Queenie drifts off to sleep, snoring softly.

Jed chuckles.

SKYLAR

That night, after running some errands and grabbing a bite to eat, Jed and I finally ease up the driveway. I sigh. This is my home. I don't want to move. What if Queenie isn't able to come home? I'm finding it hard to accept that time is moving forward and things will never be the same. How can I be ready for something so life-altering?

Jed parks, and we sit for a moment. He beats the steering wheel with his thumbs. "It's for the best."

He's said that at least three times on the drive home. *Is he trying to convince me or himself?*

"Queenie will be okay," he continues. "I'm doing this for you, too. It's time you got out of these mountains, even if it's just for a few weeks. And if she ends up having to stay…"

I jerk my door open and slam it for good measure, not wanting to entertain the possibility of her having to stay in the nursing home forever. Darrell's sitting on his back porch, watching us.

Darrell. What will happen to him? I point at him, looking at Jed.

"I'll talk to Darrell," Jed says, heading next door.

I nod and hurry inside, leaving the porch light on for Jed. I go to my room to contemplate on the hard lessons I've learned the past week. Queenie was right. When you tempt fate by casting spells, you have to be prepared for the consequences.

Taking out my tarot cards, I sit on my bed and concentrate as I shuffle. I lay out a three-card spread and turn each one over. The Moon lands in the past spot, in the present is the Nine of Swords, and in the future is the Hanged Man. I frown as I try to make sense of the reading. Secrets, anguish, and sacrifice? I pull one last card to clarify and get the Three of Swords.

I drop the remainder of the deck. This reading is far from good. It's downright scary. As I pick the cards up, I realize one has fallen under the bed. It's The Lovers.

What can this possibly mean?

CHAPTER SEVENTEEN

SKYLAR

AFTER A RESTLESS night of worry, I yawn as I walk past Jed's door in the morning. His bed is crumpled and unmade. Out of habit, I make it.

He isn't in the kitchen, so I walk out to the back porch and find his truck gone. The house seems unnaturally quiet and lonely. The coffee pot is half empty, and Jed's cereal bowl and spoon are in the sink. So much for communication—he didn't leave a note. *Typical.* I'd text him, but my phone is upstairs.

Feeling sorry for myself, I pour a cup of coffee and wander into the living area. I know I should be packing some things for Queenie, but doing so would make it real. Instead, I walk over to the old record player and put on one of the albums Jed and I used to listen to when we were kids. I skip to the song where Cher sings about turning back time.

Jed says I need to experience the real world.

What he doesn't realize is I *have.* And it's an evil place. I want to stay *here.*

Footsteps sound on the porch, followed by a knock. It's too late for Caleb to be stopping by before work. Did Jed forget his key? Peeking out the window, I see it's only Darrell. Holding my robe closed, I crack the door.

"Morning, Skylar."

I nod an acknowledgement but don't open the door any wider. He rotates his cap between his fingers, looking everywhere but at me. His avoidance of eye contact isn't unusual, but his nervousness is.

"I was wondering if you'd like to go see Mrs. Jackson. I'm headed over there and could take you."

My first instinct is to decline. But Queenie needs familiarity, and I have no idea where Jed went or when he'll return. And tomorrow she'll be moving to the nursing home. I nod and signal I'll be right there. He doesn't ask to come in and takes a seat on the swing.

I race upstairs and dress, grabbing my new phone and purse. Locking the door behind me, I follow Darrell to his car.

Worry etches his face, but the smile he gives me appears genuine. He opens the door to the ancient black Cadillac. This used to be Queenie's car, but she sold it to him years ago. I settle in the front seat and buckle up.

"Mrs. Jackson's a good woman."

He places his hat on the seat beside us. It's the one I gave him the first Christmas I came to live here. Queenie told Jed and me to either make or buy Darrell a Christmas present from our allowances. She said it was a blessing to give to others. We opted to buy him something. Dropping us off at the hardware store, Queenie permitted us to make the purchases on our own. Jed bought him a trowel and then helped me with the purchase of this hat.

That Christmas morning, Darrell opened his presents and thanked us for them. He promptly put the hat on, and Queenie's eyes narrowed as she looked at me and Jed. After he left, the resulting lecture from Queenie was blistering. At the time, I hadn't known the embroidered leaf on his cap was marijuana. I just knew Darrell liked to garden. I was

WHAT THE TREES KNOW

embarrassed, but Jed laughed so hard he cried.

"She needs to come home." Darrell interrupts my trip down memory lane.

I nod in total agreement.

He smiles, but his look turns pensive. "Soon. She'll be home soon. We can make sure of it."

I hope he's right.

Darrell doesn't say another word. After we arrive at the hospital, he politely escorts me to the orthopedic floor. An elderly man is slumped over in a wheelchair beside the nurse's desk. Another woman shuffles by with a walker. The man walking beside her holds his hand on a belt around her waist. It's like he's walking a dog on a leash.

We hurry on toward Queenie's room. Moaning comes from one room, horrid smells from another. I hate this place.

Darrell pauses and knocks on her door. I motion for him to wipe his mouth, knowing Queenie will do so. He takes out his bandana and mops away the persistent saliva.

"Come in!" Queenie calls.

Trepidation makes my heart thud. But I'm pleasantly surprised to find Queenie dressed and sitting in a chair with a walker beside her. Her face lights up with a wide smile when she sees us. She accepts the kiss I place on her cheek and cups my own.

"My beautiful girl, please don't worry. Everything will be fine."

A nurse comes in and smiles.

"Good morning. I'm Stephanie. What's your name?"

Queenie rolls her eyes. "The same thing I told you earlier."

Even Darrell cracks a smile.

"Do you know what day it is?" the nurse continues as she makes the bed.

"Any day I'm above the ground is a good day," Queenie

grumbles. "There's no need to make that bed. I'm leaving. My family is here to take me home. You'll need to change those linens for your next victim."

"Oh, you're not leaving today. The bed at the rehab won't be open until tomorrow."

Queenie sits up straighter and points her finger. "I don't know who you think you are, but you can't tell me what to do. I hired you, not the other way around. I certainly don't need rehab; I'm not a drunk. Skylar, tell me how your day's been. Where's Jedidiah?"

I sign that I don't know.

"That boy needs a job. Idle hands are the devil's workshop."

The nurse finishes straightening the room and tells us Queenie's schedule for the day.

"Ma'am, when will she be leaving tomorrow?" Darrell asks.

"The discharge paperwork should be done by ten. I believe it says she'll be transferring by private car, not ambulance, correct?"

"Yes," Darrell answers.

I wonder how he knows. I guess Jed told him.

"Great. Call me if you need anything." The nurse leaves with a wave.

SKYLAR

We leave when it's time for Queenie's physical therapy. On the way home, Darrell pulls off the road. I glance around and notice we're in the middle of nowhere. I wonder if there's something wrong with the car. Luckily, I know how to change a flat tire. Jed made me learn how to do it years ago.

Darrell turns toward me. "You can't ever leave me."

I nod but pull away when he grabs my hand.

He adds, "This is Jed's fault. He needs to go…"

Unnerved by this turn in the conversation, I twist to get out of the car.

He hits the locks and once again grabs my hand. "Wait. I'm just sayin'—"

I start shaking, and my heart rate picks up. An overwhelming need to get away sweeps over me. I yank my hand from his.

"Don't look at me like that. I love you—"

Don't look at me… The voice from my past merges with Darrell's.

I flip the lock, bolt from the car, and grab my phone to text Jed, but it's dead. I didn't remember to charge it.

As Darrell steps out of the car, I take off running, praying a car will come along to help me. If I have to, I'll dart into the woods and hide.

"Skylar, wait! I'm sorry. I didn't mean to upset you. I'm calling Jed."

I stop running and warily turn around, staying a safe distance from him. Sure enough, he's talking to someone on the phone. *Or is he?* Suspicious, I motion that I want to hear whomever he's speaking to.

He fumbles with the phone. "Hey, Jed, you're on speakerphone. She's a little upset. I'm going to put my phone down and walk away. Can you keep talking so she can hear you?" Darrell places his phone on the hood of the car and walks away with his hands up.

Cautiously, I sprint to the car, grab the phone, and run a

safe distance away. It doesn't look like my phone, and I can't see where to text.

"What the fuck is going on?" Jed yells. "Skylar, if you can hear me, let me know somehow that you're okay. Think about when we were kids."

I walk back to the car, keeping my eye on Darrell, and open the driver's door. He looks concerned but stays where he is. I could just jump in and drive off, but if I get thrown in jail for stealing, I'll be no help to Queenie. Reaching in, I honk the horn in Morse code for SOS.

"You remembered. Where are you?" Jed barks. "I don't know what the hell's going on, but Darrell's there. You'll be okay. Put his phone down on the ground and lock yourself in the car. If you have your phone, turn it on. I'll find you."

I place the phone on the ground and run back to the car, jumping in and locking the doors. Through the window, I hear Darrell telling Jed where we are and saying he'll wait by the car. He hangs up and peers in at me. His lower lip trembles, spit dripping on his shirt. I'm tempted to drive off, but I trust Jed and stay put. I refuse to look at Darrell, watching him out of the corner of my eye.

"Open the door. I won't hurt you. You're my *family*," Darrell shouts through the window.

I don't make eye contact, and he shuffles away. Sneaking a peek, I see him sitting on the side of the road, and I finally feel like I can breathe. He's crying, but I don't know if the tears are genuine.

I wish I could figure out what it is that makes me not trust him. *What is he lying about?* He's like a puzzle, and I'm missing an important piece. Fifteen minutes later, Jed pulls up and jumps out without cutting the engine on his truck. I bolt from the car and run to his arms.

"You okay, Princess?"

I nod but refuse to let go.

Darrell stands but doesn't approach us. "I took her to see Mrs. Jackson. It was just a misunderstanding. I wouldn't hurt Skylar." He starts blubbering again into the blue bandana that's always in his pocket.

Did I overreact? Or is this an act? His aura is pink. I've become almost as paranoid as Queenie and Jed.

Both men look at me to confirm what he said. I shrug, confused.

"Okay, Darrell. I'll take her home and talk to you later."

We get in the truck.

"Where is your damn phone?" Jed's look is thunderous as we buckle our seatbelts. "Do you know how worried I was? Don't you think I have enough on my damn plate? Darrell's harmless. Good God, he's practically family."

I shake my phone at him, annoyed that he's automatically assuming this is somehow my fault.

"Why didn't you use it and text me?" he grinds out, his jaw tight.

He pulls into the street, driving fast, but I don't mind. The farther we get from Darrell, the better, as far as I'm concerned.

He glances over at me, and I try to show him my phone's dead. He pulls over to the curb. Looking at the phone, he sighs and plugs it into his car charger.

"You have to keep the damn thing charged. I told you that."

I sign that he didn't leave me a note about being gone.

"*I sent you a text.* That was the purpose of getting you a phone, dammit."

I look down, and, sure enough, a text pops up from him and one from Caleb.

Jed: *Gone to store cya in a few*

Caleb: *Good morning, Skylar!*

I sign back that I was scared.

208

"Dammit, text it."

I text what Darrell said.

"That's it? For God's sake, we're talking about Darrell. He wouldn't hurt a flea. I mean, he didn't, like, put the moves on you or anything, did he? Because if he did, I'll beat the shit out of him and then call the law."

I shake my head, feeling silly. But something in my gut still doesn't trust that man completely.

CHAPTER EIGHTEEN

JED

I GLANCE OVER at Princess as I drive, concerned. She isn't handling this well. Ever since Queenie was hospitalized, she's been falling apart—before that, actually. It started with that damn sin eating. Why would she ever think Darrell would hurt her? He's done nothing but help take care of us for years, like an uncle. Maybe the stress is getting to her. Is it her past coming forward? Should I take her to see a shrink for PTSD? Is it because the lines between us have blurred? Or do my grandmother's crazy ways have her too sheltered and ill-equipped to deal with life?

I'm more convinced than ever that getting her away from this place will be the best thing for her. New surroundings, new beginnings. I take her hand and give it a squeeze.

"You have nothing to be scared of. I've got everything under control. Did you sleep at all last night? You look exhausted."

She shakes her head.

"Have you eaten?"

With a heavy sigh, she signs she isn't hungry.

"Tough. You need to eat. Here's the plan. You're going to take a nap. I'm going to go see Queenie. The rest of the day, we're going to just chill and talk about the future, okay?"

To my surprise, she nods.

When we get home, an icy breeze rains golden leaves around us. Princess looks up and smiles, her eyes closed. She turns in a circle, arms wide as if she's embracing Mother Nature.

In that moment, I *know*. And all the plans I've constructed in my head crumble.

Sky is a beautiful wood nymph who belongs here, in the mountains. I'm wrong to move her. She'll never be completely happy in a city. She is as much a part of these mountains as the trees dropping their leaves.

But despite that, I can't leave her here alone. It's my duty to protect her, take care of her because she's like my sister.

Despair washes over me. I'm lying to myself. The trees rustle. They know it, too.

I'm in love…

SKYLAR

Waking from my nap, I'm startled to see I've slept most of the day. Sniffing, I follow an enticing smell into the kitchen, where I open the simmering pot on the stove. The chicken and dumplings inside looks delicious. Dirty dishes are stacked in the sink. There's a distinct haze in the air, and flour covers the counters. A lopsided vase of flowers sits atop the set table.

Jed walks in with an armload of firewood. I question what's going on with a lift of my brow. His flour-dusted hair is pulled in a haphazard ponytail, and his shirt is filthy with dried dough.

He's never looked better.

"I wanted to do something special for you. Chicken and dumplings is still your favorite, right? I visited with Queenie. She was up walking with the physical therapist and almost made sense, although she called me Dan once."

Dan was his father's name. From the pictures I've seen, Jed looks like him. I smile and rub my stomach, pointing at the pot simmering on the stove.

"Good. I'm going to start the fire and take a quick shower before we eat. I'll do the dishes later. I want you to relax." Whistling, he bounds up the stairs.

We're as opposite as night and day, but he completes me. *I'm in love.*

I start cleaning up the kitchen. I like staying busy. If he's seen Queenie doing well, maybe he'll change his mind about the nursing home. There's a timid knock on the back door. I know it well. Opening the door, Stella's icy hand grabs mine. Her cold touch is reminiscent of her dead brother's body at the sin eating. Her cheeks are flushed.

"I finally told my baby's daddy that I'm pregnant! *And* I told Mama. Queenie was right—they're both excited! I'm glad I listened to her and didn't go to my brother's wake and funeral. I don't want nothing to happen to my baby. This is gonna be Mama's first grandchild. I know it can't lessen the pain of her findin' my fool brother hangin' in his closet, but it gives her something to look forward to, you know what I mean?"

She chatters nonstop as we walk into the sitting area where the fire is crackling. "Look! We done got married, and I was thinkin' maybe you could tell me if we're gonna have a boy or a girl. Chester wants a boy, but I'd sure like to have a pink nursery. Girls are so much more fun to dress up than boys. And I just love pink; it's my favorite color."

I go to Queenie's knitting basket and snip strands of pink

and blue yarn. Taking Stella's wedding ring, I loop both strings through it and motion for her to lie on the couch. Widdershins bats at the wedding ring dangling from the string, thinking this is a game. He meows his displeasure when I push him away.

Holding the homemade pendulum over Stella's belly, I concentrate and ask, *Boy or girl?* Jed comes tromping down the stairs as the ring swings back and forth.

"You ready to eat?" He stops and frowns. "What are you doing here, Stella?"

She hops up and grabs her ring, slipping it back on her finger, ignoring his question. "Well? Was it a girl or a boy?"

I hand her the blue string.

"Darn it. You sure?"

I nod.

"Well, shoot, there goes my pink nursery. But boys are good, I mean, passin' on the family name and all…"

Jed sighs. "Stella, go home and get a sonogram like normal people."

"I ain't paying for no sonogram. Besides, it's too early. Did you become some sort of doctor in the army, Jedidiah?" She crosses her arms, enhancing her heaving breasts. "What would you know about these things, anyway? I don't remember you being particularly interested in sex."

"Oh, I was plenty interested in sex. But I was smart enough to know you were more interested in nabbing a husband. I guess congrats are in order. You finally trapped one."

Stella's face turns bright red. She shoves a five-dollar bill in my hand and flounces out of the house. It's then I remember that Jed took her to the homecoming dance but never asked her out again. I take it she's never forgiven him. I snicker and hold up three fingers.

"Three?" he asks.

I point at my ring finger and hold up three fingers again.

This is Stella's third marriage.

Jed chuckles. "Glad I avoided that trap. Let's eat."

The dumplings are doughy, the chicken is rubbery, but the fact that he prepared this for me makes it wonderful.

"I want you to know, I'm not going to stick Queenie in the nursing home if she doesn't need to be there," he says. "I spoke to the doctor, and he thinks some of her mental issues were just a urinary tract infection combined with her meds for sleep and pain. She was up walking pretty good, but she's weak. This rehab place she's going to, they're trained to help her exercise and get stronger. I'll turn down that job, but I still need to go for a few days and pick up the rest of my things from storage. I want you to go with me. I want to show you stuff that's different from this mountain. Okay?"

I realize he's giving up a lot to be here with Queenie and me. I smile and nod. On my pad of paper, I write, *You don't have to stay here. I don't want you to go, but I understand if you need to. I* bite my lip and show it to him.

"I'm staying, but I ain't staying in that girly room. I'll fix up the cabin in the woods and sleep there. I'll be close enough, but it will be better for all of us. I need my space to battle the demons in my head."

It sounds like the perfect compromise. On impulse, I lean across the table and kiss his cheek.

After dinner, despite his protests, I help him with the dishes. I'm drying a plate when a knock on the front door makes Jed swear. I hurry to open it, knowing it's Caleb. Instead of inviting him in, I step out onto the porch, closing the door behind me.

The wind picks up, and the tree limbs dance to and fro. Storm clouds are gathering, but the smile from the man before me is bright and sunny.

"Hi, how are you? How's Queenie today?" Caleb loosens his tie and stuffs it in the pocket of his white jacket.

I sign, *Okay.*

"Did you get my text?"

I nod and tell him thank you.

"Texting is nice, but I like seeing you. Um, I was wondering…" His face turns red, and he shoves his hands in his pockets. Sensing his nervousness, I stare at the three pens in his coat pocket.

"Would you like to go get a bite to eat?"

I sign that I've already eaten, and his face falls.

"Dessert, then? While I eat a burger or something?"

Poor Caleb. I wonder if he cooks or if he still eats a lot of his meals at his parents' home with that nasty carrot cake. Caleb's lonely and always has been. I motion for him to wait a moment. At some point, I need to tell him about Jed and me. Maybe this would be the right time.

Running back inside, I find Jed standing next to the window. He looks guilty, and I'm pretty sure he was spying on us. I grab my jacket from the coatrack and write a quick note, telling him I'm going out with Caleb for a bit and will be back soon.

"I thought we were going to talk and spend the evening together…"

If I'm not mistaken, jealousy tinges his voice. I sign that I'll only be gone an hour.

"Whatever. Take your damn phone. It's charged, right?"

I nod and race upstairs to get it. While in my room, I add a little blush and gloss and run a brush through my hair. I'm out the front door in less than five minutes. I race past Jed, and Caleb smiles. Taking my hand, he escorts me to his car. I can feel Jed watching me the entire time.

No wonder I'm paranoid…

JED

Son of a bitch! Was that lip gloss she was wearing? Skylar never wears makeup; she doesn't need it. Jealousy narrows my eyes as I peer out the window, watching Caleb walk her to his car. Dammit, they're holding hands.

She's mine, she's mine, she's mine plays through my mind like a Buddhist chant. But my feelings are far from monkish where she's concerned.

Of course the polite asshole opens her door for her. He glances back toward the house, and I halfway consider flipping him off, but I take the high road and remain hidden behind the curtain, cussing under my breath.

I know these feelings of possessiveness are wrong, but I can't help it.

Taking out my phone, I text, *Curfew in 1 hr don't b late*

Immediately I get a text back with the middle finger emoji and a smiley face sticking out its tongue.

SKYLAR

Caleb takes me to a small restaurant attached to a gas station. I've eaten here with Queenie before. It isn't fancy, but the food is good. It's what Queenie calls "plain cookin'." Caleb orders the meatloaf and mashed potatoes with some green beans. While we wait, he tells me about his day—counting pills and putting up with sick people. He's a good man who genuinely cares for folks. But honestly? His job sounds boring.

The waitress brings his dinner and a glass of tea for each of us.

"How is Queenie doing following her surgery?"

Old habits die hard, and I take my pad of paper and pen out and write, *Good! We're hoping to get her home after some rehab.*

Caleb nods but doesn't say anything for a moment as he eats. Unlike Jed, he's deliberate and thinks before he speaks. "Do you honestly think this will be temporary?"

I nod and smile.

He reaches out and takes my fingers. His hands are smooth and his nails neatly trimmed, so unlike Jed's rough, work-worn hands. Just the thought of Jed's hands on my body makes my breath catch. Caleb mistakes my reaction and comes around the table to crouch next to my chair and rub my back. He looks up at me like a lost puppy.

"I'm sorry. I know this has been difficult. I wish there was something I could do to help. I care about you and Queenie. She always treated me like a normal kid, not an invalid. You know that tea she's always made to help my asthma? It's part of the reason I wanted to be a pharmacist."

I smile and nod. Queenie's been a huge influence on a number of people.

"Sky, I know I haven't been back long…but I want you to know my intentions regarding you are serious. I have deep feelings for you—"

He's almost down on one knee, and for a brief second I worry he's going to propose right here in the restaurant. I shake my head.

Thankfully, his declaration of feelings is interrupted by the waitress bringing our hot apple pie with vanilla ice cream melting on top. He sits back down and smiles at me. The sticky mess seems like an analogy for my life at the moment. I love Caleb, but not the way I love Jed. And I don't know how to tell him we can never be more than friends. The thought of hurting him makes me want to cry.

He seems to pick up on my uneasiness and doesn't press me for more than I can give right now.

After some more small talk, we stand to leave. Caleb scoops my hair out of my jacket. He's always been a perfect gentleman. Queenie once told me she knew she was in love with her husband when he did this very same thing for her. She says the way a man treats a woman is important, that it's the little considerations that matter and carry you through the bad times. Caleb is a wonderful man. If Jed hadn't returned, I could've seen myself marrying him and being happy. It would've been a comfortable life, like a merry-go-round—gentle but boring. Although I can't imagine his mama ever accepting me.

A cold rain has moved in by the time Caleb drops me back home. The light shines from the upstairs porch, and I see Jed sitting on the swing. Caleb sighs and walks me to the front door under his umbrella.

"Well, goodnight. Thank you for keeping me company," he whispers.

Jed can't see us, but I know Caleb's being quiet because sound travels. His lips brush the back of my fingers, and he presses a quick, closed-mouth kiss on my lips. It's sweet, but not toe-curling.

Leaning in close to my ear, he chuckles and says, "Maybe we should've gone parking before coming home." He moves to kiss me again, but I turn so he kisses my cheek. "I know Jed's just above us, so I understand," he whispers.

No, he really doesn't. And now that I know he has deeper

feelings for me than I do him, I feel guilty.

"We can talk more tomorrow. I know it's been a crazy few days, but you still want to go to the Fall Festival with me, right?"

No. But a promise is a promise. And he's right. We need to talk. I nod.

He wanders back to his car and yells, "G'night, Jed. See you tomorrow, Skylar."

There's no response from upstairs. I watch Caleb drive off, giving a small wave before snapping off the light and locking up the house. I'm far from drowsy, but I make my way upstairs and get ready for bed. Then I decide to check on Jed.

Stepping into my slippers, I tie my robe and visit the upstairs porch with Widdershins on my heels. Jed's still on the swing, whittling. Without looking at me, he starts humming. I haven't heard him hum since he's been back. It used to be a sign he was thinking. Softly he sings "Knockin' on Heaven's Door." I sit next to him and nudge his arm. He laughs.

"Bring back memories, Princess?"

I nod and grin. The summer after I arrived at Queenie's, we attended Vacation Bible School at Pastor Buzbee's church. On the final night, there was a program for the parents. We all sang "Amazing Grace," and then everyone was supposed to do a talent. Caleb sang "What a Friend We Have in Jesus." Another kid did a magic show. Stella did a ballet dance. Because I don't talk, Jed volunteered us to lip-sync a song. We worked hard on our moves and had it down perfect.

Just before we went to the front of the church, Mrs. Buzbee warned us it had to be a "religious" song. Jed had hedged and replied, *"It's about heaven. How much more religious can ya get?"*

That night we lip-synced "Knockin' on Heaven's Door," complete with a dramatic dying pantomime. Everyone loved it *except* Mrs. Buzbee.

I watch as Jed continues to whittle, magically turning a chunk of wood into a pretty good likeness of my cat. Widdershins purrs, moving between his legs, obviously as pleased with the carving as I am.

"How was your *date?*"

I shake my head, warning him not to go there. But, of course, he does.

"Did ya get some sugar?" Jed makes loud kissy noises and snickers when I slap his arm.

I still think he's jealous. I point at the piece he's working on.

"Keeping my hands busy helps me not want an after-supper cigarette." He chuckles. "I have a bunch of little animals I've carved for you over the years packed in a box. It's in the storage unit." From the table beside the swing, he picks up the dragonfly and hands it to me. He must've finished it while I was with Caleb. The detail is amazing.

"Have you thought about the stuff you need to pack for Asheville?"

I sign, *Not yet.*

He doesn't speak, finishing his carving. He hands me the tiny wooden cat. "I care about Queenie. We don't always see eye to eye, but I love her." He kicks back and stretches an arm across the back of the swing. I curl into him, resting my head on his shoulder as he pushes us. "I'm worried about both of you. I want her to get better; I really do. But I'm concerned about you. This superstitious nonsense isn't normal."

I take my phone out of my robe pocket and text, *The world is a scary place. I'm safe here. It's my normal.*

"You didn't find it safe the other morning."

My leg bounces, and I have no response because he's right. I text, *I didn't realize it was Darrell calling.*

"Regardless, you overreacted—just like you did this morning. Why would you think Darrell, of all people, would hurt you? I'll tell you why. Isolation fucks with your mind. You don't need to be so alone."

I can't explain why I don't trust Darrell. But I hear *Jed's* loneliness reflected in his voice. He has his faults, but sitting here, my hand resting over his heart, I know he's speaking *his* truth from his experiences. If I didn't believe in anything or have hope, I'd feel lonely, too.

I text, *We're not alone. We have each other.*

Queenie taught me to look at the bigger picture when reading cards. The illustrations have meanings, but there's more to it than that. The placement of each card is significant, and nothing is ever black-and-white. We can take control of our own destiny.

"I don't think you're getting my point," he says.

I straddle his lap and take his face in my hands. Like a blind woman, I trace his skin with my fingers, marveling at the different textures—the coarseness of his beard, the smoothness of those lips, the crevices beside his eyes—all these things make up the face of my soulmate.

Jed catches my hands in his and murmurs, "Caleb's good for you."

Caleb *is* a nice man and what most folks would deem a logical, sensible choice for a husband. He's like a rock, steadfast and true. Since he's been back in town, he's become the main focus of attention for every single woman in the county. I hear the talk on the rare occasions I do errands. It's kind of funny how folks speak freely in front of me, like I'm deaf instead of nonverbal. I care deeply for Caleb, but I know my heart could never be one-hundred-percent his.

The man in front of me is his complete opposite. Jed is like fire, sometimes contained, sometimes out of control, and always burning hot. Me? I'm water. I have the power to erode a rock or put out a fire. I lean in and press a kiss to his mouth, which opens for me to explore. He shifts against me and undoes the tie on my robe. My need to be one with this man consumes me. His warm hands roam my body, and he breathes my name like a prayer as he showers my face with kisses. And, indeed, being with Jed feels like a religious experience.

"You're mine," he growls in my ear. "And I'm knocking on heaven's door." He bucks up against me, sending a thrill through my body.

How right he is, on both counts. I fumble with his belt buckle, but he stops me, his breath sawing in my ear. Grasping my butt, he stands and carries me to his room. Widdershins must be weaving under his feet, because he swears at the poor cat. I smile into his neck when he kicks the door closed and the cat meows his displeasure from the hallway.

Unceremoniously, Jed drops me on his bed. I hear the clank of his belt buckle hitting the hardwood floor and then something ripping. The bed dips with his weight, and at last his hungry mouth finds mine. An air of desperation combined with excitement surrounds us. Somehow, we manage to rid ourselves of our clothes. Taking his time, Jed strokes down my neck and takes my breast in his hand. His tongue licks, his teeth nip, and his fingers pinch and tease until I'm on fire beneath him.

I don't think I can stand it any longer, and I pull him to me, not wanting him to be gentle. I want—no, I *need*—to feel his chaotic energy within me. Tired of his games, I somehow manage to flip him over and take control. I lower myself onto him and realize the ripping sound was a condom. He continues to caress my breasts, sending ripples of desire through me. I try to move but feel awkward and uncoordinated. Taking his hand, I finger spell, *Help me.* But he doesn't understand until I beat on his chest with my fist.

His hands move to my hips, and he guides me until I'm finally in a rhythm. "There ya go, Princess. Yesssss…"

Finally, it feels right. I rock up and down, building momentum. At last I shudder, reveling in the sensation, biting my tongue so I don't cry out. He soon follows with a shout so loud I'm sure Darrell heard him next door. I collapse on top of him, and all I can hear is labored breathing. We're sweaty and spent. His arms wrap around me, and he chuckles in my ear. "If you'd just fuckin' told me what you wanted, we could've been done sooner."

My shoulders shake as I silently giggle. *He's so silly.*

Our breathing normalizes, and he smacks my bottom. "Lemme up."

I shake my head. I don't want him leaving me again.

"I'll be right back. I promise."

I roll to the side, and he gets up and heads to the bathroom. When he comes back to bed, he pulls the covers up over us. Resting my cheek over his heart, I trap his leg with mine and wrap my arm around his waist to keep him from leaving me this time.

His hand traces figure eights on my back, and, as if reading my mind, he whispers, "Go to sleep. I'll be here when you wake up. I'm never leaving you again." His fist bumps mine, and our pinkies hook, but instead of spitting, he kisses my forehead.

And I believe him.

CHAPTER NINETEEN

JED

I TRY TO roll over, but I'm trapped underneath Skylar's body. My arm's asleep, and the place on my ass that's still healing itches. I shift her so I can move, but it backfires. She snuggles in closer, probably subconsciously fearing I'll leave her again. The sun's just rising and casts a pink glow on her beautiful face. I soak in her beauty, strangely aware of an odd calmness about me. My restless need to stay busy is gone for the moment.

Is this some kind of magic?

Or is it love?

Despite the turmoil since my return, I'm happy—like, deep-inside happy. And I'm kinda unsure what to make of it.

One thing's for sure: I need Skylar in my life, no matter what the future holds. Rationally, I don't think Queenie's going to get any better. Physically, maybe, but mentally I'm afraid it will continue to be a downhill slide if her dementia turns out to not be related to her medications and pain. I read up on Alzheimer's, and it's hard on the patient *and* the family. It will be harder for us when she no longer knows who we are. I can't have Skylar going through that alone.

Sky rolls off me but doesn't awaken. Shifting onto my side, I wiggle my numb hand and wrap a strand of her hair around my finger. I wrap it tighter and tighter, envisioning it like the noose of responsibility that makes me feel panicky at times. At least fifty times a day I've considered shirking my responsibilities and taking off. The only reason I haven't is because I worry about who'd take care of Princess and Queenie.

Caleb would gladly do it.

Shit. I feel like I've just been doused with a bucket of ice water. I wonder what Sky's feelings are for him. I know he'd be good for her, unlike me, but I can't see his sanctimonious mama ever accepting Sky into the family. Still, Caleb's a man now, living on his own.

And he doesn't come with a shitload of baggage.

He has a stable job.

He seems to have genuine feelings for her, and that pisses me off.

But she was with me last night.

The thought of losing her after what we've shared causes what feels like a PTSD episode. My heart's pounding, and sweat dots my brow. I pull Sky closer, needing her to ground me. She stirs, opens those gorgeous blue eyes, and smiles. Everything suddenly seems better. Pressing a sweet kiss to my mouth, she pushes my hair back from my face. Worry now furrows her brow; she senses my unease.

"What kind of spell have you cast upon me, Princess?" I whisper.

With her finger, she draws a heart on my chest.

I bury my face in her neck, inhaling her warm scent, taking the comfort she so freely offers. When she gets up, the bed feels cold and empty. She gives me another quick kiss and gathers her clothes.

"Don't leave," I whisper as she disappears out the door.

She pantomimes bathing and coffee.

I nod and smile, feeling foolish. *When did I become such a puss?* I haul my ass out of bed and move toward the shower. We have a lot to do today.

I stand under the water long after I'm done washing, letting the warm water work its magic until it turns tepid. Unable to stall any longer, I turn it off, slide the shower curtain back, and damn near jump out of my skin. Princess is standing there with a cup of coffee in one hand, making a slashing motion with the other. She got me again. When we were kids, *Psycho* was one of my favorite movies. Sky usually hid her face under a pillow. Her hair is damp from her own shower, and she's fully dressed in jeans and a sweatshirt that says *Feeling Witchy* with a black cat.

Does she have to advertise? "Do you have to wear that?"

She nods and texts, showing me what she's written: *It's Halloween soon, why not? We need to decorate the house. I haven't had time to do it.*

I chuckle. "In the time it took you to text all that, you could've decorated the entire house. Learn to abbreviate."

She motions for me to turn around and holds up the antibiotic gel and a large Band-Aid.

"It itches, so it must be healing."

Her soft fingers have me rock hard. When she's done, I dart back to my bedroom to get dressed before I give in to the temptation to haul her back into bed. I have too many things to get done to be distracted. First thing, I'll ask Darrell if he can help me get the house ready to either welcome Queenie home or be locked up for a bit while I get my affairs settled.

When I enter the kitchen, I find Skylar pawing through a box of Halloween decorations. Nothing she puts out will make this place look much different—there's already everyday witchy crap scattered throughout the house. She motions toward the cereal and my antibiotic. I'm not the least bit hungry, but I down a bowl of cornflakes and watch her. She's smiling as she places each item on the table. To me, they just add to the cluttered feeling in this house. Glancing at me, she writes on her tablet, *Good memories. I wish we could go back in time.*

Queenie loves Halloween. Kids always loved coming here. And why not? The house is spooky enough on a regular day, but it became a showpiece in October with the fake spider webs and stuff. On Halloween night, Queenie would sit on the porch, dressed as the witch everyone says she is, and hand out goodies and warm apple cider. The adults loved coming, too, since their cider had a special kick added to it. At fifteen, when I discovered the adult version of the spicy beverage, I snuck some for Caleb, Sky, and myself. I got shitfaced, Princess passed out, and Caleb threw up his guts. His mother chalked this experience up to another reason for him not to hang with us. Pastor Buzbee and Queenie's solution was to have us clean the church and sit in the front row the next Sunday as the good reverend preached about the toll of excess on the body and spirit.

Sky's phone dings. Her cheeks flush as she reads and quickly texts back. I assume Caleb's the one texting, and I regret buying her the damn phone.

"Was that lover boy?" I ask, hoping my tone sounds teasing and knowing I failed miserably.

She rolls her eyes and writes on the tablet, *He's my friend, not lover. The Fall Festival is tonight after the church service. I already told him I'd go with him. We're just friends.* Her face is now red and her brow wrinkled.

I try to shove my jealousy aside for her sake. "Just friends is good; he's an okay guy. Look, I know we need to work *us* out. But let's get Queenie squared away first. Then we're going to have a long discussion about you and me." For some unexplained reason, I add, "Don't give up on me, okay?"

She looks at me like I'm being stupid. Maybe I am. Pressing a kiss to my lips, she once again traces a heart over mine and then points to her own. We fist bump and pinky swear, and I find myself grinning like I haven't got a care in the world. I suddenly feel like I can take on whatever life throws at me.

"I'm going to see Dammit Darrell," I tell her. "Finish getting your hocus-pocus stuff out and be ready to go see Queenie in about half an hour. Today's the day she moves to rehab."

I put my dishes in the dishwasher, but before I make it to the back door, Sky grabs my sleeve and puckers her lips. It occurs to me that she's making eye contact more often. It's a trust I treasure and never want to break. With her, I can figure everything out. I stroke the back of my fingers down her flushed cheek and peck her soft lips.

"We're like an old married couple. I'm not sure how I feel about that," I tease.

She grins like the Cheshire cat, but there's lingering worry shadowing her face.

"I know today's going to be hard. All we can do is hope for the best, that Queenie will come home after she completes her therapy. But—and I'm not budging on this—if that happens, we're getting some professional help for her. I won't have you being a sacrificial lamb. She's put you in that role for too long."

Sky rolls her eyes. I shrug into my hoodie, determined to stand my ground. I intend to make sure Sky has a semblance of a normal life.

"I'll be back in a few." The early morning air has a nip to it; I can see my breath as I go next door. Fall is my favorite time of year in the mountains.

Dammit Darrell answers the door before I even rap on it.

"Hey, Darrell, I was gonna see if you could help me and take care of the cat while we're gone—"

His eyes narrow, and the chill in the air has nothing to do with the temperature.

"You can't do this, Jed." Darrell's throat bobbles, and his

lower lip pokes out.

I admire his loyalty, but he needs to see reason.

"Look, it's not going to be a big deal. I just—"

He crosses his beefy arms. "Skylar and I can take care of Mrs. Jackson. We done it for years, *without you*."

His attitude is pissing me off. "I'm not saying you can't, but she needs some time to—"

"No. I'm not helpin' you. It'll hurt Mrs. Jackson and Skylar."

Darrell slams the door before I can finish explaining that I plan to stay here. Fine, I'll just leave a ton of food and water out for the dumb cat.

I tromp back home and find Caleb getting out of his car, dressed up in a nice suit, holding a to-go cup of coffee and a covered plate. *Great. My day's just getting better and better.*

"Hey, Jed. You're just the person I wanted to see."

I raise one eyebrow. "Me? Not Skylar?"

He moves forward, juggling the plate and coffee with one hand and offers me his other. I shake it with a little more pressure than warranted. To his credit, he doesn't wince but looks me straight in the eye.

"Yes, sir. I wanted you to know my intentions toward Skylar." He's wheezing like the hundred-year-old organ at his church.

His intentions? Geezus. Caleb's been to college and lived in a city. His dumb statement only reinforces my thought that when you come back over the mountain, you need to set your watch back a hundred years.

I take the plate from him. "Take a deep breath. Do you have your inhaler with you? I'm *not* Sky's father; I don't need to know your intentions." *Because she's mine.*

Caleb pulls out his inhaler and takes two puffs. "What I'm trying to discern are *your feelings* for her. Do I have a chance?"

WHAT THE TREES KNOW

His face is as red and full of hope as the sunrise. I hand him the covered plate back, wondering what's in it while I weigh my answer. This needs to be handled with more finesse than I'm used to. The guy has genuine feelings, and it's ultimately Sky's choice of when, and how, to let him down.

"She's an adult. If everyone would quit treating her like a kid, she just might grow up. Personally, I think she needs to get away from here and see there's more to the world before settling down. Don't you?"

"No, I don't. This is her home. These mountains are a part of her." He looks at me. "You can't change her, Jed. She's *special.*"

"Isn't *special* the term your mother always uses for Darrell?" I reply snidely. "Is the apple not falling far from the tree?" The flame on my simmering jealousy is rapidly escalating to a full boil. *She's mine, dammit.* "Whatever happens, you better not hurt her or I'll kick your ass all the way to Asheville."

"First, I'd never hurt Skylar. Second, I'm *not* my mother. Third, you know what I meant, so quit trying to start an argument. I won't engage in it. I can see this conversation is done before it started. Just forget it." He walks up the back steps muttering, "You're still a jerk."

Yep, motherfucker, I am.

Sky opens the door, wearing a witch's hat.

"Are you a good witch or a bad witch?" the asshole teases.

I shrug past him and stomp into the kitchen. "Depends on who you ask."

Skylar signs, *Good witch, of course.* Taking Caleb's coffee cup, she tops it off.

"Thanks, Sky." He hands her the covered dish. "Mom sent some carrot cake for you. I know you don't like it, but I don't want to hurt her feelings. You can just dump it. She'll never know.

"Isn't lying a sin? I guess you'll pray about it in church this morning and be absolved," I chide.

He ignores me, and Princess shoots me a withering look.

"I, uh, wanted to see if five sounds good for me to pick you up tonight. Service and supper are at six and then the festival."

Caleb's ears are red, and he's refusing to look my way. Which is a pity, as I'm giving him my best badass glare, trying my hand at silent intimidation.

Skylar puts the carrot cake down, wrinkling her nose. I hope she doesn't toss it. If she doesn't like it, I'll eat it.

Since they both seem intent on ignoring me, I pick up the empty decoration box. "I'll take this back to the attic. Don't you need to get to church, Caleb?"

Sky frowns at my rudeness, but I don't care.

"Be ready to leave in fifteen minutes. We'll take Queenie's car—more room." I march upstairs, thinking maybe I should attend this Fall Festival. *Nah, I don't want to look desperate.*

But I feel desperate...

SKYLAR

Caleb leaves, and I turn off the coffee pot and pitch the cake in the garbage. I instantly regret doing so. I should've taken it to Queenie. She likes it, although she complains that Mrs. Buzbee bakes it to lord her blue-ribbon win over her.

Pulling out Queenie's playing cards, I throw some as I wait for Jed. Just holding them makes me feel better. The Queen of

Hearts, a Six of Spades, and a Four of Clubs. The only card that concerns me is the Six of Spades. It's a warning of some sort.

Jed tromps down the stairs, and I pick the cards up and start over.

He walks over to the table, and his face darkens. "Would you stop with the fortune-telling?"

I move the Queen, Jack, and Ten over to the King and snicker as I flip over three cards and move the Two of Hearts to the Ace.

"You're just playing solitaire?"

I cross my toes and nod. He laughs.

"You got me. Ready?" He frowns. "You threw the cake away? I was gonna eat it."

Scrunching my nose, I shrug into my coat and find my purse as Jed picks up the suitcase packed with more of Queenie's clothes and a few mementos for her new room. Once we're in the car, his phone rings. It's the hospital telling him she's ready to move.

After buckling up, he stares out the window for a minute. "This is harder than I expected," he says softly. "The not knowing how things will turn out…"

I take his hand in mine and give it a squeeze, feeling the same way. Even the cards didn't offer a clear answer.

Taking a deep breath, he pulls away and starts the car. "It's for the best. They'll get her up and moving, no matter how much she bitches about it."

When we arrive at the hospital, we can't find a parking space. I bounce my leg impatiently as Jed circles the full parking lot for the third time. I tap his arm and point at the entrance.

"Okay. I'll be up as soon as I find a space." He drops me off and pulls out.

I've been hoping for a few minutes alone with Queenie and race toward her room. This fear in the pit of my stomach feels like I've eaten some of that awful carrot cake. The door is slightly ajar, and I peek in.

Queenie looks up and smiles, holding out both hands. "Skylar, there you are, my darling girl."

She's dressed and sitting in a wheelchair, a walker next to her. Someone has packed up her things. I rush over, and she embraces me as her beloved face blurs.

"What are you crying for, silly child? I'm fine. They say I'll be up walking on my own soon."

I grab my phone and text, *The cards are ominous. Something's about to happen. I'm worried.* I show it to her, and she squints trying to read. I rifle through her things, looking for her reading glasses. Jed walks in as I find them.

"Ya know, you could've used your spell casting to find me a better parking place, Princess."

I hand Queenie her glasses, and she reads my text. When Jed leans in to kiss her cheek, I grab my phone before he sees what I wrote. Queenie cups his cheek in her hand, staring up at him.

"Are you okay?" she asks.

"Fine. You?"

She glances over at me and back at Jed. "Well, I'm not ready to go dancing yet, but I'll be fine as frog's hair as soon as I get home."

I raise my brow at Jed, hopeful. She seems more lucid than she's been in a long time. I hope he agrees.

"We're leaving this place for sure," he hedges.

It takes an hour before we have her settled in the car and headed to the nursing home. Queenie rolls down the window and closes her eyes, smiling.

"It's a little cool for the windows to be down," Jed mutters, rolling it back up.

"I like the smell," she replies. "It will get even better the closer we get to home. Nothing like good mountain air to clear what ails you."

Jed doesn't reply. I'm glad I'm in the back seat and Queenie can't see my tears. She doesn't remember she's going to rehab. His gaze meets mine in the rearview mirror, and I see the conflict he's suffering. At the red light he drums his thumbs on the steering wheel. If he turns left, we'll go home. *Turn left, turn left, turn left,* I silently plead in time with the *tick, tick, tick* of the blinker.

"Brother, do you think Mama will make us pancakes when we get home?" Queenie asks.

The light changes, and we turn right.

CHAPTER TWENTY

JED

I WALK BACK into Queenie's new room after signing umpteen papers. As I close the door, the picture of Skylar, Caleb, and me sitting in the swing when we were kids falls to the floor, and the glass shatters. Skylar gasps, her hand resting over her heart. When she looks up at me, her pupils are so big I can barely see any blue. The pulse at the base of her neck pounds.

"Death is coming! Quick, both of you—turn seven times clockwise!" Queenie shouts.

Skylar does as she's told, turning Queenie's wheelchair with her. I shake my head and cross my arms, watching the lunacy unfold before me.

"I want a word alone with you, Jedidiah." Queenie narrows her eyes. Up until this incident—aside from calling me "Brother" earlier—her mind's been sharper the past couple of days. Yesterday she readily agreed to do the therapy at this facility.

"Ma'am?" I respond out of habit, glancing over at Skylar.

"You heard me. Skylar, give us a moment, please."

Sky looks at both of us, her concern evident in her trembling lip and liquid eyes. But she steps out of the room, leaving us alone.

"Now turn around seven times."

"I don't believe this stuff. Just because a picture falls doesn't mean death is coming. Well, it *is*—we *all* have to die sometime—but this is ridiculous."

"Then humor me."

I sigh and turn around seven times clockwise.

"Good." She smiles and holds her hand out.

I take it and sit beside her.

"My black-and-white boy, always so rational. How can you not see there's more to life than what we can see?"

I shrug, not having an answer for her. "I'm pragmatic, not whimsical."

"You're in love, aren't you? Isn't that, in and of itself, a wonderful thing and not of this world? Don't fight it. She loves you, too. I know these things. But you can't take her from home, Jed. Her spirit is in the trees behind our house, and she belongs here. She's a survivor—but only because she's where she belongs. She's been marked by death. It's why she's a healer."

I roll my eyes. *And here I thought Queenie was starting to make sense.* Yet she seems to have an uncanny knowledge that I thought about taking Skylar away...

She grabs my hand and squeezes tight. "There's something in the air. I feel it. Don't you? But nothing is ever set in stone. You watch your back and keep an eye on Skylar, do you hear me? I'll be home before Thanksgiving. Mark my words."

I can't deny I've felt uneasy, but I think it has more to do with my guilt over placing my grandmother in a nursing home—even for a little while.

Skylar peeks back in the room. I motion her in, and she looks pale and shaken.

I'm surer than ever that I need to stick around...because something definitely feels off.

SKYLAR

I walk out the back door and shiver, unable to shake the feeling of doom that's overshadowed today. The cold night air bites through my shawl. I should probably wear a coat to the festival, but it wouldn't go with my fortune-teller outfit. Besides, with Caleb's allergies, I anticipate being indoors more than outside. I texted him earlier and told him I wouldn't be ready by five, so he's picking me up after church. I didn't feel like sitting through a sermon, and I don't want to leave Jed.

An owl hoots a warning. When you walk between the worlds like I do, this time of year makes you more in tune with the ancestors. The past day or so, I've felt my mother's presence more than ever, especially with Queenie not here. Fear gnaws the pit of my stomach, sort of like the feeling when you're watching a scary movie and the music turns creepy—you *know* something's going to happen and it won't be good.

Caleb should be here any minute. I should've backed out; I don't want to lead him on, but part of me is afraid of losing him, too. I'm afraid I'm a terribly selfish girl. But I'm determined to be an adult and reveal my true feelings. It isn't fair to him or Jed for me to remain ambiguous.

Oh, Queenie…how I wish you were here to guide me.

She settled into the nursing home surprisingly well this morning and only called me Charlotte once today. While Jed was completing the paperwork, she looked me straight in the eye and said, "Things have changed between you two."

WHAT THE TREES KNOW

Heat crept into my cheeks, and I stared at the gnarled hand holding mine and nodded.

"You're torn between the light and the dark. But remember, things aren't always black-and-white, my girl. Look for the signs and go with your gut."

Jed returned before I could ask her what she meant. When I'd told her the cards I'd thrown, she'd frowned and simply told me to pay attention.

I've been pondering her words all afternoon.

From the old barn, I hear the sound of sawing and hammering. I head over, pause at the doorway, and stare. Warmth floods my senses like it always does when I'm near Jed. Sweat and sawdust cover his face and bare chest. He hasn't heard me enter, and I grin as I watch him. He's singing along with Donovan's "Season of the Witch." When he sees me, he throws down his saw and walks over, holding out his hand. I take it, and, still singing softly, he pulls me close, but not close enough for me to get dirty. He smells of fresh-cut wood and sweat, and his hair is loose and down to his shoulders. Being in his arms is like being intoxicated. I try to press myself closer, needing him as surely as I need air to breathe.

He pulls back a bit. "You don't want to smell sweaty for your *date*. Shouldn't you be dressed as a witch?" he asks, giving me a twirl.

I shake my head. He knows the costumes have to be "non-scary and non-satanic," in the words of Mrs. Buzbee. The bells on my skirt jingle as we move around the barn. I sign and ask him to go with us.

"I don't think so. Three's a crowd, unless you need a chaperone." The music ends, and he softly whispers, "Wouldn't you rather stay home with me tonight?"

I bite my lip and shrug. *I want to stay, but I promised Caleb I'd go.*

"I'm gonna be totally honest with you. Going tonight is a mistake, for lots of reasons. The gossip since the wake, and...well, me and you. It isn't fair to string Caleb along."

I hadn't thought about the wake. But folks have always talked about me, so I can't imagine it will be any worse than usual. I sign that I plan to tell Caleb about us tonight. I point at the lumber he's cut, questioning.

"I'm making a ramp for Queenie, for when she comes home."

Happy, I clap my approval.

He laughs and hugs me tight for a moment, then moves me away, brushing the sawdust off my clothes. "She's still vague sometimes, but I think you're right. She seems better. Once her rehab is done, we'll move her back home and give it a chance."

I motion walking and point at him, wondering if this means he'll be leaving once she comes home. The thought makes my chest hurt.

"I told you, I'm not going anywhere without you." He runs his hand over the lumber. "I love working with wood. This may sound crazy, but I've thought about trying my hand at making furniture and stuff. Tourists come to the area; there's a store in town where I could place things on consignment. I might even call it The Devil's Workshop—think Queenie would approve?"

I grin and nod. It's a wonderful plan; he's talented. And it will keep him here, with me.

A car pulls up, and Jed sighs, looking resigned. He nods toward the door. "Your date's here. Don't be late for curfew, Cinderella."

I sign that I've never had a curfew and snicker before flouncing away, putting an extra sway in my step to make the bells jingle.

"Hey, Jed," Caleb hollers with a wave, waiting by the car. He's dressed the way he normally dresses for work: white lab coat, button-down shirt, and dress pants. All he's added is a stethoscope.

"No flowers? No box of candy? What kind of suitor is Dr. Pain-in-My-Ass?" Jed teases as he goes back to working, not returning the greeting.

I bite my lip, secretly pleased he's jealous.

"Don't you look pretty. Are you Esmeralda?" Caleb comments, opening my car door. "I can take off the lab coat and stethoscope, and I'll look just like Quasimodo."

I sign that he's being silly, and he chuckles. As handsome as he is, he'd never be mistaken for the hunchback of Notre Dame. He makes sure I'm buckled up before he starts the car.

As he drives, he keeps his hands on the wheel, staring at the road, uncharacteristically quiet. A nervous energy surrounds him.

"I, uh, spoke to Jed earlier. Or, rather, I tried to."

I stare out the window, not sure how I feel about Caleb and Jed talking about me.

"I told him how much I care for you. In turn, he told me not to hurt you or he'd kick my ass all the way back to Asheville." He smiles and glances over at me.

I'd sign my response, but we're on a backroad with no light except from the car dashboard.

"I get why he said that. He's like your older brother…" Caleb leaves the sentence hanging on an upbeat, as if waiting to see if that's how I view Jed.

Things are so complicated. I squirm in my seat. I know we have to have this conversation, but it's uncomfortable.

"I, uh, also told my parents I want to take things to the next level with you."

I blink, shocked. I bet his mother's ready to have a stroke.

"I'm telling you this because my mom…she may act a bit cool toward you tonight." His throat bobbles, and he stares straight ahead. "But my dad adores you." This time he glances over toward me and adds, "So do I."

His mother has always been cold with me, so that won't be anything new. But I really don't know what to say. It's hard to communicate in the car when he can't see me sign or read my facial expressions. I should've brought my phone, but I didn't want to be burdened with carrying a purse. This is turning into a hot mess. I wish he'd waited until we were sitting down somewhere so I could explain how much he means to me but only as a friend.

Caleb pulls into his church parking lot. Carved pumpkins lit with candles line the walkways. The hay wagon is already loaded and taking folks through the trail cut through the Garrisons' hayfield next door. And when they return to the parking lot, they'll be given hot chocolate with marshmallows in it. Inside the fellowship hall will be games for the little kids and the potluck dinner. Caleb opens my door and takes my hand. As we walk toward the church, folks smile and greet us. The smiles for him are genuine. *Everyone loves Caleb.* In turn, their gazes linger on me with questions in their eyes, some shadowed by condemnation. *Why didn't I listen to Jed and stay home?*

I lift my chin and channel Queenie's spirit. She's always told me to meet gossips head-on with my head held high.

From behind me, someone says, "Caleb's a lucky bastard. I'd tap that. Did you see her naked the other night?"

Kip Rogers guffaws in response.

I duck my head as heat floods my cheeks.

Caleb whips around. "Did you say something, Terry?"

"Just speculating on why you're with *her*," the idiot replies. "After the other night, I *know* why." He nudges Kip, looking me over like I'm a prized mare at the stock show. I pull my shawl closed and step back into a shadow.

Kip has the grace to look embarrassed. "Cut it out, Terry,"

he says.

Terry Garrison is thirty pounds heavier than Caleb and has a reputation for being mean. Back when he was married to Stella, he used to beat her on a routine basis until her brother Gary stepped in and took matters into his own hands. Terry and Stella divorced soon after. She's much better off with her current husband. I tug on Caleb's sleeve, knowing it's in his best interest to walk away. Thank goodness he isn't Jed, who would've already laid Terry out like a corpse at a wake.

"I think it best you not talk about my fiancée that way," Caleb replies, balling his fist.

I'm not sure who's more stunned by his declaration, Terry, Kip, or me.

"Caleb John Buzbee!"

Caleb and I jump at the sound of his mother's voice. He turns and moves me to stand behind him, almost as if shielding me from his mom. Judging by the look on her face, she's as dumbfounded as I am. Horrified, even.

"Yes, Mom?"

"Is this why you skipped services tonight? I think we need to talk," she hisses, her eyes narrowed. "Alone." Her attention is now directed fully toward me, and her aura has blackened.

"Not now. I don't want Skylar to miss the hayride. I'll see you tomorrow."

"Don't be ridiculous. You're allergic to hay," she snaps.

"I took an antihistamine, and I have my inhaler. I'll be fine." Caleb takes my hand and walks me toward the wagon.

From behind, I can feel the anger emanating from his mother and want nothing more than to get away, yet I know the hayride will be horrible for his asthma.

Instead, I point to the fellowship hall, and we walk inside. Several people call to Caleb. I remain by his side, aware of the curious glances cast my way. My cheeks feel hot, and I stare at the floor, wishing I'd stayed home. His mother almost magically appears again and approaches, carrying a plate of cupcakes.

Caleb whispers, "I'm sorry. Let's get out of here."

"Cupcake, son?" his mother asks.

"Uh, sure. But maybe later. We'll eat first."

"Oh, live a little. Dessert first," she encourages loudly, playing to the audience around us as she hands each of us a cupcake. She then offers them to everyone. "My prize-winning recipe. Everyone loves them."

My stomach flips at the sight of the dreaded carrot cake. But with everyone staring, I need to be polite. Mrs. Buzbee watches me, as if daring me to be rude. I refuse to back down and let her have the upper hand. I'll eat every damn bite of this nastiness just to prove she can't get to me. I take a couple of bites and smile, trying not to gag.

"Thanks, Mom. We're going to catch the hayride." Caleb has eaten about half of his cupcake.

With his hand on my back, he leads me to the back of the room, and discreetly he dumps the rest of our cupcakes in the garbage.

"I know you hate them. I'm sorry." He squeezes my hand. "Hayride?"

I nod, feeling queasy and wanting out of the hot room and away from his hateful mother. We step outside, and the cool night air is a welcome relief. Instead of heading toward the hayride, I pull him toward the rear of the church. It's quiet back there.

Pastor Buzbee has two rules for the Fall Festival: no liquor and no foolishness in the cemetery. He says it's disrespectful to the deceased. He and the other parishioners make rounds every fifteen minutes to make sure everyone follows the rules. I have no plans to be disrespectful, but I need some place to get quiet and grounded and have the difficult conversation with Caleb.

Looking around, I climb over the split-rail fence, feeling a need to put distance between me and the black energy that's heavy in the air tonight.

"Dad won't like this," Caleb whispers as he follows.

Weaving through the tombstones, I head toward the long concrete picnic table where dinners on the grounds are held. I can faintly hear the gospel music from funerals and singings. The trees whisper above us, and the presence of those who have passed reassure me it's okay; I'm safe here. Caleb lifts me to sit on the table. The cold concrete isn't entirely comfortable, but before I can hop down, he starts speaking again.

"I'm sorry about everything. Mom, well, she's Mom. Look, I know I jumped the gun telling everyone how deep my feelings run for you. I should've told you first. But I'm pretty sure you know I love you, Skylar. I've loved you since the day I met you. I want you to be my wife, my lover, and if God blesses us, the mother of our children."

I shake my head and place my fingers over his mouth, not wanting him to continue. I don't want to break his heart. But he isn't deterred. He takes my hand from his mouth and continues.

"I'm good for you, Skylar. And you're good for me. I know my mother doesn't approve, but I'm a grown man who makes his own decisions. And I love you." He cups my face in his warm hands and kisses me.

Really kisses me.

His lips are warm and tender—not nearly as possessive as Jed's, but it's a nice kiss nonetheless. Curious, I let my tongue tease his, to see if I can experience the same raw need that overwhelms me when I'm with Jed. But while Caleb's a good kisser, there's no fire incinerating me from within right now. Kissing Caleb is like an after-dinner mint—nice and sweet, but not enough to truly satisfy a craving.

"We need to stop," Caleb gasps. He breaks away but leaves

his hands cupping my face, our foreheads touching. His ragged breath mists in the cold night air.

I nod my agreement. I rub my fist over my heart, signing, *I'm sorry.* I mouth the word I know he doesn't want to hear. *Jed.*

By the light of the dusk-to-dawn light, I see the painful acceptance in Caleb's eyes. *He understands.* And my heart aches for him. It was never my intent to hurt him; he's my friend— my best friend. And I don't want to lose that.

Absorbing his suffering makes me dizzy and short of breath. Hot tears trek down my cold cheeks. My head feels too heavy for my body, and darkness surrounds me. I feel claustrophobic.

"Hey, you look like you've seen a ghost," Caleb murmurs. "Please don't cry. Shoot, I've messed this up so bad."

He whips off his coat, places it behind me on the table, and helps me lie back. "Are you going to pass out? I'm sorry. I'm sorry. Just breathe for me—slow, deep breaths," he murmurs.

I cling to his hand with both of mine, afraid to let go as his face blurs. The world above me spins, and it feels like I'm barely hanging on. Something isn't right… Silently I scream, *Save me!* My own sins are consuming me, burning like a raging forest fire within. I feel lost between the worlds. I try to sit up, but it's too exhausting. Tired of struggling, I still, succumbing to the promise of peace if I were to never return to earth.

"Jedidiah needs you." Queenie's voice resonates loudly. *Is she here?* I fight to reach her, like I did all those years ago in the hospital when she willed me to come back and not fly toward the light…

The burden of my guilt squeezes my lungs, but now I feel Jed's strong, reassuring presence. Jed will help me. Reaching out, I pull him closer to weigh me down and pin me to the present. His body will shield me from death's grip. I hear Caleb asking if I'm okay. I'm confused and scared, unable to discern where I am or who is with me. *I need Jed…*

JED

"Have you thought about going back up north, now that you've stuck your grandmother in that nursing home?" Darrell asks as he drives.

"I didn't stick her anywhere. I'm trying to do what's best for everyone," I snap.

I'm already irritated for a number of reasons. First and foremost, Sky's with Caleb. Second, she left her phone on the kitchen counter. And, finally, my damn truck battery's dead—and, of course, with my rotten luck, I don't have any jumper cables, and neither does Queenie. I asked Dammit Darrel to jump me so I could go monitor the situation at the Fall Festival. Still mad, he told me to take Queenie's car and slammed the door in my face. Silently berating myself for not thinking of that, I'd turned to leave when the door opened again. He apologized and said he'd drive me and jump me when we got home.

"Well, I can't think there's much here for you since you ain't takin' care of Queenie, and Skylar's interested in that Buzbee boy. He loves her."

I glare at Darrell, getting the distinct impression he's goading me. The comment about Caleb has struck a little too close to home. And even though I've decided to stay in this area, it's just my damn nature to be argumentative.

"Since I've got Queenie taken care of, I think I'll take Skylar to see there's more to life than this neck of the woods. It would do her some good to broaden her horizons. Who knows? Maybe she'll want to go off to school somewhere and make something of herself."

"Over my dead body," he hisses as the car swerves.

I brace myself on the dash. "Dammit, Darrell! Be careful."

Three minutes later, we arrive at the church, and Darrell slams the door of his monster Cadillac and stomps away. Maybe it would be in my best interest to see about catching a ride back with someone else. I look around for Sky.

Kids are laughing and screaming in the bouncy house as their parents wait for them, visiting with friends and neighbors. Others are bobbing for apples out of a galvanized tub. Several people stop me to ask about Queenie. The clip-clop of the horses' hooves gets closer as the wagon pulls across the parking lot from the hayfield next to the church. One child is in hysterics and throwing clumps of hay as a worried mother comforts her.

But I don't see Skylar or Caleb.

"Jed." Kip nods and crosses his arms.

"Great costume, Deputy Do-Nothing. You almost look legit." I scan the crowd for Princess.

He scowls. "I'm here in my official capacity, making sure everything is A-OK. And where's *your* costume?"

"I'm dressed as a first-class asshole. Like it?"

Kip laughs. "It's perfect."

"You watch your language, Jedidiah Jackson. This is a family-oriented event, and if you can't act like a respectable, God-fearing man, you can leave." Mrs. Buzbee's dressed as some Biblical character, possibly the Virgin Mary.

Kind of fitting. I never could see her actually having sex other than to conceive. She's never approved of this celebration. Rumor has it she only goes along because she considers it a Christian response to Queenie's usual Samhain Soirée and part of her duty to support her husband.

"I fear no god. Have you seen Sky?" I ask.

Ever since she left the house, I've had this gut feeling trouble is brewing. The wake incident and the news media camping outside our front door a few days ago are still too fresh in everyone's mind. Is it just concern over Sky's safety? *Hell no.* I have enough self-awareness to acknowledge I'm jealous as hell, too.

"I have no clue. I believe she's with Caleb." Mrs. Buzbee looks like she just ate a persimmon, but she quickly recovers and gives a fake smile to one of the church members. "Keep that language clean," she warns me before walking away.

I squash the urge to yell, *Fuck you.*

I wander over to the line waiting for the hayride but still don't see Sky and Caleb. *Did they leave already?* Meandering through the crowd, I spy Darrell at the back corner of the church, staring out into the cemetery. I remember the last Fall Festival I ever attended. Terry Garrison and I snuck back there to smoke some weed. Pastor Buzbee busted us but, thankfully, didn't turn us in to the law or tell our families. We did, however, have to clean the church grounds after the festival as part of our plea bargain.

I make my way to Darrell and cross paths with Pastor Buzbee, who's dressed as Moses, complete with Styrofoam Ten Commandments.

"Hello, Jed. How's Guinevere? With church and the setup for the festival, I haven't had a chance to check on her since she moved to the rehab facility."

"She's doing okay. Better than expected, actually. Have you seen Sky? She left her phone at home." I wave her phone, hoping my growing jealousy didn't come through in my voice.

"I saw her with Caleb about an hour ago. Come with me. You can help me monitor the cemetery."

"What if I want to light one up?" I joke.

He chuckles as we approach Darrell. "Then I'll appreciate the help cleaning the church grounds tomorrow." Across the cemetery, there's a couple sprawled out on the picnic table. "These kids never listen—" Just as he did years ago when he caught me smoking the joint, he gives a loud, two-finger whistle like he's hailing a cab in New York City.

The guy lifts his head and looks over his shoulder, and I see red. I make a move toward Caleb, but Pastor Buzbee grabs my arm.

"Don't be rash, Jed. Remember what happened last time. He cares for Skylar. *Deeply.*"

Through clenched teeth I reply, "So do I." I slap her phone into the rector's hand. "Give this to her. And tell her I may or may not be there when she gets home. I need to cool off before I do something stupid." I whip around to leave before I end up in jail.

Darrell walks with me back to the car. My heart feels like it's shattering into a million pieces. *How could she do this to me?* I slam the door and sit, fuming. "I need to get out of here. Wait, do you think Caleb's done something? Maybe I should go back…"

Darrell starts the car. "No. *He loves her.* Caleb's good for her."

The fact that he's right pisses me off, so I do the mature thing and cross my arms and sulk in silence as we head toward home.

What was she doing with Caleb? She promised… All of my insecurities roar through my now pounding head. She may belong *here*, but she belongs with *me*. Tomorrow, I'm going to take her to see Queenie, and then I'll take her on a short trip to spend a couple of days in Asheville. I can make arrangements for my belongings to be shipped home, and it will give us time alone to explore our relationship and get everything out on the table. We've been under a lot of stress since I returned. Yep, a couple of days away could be just the thing we need. *Hell, maybe we'll elope...*

Decision made, I sit up as we pull in the driveway. "I'll need you to keep a check on the house," I tell Darrell. "I'm going to take Sky away."

"You can't!" he shouts. The car slams to a halt.

"Hey, be careful," I yell back. "Yeesh, good thing this tank has seatbelts or we'd both have whiplash." I get out of the car and watch him stomp over to me. It's hard to see his face, but I can tell he's pissed. "What's your problem, Darrell?"

"You're not taking her anywhere. I won't allow it."

I've never taken well to being told what I can and cannot do. "And just what the hell do you think you're going to do about it?"

Stars explode as I topple backward. My last coherent thought is *What the fuck?*

CHAPTER TWENTY-ONE

SKYLAR

"SKYLAR, WE NEED to get out of here. My Dad's not happy *at all*. Come on."

It feels like I'm surfacing from the bottom of a well. I'm so cold my teeth chatter, and someone grips my hand. But my insides feel like a volcano erupting. I sit up and realize it isn't Jed talking to me, it's Caleb. *Where's Jed?* He was here; I felt his presence. Looking around, Caleb and I are alone in the cemetery. Standing at the entrance I see Pastor Buzbee. I bite my lip and realize this looks bad. The last thing I want is Caleb in trouble because of me.

I hop off the table, but my legs feel wobbly. If it weren't for Caleb steadying me, I'd collapse. I offer him his coat back, but he wraps it around me, kissing my forehead.

"Let's go get some coffee or hot chocolate and warm up, okay?" His voice sounds hollow, and I can feel his pain.

I squeeze his hand, wishing there was something I could do to make this easier. He wraps an arm around my shoulders as we walk toward the church and past his father. Sneaking a peek, I see Caleb's right; his father doesn't look happy. But it's mild compared to the reaction of his mother when she spies us. Instinctively, I step back, positioning Caleb between us.

"Mom, Dad, I'll see you tomorrow. Goodnight," Caleb says, taking my hand and moving me toward the car.

"Jedidiah dropped off your phone," Pastor Buzbee says, handing it to me. "He, uh, said he may not be there when you get home. He needs time to cool off."

Heat floods my cheeks, and I nod my thanks. I can't get away fast enough. Evil hangs in the air like the cobwebs of autumn. It isn't my imagination. The fear I'm feeling is so intense that if my father were to pop out from behind a tree, it wouldn't surprise me. We finally reach the car, and I jump in, ready to get home. I need to see Jed.

Caleb pulls out of the parking lot, but instead of heading toward my house, he turns left toward the center of town. "I owe you that coffee or hot chocolate."

I pat his arm and point right, wanting to go home.

He sighs. "Please? At least give me this. A few minutes to talk?"

I don't want to, but I know he's right. We need to get this resolved tonight. I shove my uneasiness aside and nod. He pulls through a fast-food drive-thru and starts to order two hot chocolates, but I motion that I want water.

"I know we could've done this back at the church, but I think we need time alone." He pulls under a light and parks.

I chug the water, feeling hot and apprehensive.

"You're different from any other girl I've ever known."

I stare at my empty cup and nod.

"Hey, I meant that in a *good* way. You're my best friend and have been since we were kids. I love you. And I want to marry you. I may be wasting my breath, but I have to say it. I'm willing to wait if you think there might be a possibility you could grow to love me, too."

I sign that I *do* love him. But the parking lot light is dim. He points at my phone in his lap.

"Text me."

My hands shake, knowing I'm not going to type what he wants to read:

I do love you and always will. You're my best friend, too. But I don't love you the way you want me to. I'm in love with Jed. I feel very selfish because I don't want to lose you.

Caleb reads and hits delete. "Does Jed love you?"

I nod.

"He doesn't deserve you."

I shake my head, disagreeing.

"I'm sorry if I made you uncomfortable, but I wanted to be honest with you." He rubs his thumb over my ring finger, silent for a moment. "Thank you for being truthful with me, too." He sighs. "Guess I need to give him the same talk he gave me. If he ever hurts you, I'll kick his ass."

I want to hug him, but with the complicated emotions between us, I don't know what's right. He places his hot chocolate in the cup holder and starts the car, headed toward home. It's an awkward, silent ride. As we get closer, my knee bounces, and fear washes over me as if I've been doused by a bucket of water. *Something is terribly wrong. Is it Queenie?* I now understand why Jed wants me to have my phone with me. I check, but there's no text from him. It's all I can do to not urge Caleb to drive faster. I text Jed, *I'll be home in a few minutes.*

The house is dark except for the porch light. I look up to the second-floor porch, hoping Jed is there, wanting to hear his teasing remarks. But it's empty. I'm out the door before Caleb cuts the ignition.

"Whoa, hold on—are you that mad at me?" He's only a second behind me and follows me up the steps.

The door's been left unlocked, which isn't unusual if Jed's here, but I hang back from entering. Caleb grasps my hand, his worried gaze darting from me to the cracked door.

"What's the matter? Scared Jed's gonna kick my butt?" he whispers. "Tell you what, I'll concede you're his before he does, so no worries."

I bite my lip and shake my head. I point to the door and sign that I want him to come in with me.

He hesitates and glances out into the yard. "Honestly, I really don't want to see him. I need some time to think about everything…"

I hang my head, feeling terrible about hurting him.

Using his finger, he tilts my head up. His eyes are shiny. A hot tear slips down my cheek. "You're still my best friend and always will be." He kisses my cheek and steps away. With a small wave, he bounds down the steps toward his car.

I want to stop him and beg him to go inside with me, but I don't. I don't have the right to test his friendship and feelings this soon after rejecting his love. *I need to be brave.*

Something brushes my ankles, and I jump. Widdershins weaves around my feet, purring loudly. I reach down and scratch his ears as I switch on the lights. There's an eerie stillness settled around the house. I know Jed isn't here, and the knot of worry in the pit of my stomach tightens. I walk to the kitchen and peer through the curtains. His truck is gone. There's no note on the table.

I lock up the house and hurry upstairs, stopping by Jed's room. It's a mess, as if he was in a hurry. The closet door and drawers are wide open and empty. He's gone. He brought my phone to the church… Was it to say goodbye? A sense of urgency hangs over the room. *Jed must've seen me with Caleb.* I look around, and nothing is left except the dream catcher I made him. I sink to the bed, stunned. It's like drowning all over again. It hurts that Jed doesn't trust me.

I can't catch my breath, and I feel helpless—for about three seconds.

Angry, I stomp upstairs with the cat fast on my heels. My phone dings with a text.

I cannot stay here. Do not come looking for me. Take care of Queenie. Darrell will help you. —Jed

Where are you? I text back.

It says delivered, but there's no response.

Four hours later, there's still no response. I've stared at the screen until my eyes hurt. Turning off the phone, I cry myself to sleep, resolving it will be the last time Jedidiah Jackson makes me cry.

JED

I can't see, I can't hear, I can't move, and I damn sure can't say anything with the gag in my mouth. My head throbs, and lying here trussed up has my muscles screaming for relief. It smells musty, and I'm cold. And I can't even think about how badly I need to take a leak. I hear shuffling and a chain rattling. A blast of cold air follows. Despite the chill, I break out sweating, and my heart hammers so hard my chest feels ready to implode.

What the fuck is going on?

Someone grabs my arms and pulls me to a sitting position. The cold barrel of a gun presses against my forehead, and there's the unmistakable sound of a trigger being cocked. A multitude of feelings and thoughts invade my panicked brain. Anger, fear, sadness… Despite past thoughts about suicide, right now I want to live. I *have* to live. My family needs me, and I need them. I remain still and cooperate, knowing it's my best bet to survive.

"I've brought ya some breakfast and water, but if you say a word or try anything, I'll shoot."

Darrell?

He takes the gag out of my mouth, but I'm still tied up and blindfolded.

"What the hell?" I sputter.

"Don't cuss. It ain't nice, Jed."

"What are you doing? I gotta take a leak."

He yanks me to my shackled feet and roughly shuffles me out the door. To my embarrassment, once we're outside, he starts fumbling with my belt. "Hey, cut that out. At least give me the courtesy of untying one hand so I don't piss all over myself."

"Turn around. If you try anything, I'll kill you."

I'm trying to judge if he really would. He's a good shot—no doubt about it. He's the one who taught me how to hunt. The chilling memory surfaces of him smearing deer blood on my face right after my first kill. Maybe it's just my overactive imagination, but there'd been a gleam in his eye…

Yet I'm younger than him, and maybe if I surprise him, I can gain control of this situation. He unties my right hand, but before I can turn to try to deck him, the gun nudges my back. Instead, I conduct my business and zip up. He's like a member of the family. Why would he hurt me?

"So what's this all about, Darrell?" I'm acting a lot more nonchalant than I feel with the barrel of a gun pressing into my back. He reties my hands, damn near cutting off the circulation.

"Get back in the cabin, Jed."

The cabin. It makes sense he brought me here; it's an isolated place. He pushes me onto the side of the bed.

"Will you take the blindfold off?"

Instead of answering, he shoves a bite of a bologna sandwich in my mouth. Not my first choice for what I assume is breakfast, but beggars can't be choosy. I swallow, and he puts a bottle to my lips. It's water, and about half of it dribbles down my chin.

"Why are you doing this?" I ask, only to have another bite of sandwich shut me up.

"I have to," he answers cryptically. He gives me another drink of water, and I open my mouth for a bite of sandwich. Instead, something nasty is squirted down my throat, followed by water.

"Swallow," he commands, the gun now at my temple.

Reluctantly, I do as I'm told. He shoves the gag back in my mouth and pushes me prone on the bed. The door closes, and I'm left alone, wondering why the hell he'd do this to me. And what will happen to Sky?

CHAPTER TWENTY-TWO

SKYLAR

A SOFT RAIN makes the early morning as dreary as I feel. I checked my phone when I woke up, but there's still nothing more from Jed. I've thrown some cards in a past-present-future spread. In the past is The Lovers, the present is The Moon, and in the future, The Tower. This is scary. I read it as meaning in the past Jed and I were lovers, the present is full of illusion and deception, and the future holds major change, and possibly not in a good way. I feed Widdershins, who doesn't seem the least bit concerned that my world is falling apart. As long as he's fed, he's happy.

I look out the window, hoping to see Jed's truck pull up, but instead I see Darrell coming out of the woods. He's carrying a gun, which isn't unusual, but I wonder what he was doing out so early. *Maybe he's heard from Jed...* I step out on the porch and hold up my coffee cup, pointing to it. He hesitates but comes to the house and into the kitchen. I offer him a cup of black coffee, which he accepts.

Have you seen or heard from Jed? I write on my tablet.

He looks at the floor. "No. His truck's gone. I, uh, was setting traps in the woods, 'cause, uh, we've got coyotes."

Sipping his coffee, his posture is stiff. "You want to go see Mrs. Jackson this morning? I can take you."

I sigh, not having any other option now that Jed's left me and I've broken Caleb's heart. I'd ask Pastor Buzbee for a ride, but I can't imagine he'd be too keen on helping me after last night. And the nursing home is too far away for me to feel comfortable driving myself.

But as much as I want to see Queenie, something doesn't feel right. *What if Jed returns? I need to stay here.* I shake my head.

"But she needs you." Darrell slams his coffee cup down and rubs his hand on his worn jeans. His nervousness makes me suspicious. I kind of wish I hadn't invited him in. Abruptly he stands and grabs my hand. "We need to go get Mrs. Jackson!"

He looks like a lost child, but there's no way I'm going with him. I need to get him out of the house. I point toward the tablet, and, thankfully, he lets go.

Big, fat tears slip down his cheeks. "We're all she has. *I need her.*" Darrell collapses in the kitchen chair and starts sobbing.

Pity overrules my wariness, and I sit next to him and pat him on the shoulder, trying to comfort him. I know he's been worried about Queenie, and despite my personal feelings regarding him, she trusts Darrell and always has. I write, *Maybe later? I want to wait and see if Jed calls or comes home.*

"He won't." Darrell jumps to his feet. "I'll check back with you this afternoon." He leaves before I can respond. His behavior is even odder than usual.

I run upstairs and check my phone. Jed still hasn't read my message. Bored and missing him, I wander outside to the barn where he was working on the ramp for Queenie. It's stopped raining, but I hear a rumble of thunder in the distance. Jed's left the barn a mess, with his tools scattered everywhere. I pick up his hammer, and it vibrates. Maybe he went to Asheville to tell them he isn't taking the job? But wouldn't he just call? Or did he go to pick up some of his things? If he was gone for good, he wouldn't have left his tools.

I leave the barn, and the wind shifts. It feels like a warning: the cold hand of death is near. I close my eyes, trying to tap into Jed's energy, and see a vision of a derelict cabin. I think it's the one he used to hide out in as a kid.

Determined to find him, I locate the trail and make my way over the hill. I pause when I hear the roar of the river. It still makes me nervous to be near water. In front of me is a huge oak tree. Closing my eyes, I hug the tree, asking it to lend me some of its strength. A quiet stillness settles my racing heart, and I open my eyes. The brown leaves whisper Jed's name as they drift around me, but they don't give me the answer I need.

Which way do I go to find the cabin? I've never been alone in the forest.

Above me, a squirrel chatters, and a branch just misses my head, falling at my feet. It's Y-shaped, and I remember Queenie water-witching with an oak branch right after I'd come to live with her. I pick it up and point it toward the ground. The divining rod vibrates and pulls me to my right. The underbrush snags my clothes, but I don't care. I'm determined to find Jed. As I walk, the stick twitches and moves until I finally end up back on a well-beaten path. The pull becomes stronger. I'm close, so I pick up my pace, running until I see the run-down cabin hidden among the trees.

The front door is locked with a padlock and heavy chain that's wrapped around the porch railing. However, there are footprints going in and out, and it looks like something's been dragged through the dirt and leaves. I circle the cabin, and all of the windows are boarded up except for one small one. Standing on tiptoe, I try to peek in, but I'm too short. I knock on the bottom of the windowpane and wait, straining to listen. Just as

I'm about to leave, I hear a faint sound from inside. I know that snore. *It's Jed.* Again, I bang on the window, but he doesn't rouse. Looking around, I search for a stump—anything for me to step on to see better—but there isn't anything that will work. I keep knocking on the window, my worry escalating.

This isn't like Jed; he's a light sleeper. He blames it on his years in the service.

Something's wrong.

I have to get help, or at the very least get a stepladder so I can climb in through the window. I hurry back through the trees, trying to follow the path that leads home, but everything in the woods looks the same. *Where's the big oak tree? Is that it? No…* Lost and discombobulated, my rising panic has me near tears.

What if I can't find my way back to Jed? I don't have crumbs to leave behind like Hansel and Gretel. Besides, Jed always said it was a dumb story; the squirrels would eat the crumbs. Instead, I remove the ribbon from my hair and tie it on a limb. Every few feet I look back, and when I can't see the ribbon anymore, I shed my coat and drape it over a branch. Next, I peel off my sweatshirt, regretting not wearing a bra or socks today. My jeans and panties follow, and last are my tennis shoes.

Ready to cry with frustration, I finally find the main path that leads to the scary river. I turn left, racing toward home. Just as I come out of the woods, Mrs. Buzbee steps out of her car. The woman's mouth drops, and she looks ready to have a stroke. *And why not?* Once again, I'm inappropriately naked in her presence. At least this time I'm in my right mind.

I don't care how she judges me; she can help me rescue Jed.

I wave my arms and point toward the woods, but instead of coming to me, she gets back in her car. *I should've known she'd never help* me. I head into the barn and grab a stepladder.

Spying one of Jed's blue flannel shirts, I shrug into it. It smells like him and fuels my need to reach him. Spying a roll of duct tape, I slip it on my wrist like a bracelet. I can use it to mark my way back and collect my clothes. It takes me two tries to loosen the ax from the woodpile, but I now have it and the stepladder. I rush toward Mrs. Buzbee's car, but she locks the doors and closes her eyes, raising her hands as if she's in the midst of a prayer meeting. She's probably praying for my soul.

I don't care if I look like a crazy wild woman; she could have the decency to see what I need. I just hope she's called the law on me. Much as I don't like Kip, at least he'll help me get Jed out of that cabin.

Running back into the forest, I find the trail and see my first tennis shoe. I grab it and the next one and slip my shoes on so I can run faster. As I make my way back, I tear off strips of duct tape to mark my way, opting not to take the time to get into my clothes; I can get them later. Arriving at the cabin, I go straight to the small window that hasn't been boarded up and climb the stepladder. Using my sleeve, I wipe the dirt off the pane, but it's still too dark to see inside. No matter how hard I try, I can't seem to budge the window open. I take the ax and knock out the glass. It's going to be a tight fit, and I have no idea how I'll get Jed out if we have to go through the window.

It takes a couple of hops before I can hoist myself through, but, thankfully, there's a table I land on, knocking things over in the process. I find a candle and a book of matches. My hands shake so hard it takes me three tries to strike a match before the flame flickers to life. Unfortunately, it's also the last match in the book. The cabin is dusty and pretty bare. In the corner, I see Jed tied up, gagged and blindfolded. I rush over to him, careful not to extinguish the candle.

My fingers fumble, trying to untie the blindfold first.

Jed sits up abruptly, headbutting me so hard I see stars. I fall backward, knocking the candle over. We're plunged into darkness, except for the light from the small window. I crawl back to him and pat him, but he's kicking and fighting.

"Shhhh," I whisper, reaching out and stroking his arm.

He swings his feet and kicks me away. Jed's breathing hard, like an injured animal, and his fear is palpable even in the dark. I have to calm him down so I can get him out of here.

My past slams into the here and now. Fear has silenced me for years. I might not have drowned in that lake, but my courage sank to the bottom of that deep, dark water, killed by a monster.

Yet in this moment, I know I'm not a child anymore. I have to overcome my fear and be brave. Jed needs me.

It takes effort, but I manage to croak, "Jed. It's m-me, Skylar." My throat feels funny, and my voice sounds hoarse, out of place.

He stills, and his voice sounds muffled and confused around the gag.

"I'm coming toward you," I whisper, crawling to him.

His breathing saws, and my fingers find his face and the gag in his mouth. It takes some pulling, but I finally get the gag moved down to his neck.

"Get the blindfold off, too. Sky?"

"Yes," I whisper.

"Son of a bitch. I always knew you could talk. Get me untied."

"What happened?" As hard as I try, I can't speak above a whisper. I struggle to undo the knots, but I can't. I try shoving the blindfold up, but it's tied too tight. "I can't get them off. Who did this to you?"

"Darrell, and I have no idea why. Dammit, go get a knife."

"Darrell?" Part of me is surprised, part of me isn't. "I have an ax—"

"No thanks, Lizzie Borden. God, my mouth is so dry, and I feel weird. I'm pretty sure he drugged me. Let's get out of here. Help me up."

"The door is padlocked, and the front windows are boarded. I came in through the side window. I'll call Kip... Shoot, my phone's in my room." My hoarse-sounding voice has an odd squeak at the end even though I'm talking as loudly as I can.

"It's weird hearing you speak, even if your voice is kinda sexy-soft. And how many times have I told you to carry your phone with you? Don't call Kip. I refuse to be the laughingstock of the county. There's a knife in my room."

"No, your stuff is gone. So is your truck. I never trusted Darrell."

"It doesn't add up. Go home and look for my utility knife in the barn. Then come back and cut me loose. But hurry. And when this is all over, you have a lot of explaining to do, Chatty Cathy."

"I don't want to leave you. I'm scared," I whisper, grabbing his upper arm. Something bad is about to happen; I can feel it.

"For once, I'm not going to argue with you, but I'm not much good tied up. Go. You're the bravest girl I know. You can do this."

"But what if he sees me? I marked the way to get here with duct tape because the path is overgrown."

"You must've come the long way. There are three different ways to get here. Look, when you go out the window, turn left and head to the back of the cabin. There's an alternate route that's quicker, but it's steep. Darrell never uses it because it's a hard climb up and down the mountain."

I grab his face and kiss him. "I love you."

He chuckles. "I love you, too. Hurry, we don't know when Darrell will return."

"Okay." I'm reluctant to leave, but I have to get him out of here. I grab the duct-tape roll and slip it on my arm. *I knew Darrell couldn't be trusted…*

As I'm climbing through the window, I look back toward Jed. I can't see him, but as I jump down to the stepladder, he says, "Be safe. I love you, Princess."

I find the tiny path behind the cabin. Jed's right—it's a steep drop down the mountain, and I can barely make out the path. Just to be sure, I leave a small duct-tape trail by wrapping a branch every so often so it's less noticeable than the dangly strips I left on the other trail. But now I'm worried. If Darrell uses the other trail, he'll see my clothes and the tape and know I've been there. *I have to hurry.*

I hear noises in the brush, like something's out there. *Is it Darrell or some critter?* I still and hold my breath, listening. I can't tell what it is, but it's moving away from me. Forcing myself to take deep breaths and calm down, I walk quietly, trying to make as little noise as possible, leaving very tiny duct-tape markers behind until I see the back of the barn. Again, I look toward Darrell's, but I can't see the back of his house, so I assume he can't see me either.

Inside the barn, I find the knife. Should I get my phone and Queenie's gun, too? Trying to act nonchalant, I hurry toward the house, watching Darrell's with a side-glance. Once inside, I race upstairs and grab my phone. Outside, I hear the crunch of a car coming up the driveway. *Please don't let it be Darrell. No, he'd simply walk over.* I pull on my baggy pajama pants because they fit over my shoes, quickly button Jed's shirt, and tiptoe down the stairs. Looking out the front window, I see Mrs. Buzbee's car parked on the side, but she isn't in it. A knock sounds on the back door at the same time Widdershins decides to circle my feet, purring loudly.

I tiptoe into the kitchen, and peeking through the window, I see Caleb's car. *Oh, thank God.* I open the door, surprised to find Pastor Buzbee is with him.

"Where's my mother?" Caleb asks. His color is pale, and Pastor Buzbee looks disheveled, very unlike himself.

I shrug and point toward the woods, urging them to follow me. She's the least of my worries.

"Skylar, this is serious. Eleanor isn't well. Her car is here. Where is she?"

I stomp my foot, not caring she isn't well. Jed needs us. Taking a risk, I whisper as loud as I can, "Something's happened to Jed. Come."

"You can talk?" Caleb asks, looking dumbstruck.

"What happened to Jed?" his father asks.

I brush past them out the back door.

"Did Jed get hurt hunting?" Pastor asks.

"Do you have any idea which way to go?" Caleb's huffing and puffing to keep up.

If I weren't so worried about Jed, I'd slow down. Vaguely I point at my tiny duct-tape markers. The distinct smell of burning wood is in the air.

"I smell fire!" Pastor Buzbee shouts.

I think he must've stopped behind us to call and report it. I whip around when I hear him mention Darrell's name. *He phoned Darrell?* I race up the hill through a haze of damp smoke. The side of the cabin is smoldering where the broken window is, and Mrs. Buzbee is standing with her back to us, arms raised.

"Mom!"

She whips around at the sound of Caleb's voice and pales. She points at me, and her face contorts into an ugly mask of hatred. Her eyes appear black and soulless. "What are you doing out here? Witch! It's black magic! *Thou shalt not suffer a witch to live!*"

I grab the ax and run up the steps to break through the door. But my effort is futile. Caleb's behind me and takes over. His breathing sounds like a dying accordion, and he's barely chipping the door because it's so thick. The fire's spreading, and I silently pray for rain.

Behind us, Pastor Buzbee and his wife are arguing. He's holding her to keep her from doing God knows what.

Darrell bursts up behind them, and I scream, "No!" But it comes out as a hoarse squeak.

He hurries forward, shoving Caleb out of the way, and begins unlocking the padlock. The chain clatters to the wooden floor. I wrench the door open, and smoke billows out. Strong arms pull me back down the steps, preventing me from entering the burning building.

"I'll get Jed," Caleb shouts.

I wrestle against Darrell's hold on me. "Let me go! I have to get to Jed." My attempt to break free is as useless as my atrophied vocal cords.

Jed stumbles through the thick smoke, still blindfolded and bound. He trips and falls to the floor. Darrell lets go of me and drags him off the porch. *Where's Caleb?* I dart past Darrell, who now has Jed over his shoulder. He reaches for me, but I evade him. I race inside and almost trip over Caleb's body. The entire cabin is now engulfed in flames. A beam falls just behind us as I try to drag his dead weight outside. His mother's hysterical cries from the yard mix with a boom of thunder. Someone enters behind me and shoves me out the door. I race to go back in to save Caleb, but Darrell once again grabs me.

From the doorway Pastor Buzbee yells, "I've got him."

Darrell cuts the tape binding Jed's hands, and Jed grabs the knife to cut his feet free. Mrs. Buzbee falls to her knees, praying and sobbing. I look up, and, using every last ounce of power within me, I try to summon the rain. The wind picks up, and the drops come down in earnest. As soon as Jed's free, he jumps up and holds me tight. I bury my face in his wet shirt and cling to him as the cold drops pelt us. I look over to see Caleb lying on the ground, coughing. His color is gray beneath the soot. His eyes look wild and unfocused, and he keeps coughing.

Pastor Buzbee yells, "Breathe, Caleb!" He's crying as he tries to administer Caleb's inhaler.

"Come on, buddy, take a slow breath." Jed runs and kneels beside Caleb, checking for a pulse as Mrs. Buzbee crawls toward him in hysterics.

But all Caleb can do is cough, cough, cough. His lips turn blue in his gray face, and he clutches his chest, staring at me. I also drop to my knees, croaking, "It's okay, Caleb. Relax and breathe." But I'm not sure he can hear me over the rain and his mother's wailing.

"Get away from my son, witch! You were supposed to be in the cabin!" Mrs. Buzbee tries to shove me away, but Caleb reaches for my hand.

Still coughing, he signs, *I love you.*

"I love you, too," I reply, kissing his hand. He closes his eyes and smiles.

The sound of the crackling fire and downpour mix with his mother's weeping.

"Son!" Pastor Buzbee again tries to administer the inhaler.

Staring above, peace relaxes Caleb's face as his soul slips away, flying free, soaring above the treetops.

CHAPTER TWENTY-THREE

JED

THIS CAN'T BE happening. I check Caleb's pulse: nothing. No breaths. Pastor Buzbee and I start CPR, but the breaths don't go in, and the compressions are useless. We switch every fifteen minutes or so, and after forty-five minutes, we're both exhausted.

It's Caleb's father who stops first. "Enough," he says. "He's gone."

Mrs. Buzbee collapses on Caleb's still body, sobbing. "No, no, no! The witch was supposed to die. My son's a righteous man. He can't be unequally yoked. I was trying to save him…"

I look at Pastor Buzbee, trying to comprehend what's just happened. *Darrell locked me in the cabin. But Mrs. Buzbee set the place on fire?* None of this makes any sense.

"I'm sorry, Jedidiah. You were going to take Skylar away…" Darrell starts blubbering. "She's my family. She and Mrs. Jackson are all I have. I didn't mean to hurt you. You're my friend."

Pastor Buzbee supports his wife as they cry over Caleb's body. Princess simply looks shell-shocked. This is surreal, a nightmare. *Surely I'm going to wake up any minute…*

The last wall of the cabin collapses, and Sky shivers. None of us is wearing a coat.

I place a hand on the grieving father's shoulder. "Sir, we need to get out of here in case the fire spreads…"

He nods and stands. "Come, Eleanor. Caleb's gone."

"Noooo, he can't be. It was supposed to be her. I wanted her to *die!*"

SKYLAR

Caleb's mother points at me and sneers, "You and Guinevere are in league with Satan. This is all your fault. You're evil, and you deserve to be punished. I was doing God's will."

"Eleanor, stop. You're not thinking straight." Pastor Buzbee looks as bewildered as I feel.

"I'm thinking plenty straight. Guinevere ensnared you in her trap years ago. Do you think I'm ignorant? That Jezebel bewitched you. And this one was trying to do the same with my boy. I tried to show everyone she was evil; you saw how she ran around naked, showing off her body. And it wasn't just the jimsonweed that made her do it. She did it again today. I saw her! I couldn't risk Caleb's soul. I had to destroy the witch. The Bible says so—"

"Dear God, Eleanor. What are you talking about?"

Darrell reaches down and hoists Caleb into his arms.

"Put him down! You're as bad as they are. You aren't normal!" Her eyes blaze with the fanaticism of someone who's lost touch with reality.

Jed takes Caleb from Darrell and nods toward me. "Walk with Sky."

Darrell grabs my hand, but I try to wrench free, shaking my head. "No, Darrell hurt you!" I whisper.

Tears spill down Darrell's face. "I'm sorry, Jed. I didn't mean to. I had to do something to keep you here." He turns to me and whimpers, "I love you, Birdie."

I stop fighting him, and for a moment everything goes still. The dark shroud that's hidden a niggling memory for years rips away. It feels like I'm in a tunnel, and the light grows brighter and brighter as my fractured mind pieces itself together.

The night my father killed my mother, she'd argued with him, but that was nothing new. And he'd beaten her, but that wasn't different from any other day either. But he didn't stop, even when I begged him to. Then he shot her and she didn't move. I tried to push him away, but he grabbed me by the neck and told me to shut the hell up. I thought he was going to tear my head off, it hurt so bad, and I couldn't breathe. I must've passed out, because the next thing I knew, we were in a boat. My throat was sore, and I had to pee, but I was too scared to move. Above me was a full moon, and under the eerie light, Mama's purple-and-blue face looked like a mask. Her eyes and mouth were open, fear stamped on her face. I nudged her with my hand, but she didn't move. On top of her were three cement blocks.

I looked up at him, terrified.

"Quit looking at me," he hissed. *"You're hideous like your whore mother."*

I did as he'd said and squeezed my eyes shut. He grunted and tugged, and then there was a splash. The boat rocked, and I was terrified we were going to turn over. I didn't know how to swim. With a final grunt, he sat back down and started rowing.

"What am I going to do with you?" he snarled, yanking me

out of the boat by my hair. *"You can't say anything…"*

"*Mama,*" I whimpered, but my voice sounded far away.

"You never listen, you little brat. I said not to say anything!" He pushed me under the water, his hands tight around my throat…

I have only one other recollection of the time before I woke up in the hospital: big hands pushing on my back as I vomited water. My throat felt like it was on fire, and from far away I heard a man say, *"I won't ever let him hurt you again, Birdie…"*

I blink and watch as Jed carries Caleb's body down the mountainside, with his parents following.

I turn to stare at Darrell. "Who are you?" I croak.

"Your mother was my baby sister." He sits down in the pouring rain and covers his face, rocking and keening. "I've done bad things, but I didn't mean to…" His shoulders shake as he bawls and apologizes over and over.

I sink down beside him and stare at the man I've always mistrusted. But his aura is no longer murky. "W-what bad things, Darrell? Tell me."

"I had hate in my heart. I never liked your daddy. Rodney was mean to Sissy. She called me one night and said he was drinking a lot. She was scared. It took me two days to get there." He wipes his eyes. "I didn't have the money for the bus ticket. I had to borrow it, and I was too late. I didn't get there in time. I got to the house, and it was dark, but I heard noise down toward the dock. He was hurting you. I had to make him stop. I didn't mean to kill him, but I had to make him stop."

"Why didn't you ever tell me who you are?" I ask softly.

"It was a secret. I promised Mrs. Jackson not to tell. She volunteered at the hospital where I cleaned rooms. She always treated me real nice. I told her what I done, and she told me she'd handle things. She's gonna be mad at me now. I need her. We have to get her home. Please?"

It's a lot to take in. But I realize my fears have been

unfounded. The secretiveness I mistrusted all these years was because he loved me and trusted Queenie to keep her word. This man saved my life. I stand and urge Darrell to get up. "We'll get this straightened out. Jed will help."

Darrell stands and shakes his head. "No, Jed's mad at me. I'm not a good friend. I gave him your grandmother's sleeping medicine. I needed time to get Mrs. Jackson home... I love Jed. I didn't want to do it."

"He won't be mad when you explain. We need to go home. Come."

"Don't leave me. Promise?"

"I promise."

He wipes his nose on his sleeve. "You sound funny when you talk," he says with a sniffle.

"I know."

It sounds funny to me, too. I squeeze his hand, and together we head down the mountain. Thankfully, the cabin fire is dying down, and with the torrential rain the woods around it didn't catch fire. As we maneuver down the path toward home, my heart feels broken with the loss of Caleb. Life seems bleak without him. Several firemen run toward us, carrying shovels, axes, and other equipment. Darrell points out the path to them.

It's a somber scene when Darrell and I come out of the woods. There are lots of vehicles and people in our yard, seemingly oblivious to the pouring rain. Paramedics load Caleb's sheet-covered body into the back of the ambulance. Kip has placed Mrs. Buzbee in the back of the police car. She's ranting incoherently as Pastor Buzbee—looking haggard and bewildered—speaks with Sheriff Rogers and someone from the fire department. Jed has his hand on the minister's back as they talk. One of the church elders gets out of a car, opens his umbrella, and hurries toward the minister. Sheriff Rogers nods, and the elder escorts Pastor Buzbee away.

WHAT THE TREES KNOW

"I'm scared," Darrell whispers.

"Don't be." I squeeze his hand as we walk toward them.

Sheriff Rogers turns toward us. "I need to ask Darrell and Skylar some questions," he tells Jed.

"Look, what Darrell did was just a prank that went wrong—"

Darrell's blubbering intensifies. "I'm sorry, Jed."

"It's okay, buddy. It was just a joke. I'm fine. How about we go inside, Sheriff? Skylar can write her answers to your questions. We're all tired and cold."

His sad gaze meets mine, and he glances toward Darrell, who looks like a lost child. I blink my acknowledgment, relieved that he realizes Darrell did something wrong for the right reason. An unspoken bond to protect Darrell cements itself between us.

CHAPTER TWENTY-FOUR

JED

I STAND IN the hot shower, letting the water work out the kinks. I'm stiff and feel a bit hungover. It's been one hell of a day. I'm still trying to process what happened. Darrell thought he was protecting Sky, Mrs. Buzbee lost her mind, and Caleb died. The one I truly feel sorry for is Pastor Buzbee.

I should've gone to check on Queenie, but I just didn't have it in me, and neither did Princess.

The curtain pushes back, and Skylar steps in, surprising me. No slashing movements. Instead, she wraps her arms around my waist and tucks her head into my neck. I tighten my hold around her, needing her every bit as much as she needs me. Together we cry over the loss of our friend as the water cleanses away the dirt, if not our sorrow.

"I tried to save him," I choke hoarsely. "I tried."

She nods and kisses my chest.

"He died saving *me*." Two days ago, I never would've classified Caleb Buzbee as the heroic type. How wrong I've been about him, and how I wish I could turn back time. He had to have known he was putting himself at risk with his asthma and the smoke. But he did it selflessly. Guilt weighs heavily on me even though there was nothing I could do about it.

I wash Skylar's hair and soap her down before rinsing her off. She hasn't spoken a word, but it's okay. She'll talk again when she's ready.

Despite the shower, the lingering scent of smoke remains. I reckon it will take a few more showers to get it out of our pores. I turn the water off and wrap a towel around my waist. She steps out from behind me, and I dry her off as she wraps her wet hair in a towel. Her eyes are luminous with tears.

"I'm sorry," I say, wishing I could take the pain from her.

"I know," she says in that breathless voice I've longed to hear for so many years. "Me, too."

Her finger traces the almost-healed place on my ass where the bullet grazed me. That seems like ages ago, though it's been just over a week. She rubs some ointment on my wrists where the rope chafed them. Silently, we dress.

"I love you," she whispers.

I kiss her petal-soft lips and murmur, "I love you, too. I need to hold you."

I feel vulnerable, admitting this, but she nods and leads me to my room. We collapse on the bed and snuggle, listening to the rain tap against the window.

"I should check on Darrell," I comment after a moment, making lazy circles on her back, torn between duty and staying here with her. We insisted he stay with us tonight, and he's bunking in Queenie's room downstairs.

Sky pats my chest, signaling he's fine. And, sure enough, as if she knew, I hear Darrell playing his guitar downstairs and softly singing "Ain't No Grave." I swallow the lump in my throat. It was one of Caleb's favorites. I used to make fun of him for liking this kind of music. What I wouldn't do to make fun of him now…

A tear slips down my cheek, only to be captured by Sky's lips.

"Sorry to be so emo," I mumble.

"I'm going to miss him, too," she whispers against my ear, stroking my face.

"I feel so helpless…" I stare at the dream catcher over my bed. "When I was overseas, I saw a little kid blow himself up. He took the grenade, pulled the pin, and there wasn't a damn thing I could do about it…"

She props her head on her hand, listening, and nods. "I felt that way the night my mama was murdered."

"Ah. Is that what happened? Pretty traumatic for a little girl. I'm sorry."

"My father shot her and dumped her body in the lake behind our house. Then he tried to kill me. It was Darrell who saved me from drowning. He's my uncle. H-he killed my dad."

My eyebrows shoot up. "The fuck you say…" I try to absorb this information. I'm not sure I can. "I want you to tell me all of it—if you want to and when you're ready. It doesn't have to be right now."

She nods and lays her head back down. She's done talking for now.

After a moment, I sigh. "When I was tied up like a Thanksgiving turkey ready for the oven, I didn't understand why Darrell was doing this. I guess it makes a little more sense now. I was crazy with worry. I knew I had to get out of there, for you and for Queenie. But he drugged me."

She rubs my chest. "He mashed up one of Queenie's sleeping pills in your water. I think he was just trying to buy time. All he wanted was for me to stay here and Queenie to come home."

"I shouldn't have been so stubborn. I should've told him I'd changed my mind about taking you away permanently. But I felt like he was questioning whether I was doing the right thing. You know me and authority. And I was too focused on my jealousy over Caleb to realize how distressed he was. When I saw you and Caleb making out in the cemetery, I lost my shit…"

"We weren't making out. I didn't feel well. I'd eaten a couple bites of Mrs. Buzbee's carrot cake. I was actually telling him I love *you*."

My relief is immediate, and some of my worry lifts. "That explains quite a bit. Apparently, Mrs. Buzbee's been crazy for a while. She told Sheriff Rogers she'd been putting jimsonweed in the carrot cake for you and Queenie to show Caleb you two weren't normal."

"The only time I ate it was when I had to at the wake, and then a couple of bites at the festival to be polite." She pauses a moment. "But Queenie's always liked it…"

"Yup. I'm thinking that might be the source of a lot of her issues. I feel bad for Pastor Buzbee. He's lost his son *and* his wife. He thought she was just too zealous. He told me she called him and was jabbering that you were running around naked in the woods in a satanic ritual, and she was called by God to rid the world of evil."

"So that's why he and Caleb came over. I thought you'd left. I found your clothes gone; your truck was gone. And you sent me a text…" She pauses. "Wait, the text. It was complete sentences. I should've known it wasn't from you."

"Nope. Darrell jumped my truck and hid it in his garage. He must've emptied my room of my stuff to make it look like I'd left."

"So much miscommunication… We've all been drowning in silence. Poor Caleb, if only everyone had been more honest." She puts her head down and sobs.

"He loved you." I swallow the lump in my throat. "And he loved me. I never gave him a fair shake."

She sighs. "I feel guilty, too. I broke his heart at the Fall Festival. And I misread the cards. I knew something bad was going to happen, but I thought it was you who was in trouble."

I turn toward her, taking her hand to kiss it. "He wouldn't want us being sad. He believed in heaven and a better place. He'll always be here with us, in our hearts."

She nods, wiping her tears. "I know. But I'm sure going to miss him. I need to tell the bees…"

I nod and brush her hair back, caressing her cheek. "Okay. But first, I want to say something."

She looks at me and waits.

"I love you. And I swear I won't let Caleb die in vain. I'm going to learn from my past mistakes. I'll live each day from now on thankful for what I have, to honor his memory."

And I mean it. Because holding this woman in my arms, I realize I have everything. *I always have.* I feel like Dorothy in the *Wizard of Oz*, finally understanding there's no place like home.

Sky smiles and wipes the tears from her eyes. She nods. With another kiss, we go downstairs to check on Darrell.

SKYLAR

In the kitchen, Darrell's playing his guitar and singing another poignant gospel song. He stops playing and bursts into tears when Jed enters the room.

Jed squeezes his shoulder. "We're good. I love you and forgive you, okay? Sky needs to go tell the bees about Caleb."

"Okay." He sniffles, continuing to play as I gather three pieces of black cloth and embroider Caleb's name on each one.

When I'm done, I grab the sugar bowl and an umbrella. Jed and Darrell follow me outside but stay on the porch. They know I need to do this by myself. I approach the beehives and respectfully knock three times on each box before draping the cloths over the top and sprinkling the sugar offering.

For the first time, I speak the sad truth out loud. "Do not fear; we're still here. Caleb's gone; we'll persevere."

From inside the box, the bees buzz an acknowledgment. I wonder if they're as shocked as everyone else that I can speak. I can't wait to see Queenie and tell her out loud how much I love her. When I turn and walk back toward the house, I swear I see Queenie standing with Jed and Darrell for a brief moment. I smile. It's a sign. She'll be home soon; I know it.

Above me, an eagle soars above the treetops, and, despite the sadness I feel losing Caleb, my heart is filled with hope. The world is full of change and loss. But it's a beautiful, magical place.

EPILOGUE

2020, ONE YEAR LATER
JED

"No, THAT LOOKS ridiculous. You placed the tombstones like a military cemetery. Mix them up more; it's supposed to be haunted. And you need to move the cauldron into the yard. It won't be the same this year, but we can still make it look right." Princess drops the curtain, fussing in that whispery voice that's no less effective than the barked commands of my ex-drill sergeant. "Darrell, have you put the hay bales in the yard? I'll put the mums on them later. The children can't trick-or-treat, but they're going to leave their carved pumpkins in the yard for Queenie to judge."

Darrell nods. "Yes, *ma'am*, Ms. Birdie."

I snicker. He usually only says "yes, ma'am" to Queenie. And he's the only one who calls Skylar by her birth name.

"Everything has to be perfect—this pandemic has ruined so much. I hear the new preacher was going to cancel the Fall Festival even before this mess…" She bites her lip, looking sad.

Caleb's been on all of our minds this week. It still seems strange he's gone; so much has happened in the last year. Princess twists her plain gold wedding band. It isn't anything fancy. The Christmas after Caleb died, we had a small wedding. Pastor Buzbee married us before he moved to be closer to where his wife has been institutionalized.

I pull Sky to me, knocking her silly witch hat off in the process.

"No sadness. Caleb wouldn't want it."

She nods, and I kiss her. It's been so long since we've been intimate, and those full breasts pressing against my chest make me wish we were alone and naked.

"Not now. We have too much to do. Really? This is your costume?" She straightens my tie.

"What? I'm Darren, you're Samantha. It's just us anyways."

Shaking her head, she bends over and picks up her hat, that sweet ass tempting me. I give it a good swat. She stands upright, grinning as she rubs it. She's the sexiest witch I know.

"Jedidiah!" Queenie makes her way into the room, using her four-prong cane. She's dressed as Endora from *Bewitched*. "Don't you have better things to do than harass Skylar?"

"Not really." The urge to back talk remains strong. I've worked on self-improvement and patience, but sometimes I slip. Besides, Queenie expects nothing less from me.

"Have you finished your chores, young man?"

"No, apparently I need to rearrange tombstones and move a cauldron."

"Then get to it and quit dawdling or I'll tan your hide."

I let out a deep breath. I'll always be eleven years old in her eyes.

"Come on, Darrell. Let's get things done so we can eat before *you know what.*" I motion to my buddy. We both snitch a candy bar from the bowl by the front door on our way out. There's no trick-or-treating, but Sky made sure to have all of our favorite candy.

"Stop it, you two. You'll ruin your supper," Sky fusses.

"I kinda miss the days when you silently nagged," I tease as I shut the front door.

"You gonna hear about that one, Jed. Birdie's got her mama's temper at times," Darrell says with a chuckle.

Dead leaves crunch under our footsteps even though he raked this morning.

"I know it. Making up's the fun part, though."

The sun is sinking behind the trees. I feel antsy; my surprise for Sky's birthday should arrive soon.

We get the cauldron in the yard. Instead of apples for bobbing, this year it has a huge yellow mum in it. Shortly after that, the tombstones are scattered, hopefully to Princess's liking.

"Mrs. Jackson's having a pretty good day today. She only called Birdie by your aunt's name once," Darrell comments as he collapses in the rocker, staring out into the yard.

He's been quiet this week, and I'm waiting for his daily apology. It's part of his personal penance. It used to annoy me, but now I just give him the reassurance he needs.

"That new medicine the doc put her on for her memory has helped. She still gets more confused at night, but hopefully our visitor won't be too much for her. Skylar thought having things as much like normal would be good for her."

Darrell nods. "She checked the cards. It'll be okay."

I roll my eyes and sit next to him. I still think the hocus-pocus stuff is nonsense. And yet...I've found myself taking the time to enjoy each moment and give thanks for the blessings in my life. The wind shifts, and smoke from the fireplace whispers across the porch. I shiver. It's the first fire we've built since the cabin burned. The smell makes me a little queasy.

"I'm sorry for what I did." Darrell looks ready to cry, again, and mops his mouth with his bandana. "I hope you can forgive me."

"I know you are. We're good." I bump fists with him, and

he sniffles and wipes his eyes.

A car approaches, and I nudge Darrell. "He's here."

SKYLAR

"Is my hat on straight?" Queenie asks.

Even though I don't remember Endora wearing a witch's hat, Queenie's insisted on a purple one to match her dress. It has a feather plume and black veil with fake spiders on it.

"It is. You look perfect."

She cups my cheek in her gnarled hand. "My sweet girl, I know this has been a hard week. I still sometimes think Caleb will be by to ask questions about medicinal herbs." Tears fill her eyes. "I can't believe his spiteful mother laced her carrot cake. Damn foolish woman. Personally, I think they should've revoked her blue ribbon."

It *has* been a hard week, but I've sensed Caleb's spirit. And since his death, there's an eagle that nests on the mountain behind the house. I love watching it soar through the trees. I'm convinced the bird's a messenger from Caleb. I straighten the candy bowl, feeling nervous. Jed's been keeping a secret, but it's my birthday, so it's to be expected. Yet it feels bigger than a birthday present. My emotions have been all over the place for weeks now, though, so I'm trying to take things in stride.

The front door opens, and I cover my mouth, surprised, and promptly burst into tears. His hair is grayer, and permanent sadness etches his kind eyes, but behind his mask, I can tell he's smiling. My heart's so full it feels ready to burst.

"He's self-quarantined for a couple of weeks and doesn't have a fever," Jed says. "Tell him he can take off the mask, Sky. He's actually gonna stay with us for about a week."

"Yes, yes, of course."

Pastor Buzbee removes it and opens his arms. I run to him and hug his neck.

"I didn't know you were coming!"

He pats my back and chuckles. "Well, that's a surprise. I figured either Queenie would have read it in the tea leaves, you in your tarot cards, or, more likely, Jed would've blabbed. He was never very good at keeping secrets." He pulls back, holding me by the upper arms, and peers into my face. "You look beautiful, my dear."

Actually, Jed's very good at keeping secrets, but I don't disagree with this dear man. "Thank you." I look down but then back up again. I'm doing better at making eye contact.

Jed wraps his arm around my shoulders and kisses my temple. "Happy birthday, Princess."

"It's the best present ever." I beam up at him.

Darrell nods, and Queenie takes her cane and taps the floor. "Hello, Preacher. Stopping by to see the competition? You keep a tally of who comes to your Fall Festival, and I'll do the same with my Samhain Soirée. Whoever has the most visitors wins. We'll compare over tea tomorrow."

An awkward silence ensues. Obviously, at the moment Queenie doesn't remember Pastor Buzbee no longer lives here, and there isn't a Fall Festival this year or our annual Samhain Soirée.

"I've given up trying to compete, Guinevere. No one can compare to you. And tea tomorrow would be lovely."

Queenie turns her attention to Jed and me. "Well, go on, you two. Show him what you've been up to."

I take Pastor Buzbee's hand, and we follow Jed upstairs. "I still can't believe you're here."

"I was happy for the invitation from Jed."

"Hurry up, slowpokes! Just wait until you see..." Jed takes the steps two at a time, for once not caring that he's made them squeak. We reach the bedroom, and Jed turns around, a huge smile on his face. In his arms, he holds our newborn son.

"He couldn't wait to get here and came a month early. I think he gets his impatience from me. But he's beautiful like his mama. Meet Caleb Darrell Jackson."

Caleb stretches his little arms and scrunches his face as Pastor Buzbee takes him and holds him to his heart, kissing the top of his head. "I can't begin to express my happiness..." he chokes out, tears running down his face. Caleb's tiny hand grasps the reverend's finger. "This is truly a blessing."

"Yes, sir, it is. I only hope I can raise my son to be as fine a man as your Caleb was."

Pastor Buzbee smiles. "Thank you. And you're happy, staying here?"

Jed takes my hand in his and smiles. "Yes, sir. I've come to realize that home is where people love you and accept your imperfections."

Pastor Buzbee nods. "And therein lies the true magic."

THE END

ACKNOWLEDGMENTS

Thank you, Katherine, Jamie and Martha Jane, for your feedback and help with the first draft and for allowing me to brainstorm ideas. I'm sure my Google search has raised some eyebrows.

As always, editing is my favorite part of the process thanks to my amazing editor, Jessica Royer Ocken. Her sense of humor and gentle guidance make this aspect of book publishing fun.

Colleen Keough Wagner, your Buffy inserts as you line edited made me laugh out loud. I can't promise I'll ever understand commas, but you explain them very well!

Gina Dickerson of RoseWolf Design, thank you for the lovely cover and making the inside of my book as beautiful as the outside.

Stephanie Phillips of SBR Media, you are the best agent ever! Thank you for always believing in me and picking me up when I'm down.

My family has been there during the tears and laughter of this long journey. I couldn't have done it without their support.

And to my readers. Thank you for reading and loving my characters as much as I do. I write because I have to. I publish for you.

About the Author

Nancee is a retired nurse and addiction counselor. Nights are spent writing magical realism and romance books with a serrated edge.

Website: nanceecain.com
Goodreads: goodreads.com/Nancee_Cain
Facebook: facebook.com/NanceeCainAuthor
Reader's Group (Cain Raisers): facebook.com/groups/Cain.Raisers
Twitter: twitter.com/Nancee_Cain
Pinterest: pinterest.com/nanceecain
Instagram: instagram.com/nanceecain
BookBub: bookbub.com/authors/nancee-cain
Spotify Playlists: open.spotify.com/user/12184539074

BOOKS BY NANCEE CAIN

Paranormal Romance (Angels)
Saving Evangeline, Tempting Jo, Loving Lili (novella)

Contemporary Romance (Pine Bluff Novels)
The Resurrection of Dylan McAthie, The Redemption of Emma Devine, The Rehabilitation of Angel Sinclair, The Redirection of Damien Sinclair, The Reinvention of Jinx Howell, The Reintroduction of Sammie Morgan, The Realization of Grayson Deschanelle

pine|bluff

Contemporary Romances

Although each of the titles in this series can be read as standalone stories, this is the preferred reading order:

The Resurrection of Dylan McAthie, The Redemption of Emma Devine, The Rehabilitation of Angel Sinclair, The Redirection of Damien Sinclair, The Reinvention of Jinx Howell, The Reintroduction of Sammie Morgan, The Realization of Grayson Deschanelle

The Resurrection of Dylan McAthie

A Pine Bluff Novel

Maybe You Can Go Home Again

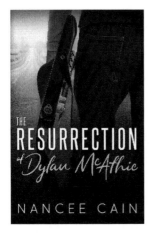

Hounded by paparazzi, Dylan McAthie — the former lead guitarist for Crucified, Dead and Buried — craves quiet anonymity to regroup and sort out his life. An accident leaves him dependent on the family he once ran from, with no choice but to return to the small town of Pine Bluff, Alabama.

Hired by Dylan's estranged brother, private-duty nurse Jennifer Adams remembers the charming boy Dylan was before fame and misfortune. And she notices he's developed a knack for blaming everyone else for his problems, rather than bothering with introspection. She's not having it.

Despite their clashes, as her patient heals, the chemistry between them grows undeniable — until scandal finds Dylan again, threatening to destroy the progress he's made and the couple's growing respect and affection. Can Dylan fix what fame has so easily broken? Or will his public resurrection mean the death of any relationship with Jennifer?

The Redemption of Emma Devine

A Pine Bluff Novel

A Little Shake-Up in Life Can Be Devine

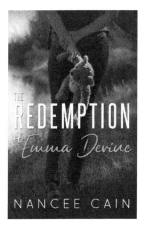

Emma Devine is on the run and fighting to survive. Her tortured past makes trust difficult, especially where men are concerned. But she has no choice other than accepting the help of the man who catches her shoplifting on Christmas Eve.

When not stopping shoplifters, David Patterson leads a quiet life in Pine Bluff, Alabama, working as a high school teacher. His random act of Christmas kindness brings unexpected joy to his life, as he finds himself drawn to the mysterious Emma. When she leaves, his world is turned upside down, and his dreams are changed forever.

Four years later, Emma returns in search of long-overdue redemption. But despite an undeniable attraction between the two, trust is an even greater issue now — for both of them. Can they find their way to a place of understanding? Or have yesterday's mistakes destroyed their chance for a future together?

The Rehabilitation of Angel Sinclair

A Pine Bluff Novel

Love — the Hardest Addiction to Kick

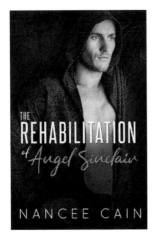

Angel Sinclair arrives in Pine Bluff, Alabama, determined to make amends for his past and move on. But that changes after a chance encounter with a beautiful inn owner, and instead he finds himself pursuing two things that haven't been in his life for years: love and trust.

Still reeling from a bitter divorce, Maggie Robertson wants to focus on making her business a success. Getting involved with anyone in this gossipy little town is the farthest thing from her mind...until she finds herself tempted by a younger man.

Neither Angel nor Maggie can ignore the sizzling heat between them. But Angel's secretive nature soon fills Maggie with doubts about the man she's allowed into her heart.

Was she wrong to believe love could conquer all? Is their age difference an obstacle they can't overcome?

The Redirection of Damien Sinclair

A Pine Bluff Novel

Sometimes You Get What You Need

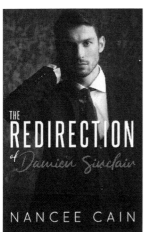

Acclaimed divorce attorney Damien Sinclair has witnessed more than his share of love's ugly aftermath. He keeps things black and white, preventing anyone from getting too close. But his illusion of control fades when an attempt on his life leaves him struggling with PTSD.

Enter Damien's childhood friend, the free-spirited Harley Taylor. Shrugging off the awkwardness of their teenaged fling and her broken heart, she appoints herself his caregiver. The man needs to learn not to take himself so seriously, and she's hellbent on snapping him out of his brooding funk.

After a decade apart, Harley and Damien find their attraction is stronger than ever. Could Harley's sunny disposition be the bright spot Damien needs in his life? Or will their differences overshadow any hopes of a future together?

The Reinvention of Jinx Howell

A Pine Bluff Novel

Can Love Unmask Their True Selves?

Hiding behind her wigs and heavy makeup, Jinx Howell masks her insecurities — which even she doesn't understand — with bravado, slashing through life with reckless abandon. Lonely, but unwilling to get close to anyone, she finds the ideal solution: a hook-up with the campus's most notorious heartbreaker.

In similar fashion, Mark "Two- Time" MacGregor protects his heart and keeps himself unencumbered through a string of one-night stands. A chance meeting with the edgy Jinx in a dark alley seems like destiny. She claims to want sex with no ties, making her perfect. *Like attracts like.* But this girl with a switchblade has more hang-ups than he does, which is a hell of a lot.

When tragedy strikes, Mark's hit-and-run lifestyle takes a backseat to his need to protect the broken girl whose secrets are unraveling. Along the way, both of them will find their truths unmasked. Can they forge a real relationship, or will they give up on their romance as jinxed?

The Reintroduction of Sammie Morgan

A Pine Bluff Novel

Can Life Get Any Crazier?

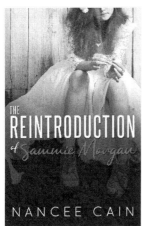

Still reeling from the tragic deaths of his wife and daughter, Matt Tyler trudges through life, caring for his young son, managing his cantankerous father, and working as much as he can. Despite his best efforts, bills are piling up and his vindictive in-laws seem determined to take Luke away from him.

Things change when he stumbles upon Sammie Morgan — with a car that won't run and her mother's ashes in the backseat. Best friends growing up, Matt and Sammie have spent years apart following very different paths. Now they've both run out of options. Without a dime in her pocket, Sammie has nowhere to go. And Matt lacks the stable home life he needs to fight his former in-laws.

Their hasty solution? *A marriage of convenience.*

But how convenient will this reintroduction be if it means Matt and Sammie have to relive the most painful parts of their past?

The Realization of Grayson Deschanelle

A Pine Bluff Novel

Sex, No Strings Attached

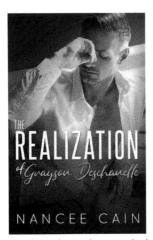

Despite a high-profile clientele, fashion photographer Grayson Deschanelle prefers being behind the lens, away from public scrutiny. After his movie star girlfriend dumps him, he flees to his stepbrother's remote cabin to hide from the paparazzi.

Related to Grayson by marriage, Lissy Carlton decides his plan to run from his problems might work for her, too. And perhaps he can help her out of the predicament that tanked her grades this semester of college as well.

Caught by surprise, Grayson finds Lissy much different than the girl he's known for years. She's no longer a child—though her teenaged crush is still very much intact. Snowed in with her, he tries to fight his growing attraction. But being with Lissy brings what his life is lacking into sharp focus.

The ice melts, and they return home. When their families discover their secret, Grayson must decide what kind of life he truly wants—and whether he'll fight to keep Lissy by his side.

Paranormal Angel Romances

Although each of the titles in this series can be read as standalone stories, this is the preferred reading order:

Saving Evangeline, Tempting Jo, Loving Lili (novella)

Saving Evangeline

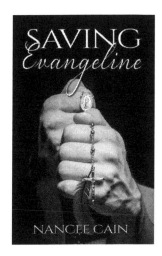

Evangeline is the town pariah. Everyone knows she's crazy and was responsible for the death of her last boyfriend. Even her mother left her and moved cross-country. Lonely and desperate, Evie decides to end her life.

Rogue angel Remiel longs to return to Earth, but there's just one problem. He tends to invite trouble and hasn't been allowed back since Woodstock. The Boss sends him to save Evangeline, but there's a catch: he can't reveal his angelic nature, and he must complete the task as Father Remiel Blackson.

Forced together on a cross-country trip, a forbidden romance ignites and love unfolds. A host of heavenly messengers tries to intervene, but Remiel and Evangeline are headed on a collision course to disaster. Will his love save her, or will they both be lost forever?

Tempting Jo

Forbidden love is hell...

Confident and quirky, Jo Sanford thinks her boss is God's gift to women — and she couldn't be further from the truth. Devilishly handsome, Luc DeVille will stop at nothing to lure his administrative assistant right into his arms — and bed.

Over Rafe Goodman's dead body...

Rafe, Jo's best friend, refuses to sit by and watch as Luc tries to win the heart of the woman he's always protected. After all, Rafe is her guardian angel. Suddenly, Jo's caught in the middle of a battle between good and evil. But the closer she gets to the fire, the hotter it burns. Now, Jo's going to learn that when love battles lust, Heaven and Hell collide.

Loving Lili (novella)

Their lovemaking is hot and dirty. Their break ups are nasty and epic.

Tired of taking the blame for every wicked thing that happens on Earth, fallen angel Luc DeVille decides to write a tell-all-book exposing The Boss.

Sharing a long and passionate history, Luc is shocked when Lili Nix arrives to interview for the job as editor. Immediately the verbal sparring begins, but the sexual chemistry remains combustible. Fascinated by this heavenly creature, Luc changes his game plan. After all, she's the only angel who has ever held his attention and understood his intentions.

Being in this world, but not of this world, is a lonely business. Can two lost angels connect and make it last this time?

Made in the USA
Monee, IL
27 October 2021